"Whatever you m   I'm not the enem

Another forward step brought him close to Paxton. After a second quick glance at the moon, he lowered his voice. "No one here is out to hurt you. Please remember that."

Daring to touch her, Grant placed a finger against her lips, fighting an overwhelming urge to replace those fingers with his mouth. But that kind of unanticipated aggression would have ended any future dealings they might have. He got that.

Her lips were soft against his fingertips though. And Paxton didn't back away from his touch.

Damn those haunted eyes of yours.

Damn those lips.

He almost said those things out loud.

Hiding a shudder similar to the one he saw pass through her, Grant spoke again. "Good night. Sleep well."

It took all of his willpower—every last ounce of it—to leave her there...and keep walking.

Linda Thomas-Sundstrom writes contemporary and paranormal romance novels for Harlequin. A teacher by day and a writer by night, Linda lives in the West, juggling teaching, writing, family and caring for a big stretch of land. She swears she has a resident muse who sings so loudly, she often wears earplugs in order to get anything else done. But she has big plans to eventually get to all those ideas. Visit Linda at lindathomas-sundstrom.com or on Facebook.

Books by Linda Thomas-Sundstrom

Harlequin Nocturne

Red Wolf
Wolf Trap
Golden Vampire
Guardian of the Night
Immortal Obsession
Wolf Born
Wolf Hunter
Seduced by the Moon
Immortal Redeemed
Half Wolf
Angel Unleashed
Desert Wolf

Harlequin Desire

The Boss's Mistletoe Maneuvers

Visit the Author Profile page at Harlequin.com
for more titles.

DESERT WOLF

—————

LINDA THOMAS-SUNDSTROM

Recycling programs
for this product may
not exist in your area.

ISBN-13: 978-0-373-13992-7

Desert Wolf

Copyright © 2017 by Linda Thomas-Sundstrom

Printed in U.S.A.

Dear Reader,

Arizona. Hot desert night lit by a full moon. A scent of danger is in the air, and a sexy, auburn-haired former Texas Ranger might become something less human after sundown. Welcome to Desperado, where a desert pack of werewolves have taken over an old ghost town, and their Alpha is about to meet his match in a woman from the East.

This is *Desert Wolf*.

What's not to love about a mix where East meets West, girl meets boy and human meets Were on a grand scale? Add in the unique beauty of a warm Arizona desert landscape, and well...the whole thing can lead to a trippy, dangerous, high-octane romance.

Imagining stories like this one are the reason why I enjoy writing about the werewolf world. I always look forward to finding out what these tall, edgy, gloriously sexy Weres can do to make my blood boil. And then I hunt, as they do, for just the right adversary in the form of a strong, independent woman who might turn out to be a perfect match.

Whether genetic Lycans or newly initiated into the werewolf clan, my heroes are take-charge guys that are a bit beastly at night, during the full moon phases. But my wolves *always* possess certain qualities that make me fall for them. High on that list are intelligence, loyalty, nobleness of heart and the desire to help others in need.

Don't you love those same qualities?

Please do check out my website to keep track of what's coming up next. Connect with me on my Facebook author page. Stop by and say hello. I'd love to hear from you.

Cheers and happy reading!

Linda

www.LindaThomas-Sundstrom.com

www.Facebook.com/LindaThomasSundstrom

To my family, those here and those gone, who always believed I had a story to tell.

*The Desperado ghost town is far from empty...
but its inhabitants aren't ghosts.*

Chapter 1

There was no man in the moon.

Every werewolf knew this.

The moon was female and a temptress. Her kiss was cool and her love ran hot. For Weres, Madame Moon was everything—lover, mistress, redeemer, betrayer. She bestowed power, strength, enhanced senses, lightning-fast reflexes and pain...terrible racking pain that long ago had turned former Texas Ranger Grant Wade inside out, but seemed normal to him now.

Tonight, the moon took up a good portion of the wide expanse of the star-filled Arizona sky and called to Grant with a seductive, silvery promise that made his shoulders twitch.

Only two other things Grant knew of felt anything remotely like this gut reaction: beautiful women and fine, aged whiskey...neither of which were present at the moment.

"Wait." Holding back tremors that were bubbling up inside, he addressed the moon. "Not yet. Soon."

The night was still warm after that day's unforgiving desert sun. Shirtless, wearing only jeans and boots, Grant rolled his shoulders to ease the growing aches of his imminent shape-shift. As a pure-blooded Lycan version of the werewolf species, shifting was part of his heritage. He liked it.

But he needed a little more time before he could do so, and he needed to keep his voice for a while longer. Long enough to corral the trespasser he was hunting out here, a rogue who brought trouble too close to home and was slippery as hell.

"Where are you?" Grant whispered to his prey. "What are you?"

The interloper whose arrival he anticipated could be human, though Grant doubted it. As a rule, humans weren't partial to acts as grisly as this crazy son of a bitch's grotesque taste for the raw meat of neighboring cattle. Disappearing animals had garnered the attention of angry ranchers with rifles, and those ranchers would be on the prowl tonight to protect their herds.

No. He suspected it was a half-crazed werewolf doing the damage. And if that scenario turned out to be true, the rogue had to be removed from human radar as quickly as possible. Werewolves had kept their presence and identities safe for over a thousand years and couldn't afford to blow it all now.

But damn...

The whole raw meat thing surrounding the freak he was after was a strange twist on abnormal. No werewolf Grant knew of went after cattle on the hoof. Most Weres, including him, preferred their burgers well done and on a bun.

These days, most Weres were as civilized as their human counterparts—at least 99 percent of the time. Humans just wouldn't like the fact that some police officers, nurses and even ER techs could actually be more than they seemed each time a full moon rolled around.

This trespasser was messing with those secrets. Grant couldn't afford to let angry ranchers get too close to his place of business. Keeping neighbors out of his hair and away from Desperado was imperative to protect the special beings harbored behind the old ghost town's shuttered windows.

Grant raised his head, sniffed the air.

A bittersweet scent left a tang on his tongue. Moonlight ruled the desert tonight in an almost-full phase. His inner wolf was expanding, waiting in anticipation, as the moon rose above the trees.

Unlike most Weres, Grant didn't have to give in to the moon's mystical allure. He could refuse the call if he chose to. A special gift had been twisted into his heritage, giving him the ability to shift with or without the moon calling the shots, when resistance for many others of his kind was futile.

"Just a few minutes more," he mused, almost ready for his transformation. Wolf blood made him faster and more flexible. It also made him lethal.

The first claw popped out as his fingers uncurled. The rest of them followed in rapid succession, long and razor sharp.

Pressure inside him was building. Ten seconds was all it would take to complete a full shape-shift. His unique abilities, combined with the purity of his bloodline, made him alpha of his own desert pack. Rattlesnakes and crazed lunatics aside, he was probably the most dangerous creature in the area.

"As for you," he said, speaking to the interloper he waited for. "Are you an unlucky bastard who'd been in the wrong place at the wrong time? Were you infected by a bite or scratch from a bad wolf and surprised when the next full moon came around? Because it seems no one has taught you how to behave."

Even after a bad bite or scratch, Grant knew, if a human being had been a good human before, he or she would be a good Were now. And good guys weren't cattle rustlers.

"You would have garnered sympathy if you had come knocking. Now look. The problems you've been causing have to be dealt with." The secrets hidden inside the town called Desperado were at stake and Grant was uncomfortable with how close to Desperado's gates he was standing. "So, come on. What are you waiting for?"

He searched the area for a hint of the trespasser and spoke again. "I am leader, watcher, gatekeeper, secret holder, guardian and reluctant ruler of a pack of like-bodied, like-minded Weres. Do you purposefully taunt me?"

His patience was wearing thin. Grant glanced once more at the moon then did a quick scan of the mountain range, sifting through the night smells in search of anomalies.

The air was loaded with unique fragrances only found in the West: a combination of sand, brush, overheated rock, animals, cactus and the trees that tenaciously clung to the hillside despite a general lack of water. All those smells fit neatly into his mental data banks.

Except for one.

That one stood out like a shout.

Wrapped in the breeze was the unmistakable odor of

blood. There had been another fresh kill, the third in as many passing months. That pissed him off.

"Damn fool." His voice rumbled. "Who the hell do you think you are to put all of us in jeopardy? It's only a matter of time before we find you."

The fact that the creature out there had so far eluded capture was also an anomaly with a wolf pack on the prowl. The only question to consider was whether this trespassing idiot would turn out to be adaptable if offered a choice.

Grant turned upwind. His shoulders twitched again. *"If you're a Were, and in the vicinity, you should be able to pick up my thoughts."* Grant silently sent the message over the telepathic channel most werewolves used to communicate. "Barring that, maybe you can hear my voice."

He detected no response at all.

"Okay. All right." Grant raised his face to let the moonlight soak in. "It's time to up the ante."

Waves of cold penetrated his bronzed skin and sifted downward, layer by layer, to take control of muscles and nerves. The pain the cold brought was immediate and terrible, but was quickly replaced by a searing heat that would fuel mounds of muscle.

Grant welcomed the discomfort. He welcomed the wolf. Vestiges of his human shape began to shred as he became one with the song that sang to him now. Wolf music. The call of the wild.

I am Lycan, alpha and a servant of the moon. Whatever the hell is going on around here needs to be set straight.

Muscles trembled as they began to expand. Grant's jeans felt tight. His boots felt cramped and his face stung. With his last speaking breath, he warned, "Time to face the consequences of your actions, whoever you are," knowing that any rogue wolf with half a brain would run the other way.

Cheekbones rearranged with a rub of ligaments. Vertebrae crackled with sounds no human would ever want to hear. Rabbits scurried. Coyotes whimpered and tucked their tails as Grant Wade, now half man and half wolf, straightened up in the light…his transition punctuated by gunshots in the distance.

Hell, had ranchers found that rogue?

Voiceless now, his body corded with tense, fine-tuned muscle, Grant issued a roar that echoed along the red-rock canyon walls behind him…and began the steep slide downhill.

Chapter 2

Paxton Hall wrinkled her nose as she stepped off the plane.

She pressed her blond fringe of bangs off her forehead and squinted at the scene in front of her. The jet had parked its little tin-covered ass in the middle of nowhere, it seemed to her. Unlike private airports in the East, this Arizona stopover would require a long-distance sprint across an acre of molten tarmac in the blazing sun to get to the terminal. And she was wearing heels.

"We'll unload the luggage," someone said from behind her. "You can pick up your bags at the gate."

Swell. Her bags were going to get a ride. Maybe she could hitch a trip to the terminal along with them.

"Thanks," she said, watching heat rise from the asphalt like a wavering mirage. She hadn't forgotten the extremes of Arizona weather and the scorching wind that made everything look barren, but being born here wasn't an automatic passport to feeling familiar with it now.

Paxton didn't reach for the metal stair rail, which would have been a sure way to scald her fingers. She was seriously reconsidering the viability of this trip, not quite sure why she was in Arizona. She had her own gig in the East and a nice rented town house. Her income was steady, if not fabulous, and good enough to support her current lifestyle.

So, why did she really need this Arizona property her father had left her, other than for a trip down Nostalgia Lane and the small chunk of change a couple of hundred acres in the middle of nowhere might bring when it sold?

Except that she couldn't actually sell it, as things were, since her father, God rest his soul, had left the old tourist attraction that sat smack in the center of all that land she had inherited to someone else. Someone unrelated to the family. An unfamiliar name in the will.

Who the hell was Grant Wade, anyway?

How was she supposed to sell a parcel of land that circled, but didn't include, the central piece?

"Safe journey," the attendant said politely, interrupting her thoughts. "Will you need anything else, Ms. Hall?"

"No. Thanks," Paxton returned absently as she headed down the steps with a tight grip on her briefcase.

That man...Grant Wade...would either have to buy her out or turn the Desperado ghost town over to her so she could sell the place and be out of here—back to civilization, green grass and cool breezes. When she was in Maryland, coming here had seemed like the thing to do. Now that she was here, Paxton hoped she hadn't been wrong about that.

She'd worn a skirt, which allowed hot air to flow up and over her thighs as she stepped onto asphalt so overheated her heels seemed to sink in. With that hot caress on her naked legs came flashbacks…memories of sweltering desert heat on her face when she was a kid and how much she had liked the soaring temperatures back then. A very long time ago.

She remembered the distinct smells of heat-scorched land and the way her young skin had first burned before becoming a sun-kissed gold as summers wore on. Here in Arizona is where her wildness had first blossomed and where she had learned to ride and run. It's where her mother had died, right before little Paxton had been sent away to a distant relative on the East Coast, away from this place and far from her dad.

Those old memories were more reminiscent of bad dreams now. But the tingle at the base of her neck signified something more complex than just reminisces and the firing up of a few random nerve endings. It brought home the fact that she had never seen her dad again after leaving this place. Not even once. She hadn't heard from him—no birthday cards, Christmas packages or calls—in all that time.

Twenty frigging years.

And now Andrew Hall was dead, and she was back where she started. The land of sand and sun. Because of that, Paxton was determined to be trouble incarnate if Mr. Grant Wade didn't listen to reason. She was going to bury her fear of confrontations and make Grant Wade assume *trouble* was her middle name.

Got that, Wade?

Besides, the man had to be at least sixty-five years

old if he had been her father's friend. That land might be a burden for an old guy. She'd done some research, of course, but the only person the internet had turned up with that name in this part of the United States was a Texas Ranger nowhere near an advanced age. So her Grant Wade had to be an old guy who had inconveniently stayed off everyone's front page.

Paxton squinted as she scanned the tarmac, where the damn heat waves were manifesting into the form of a man—one lone man in all that wide-open space, seemingly walking toward her.

Shielding her eyes with a hand, Paxton wondered whether to keep walking and meet this guy or stay in place and fry in black silk on the hot asphalt.

She kept walking.

Behind her, she heard the luggage cart pull away from the plane. From somewhere far off came the static sound of a speaker. Those things were inconsequential. Her eyes were trained on the man who walked with the casual, apparently single-minded intention of meeting up with her. Had to be her, because at the moment she was the only one out here and he wasn't headed to a parked plane.

Who was this guy?

The stranger was tall, lean, and wore a wide-brimmed hat. Broad shoulders balanced a narrow waist. Long legs were clad in jeans, and his boots made soft thudding sounds on the pavement. A silver buckle on his belt flashed in the sun the way diamonds flared beneath jewelry store lighting.

Those things screamed the word *cowboy.*

A white shirt with the sleeves rolled up to his elbows showed off sun-bronzed skin. As he approached, Paxton saw that enough top buttons on the shirt were open to lay bare a triangle of skin that attracted her attention for a little too long. When she looked up, he was close enough for her to see his wide, engaging smile.

And his face...

Christ almighty. It was chiseled, angular, with taut skin that fell somewhere on the golden spectrum. This guy, whoever he was, seemed to have inherited a lucky combination of genes that made him both elegant and rugged. The whole package suggested a new classification of the term *handsome*. Even if he was a cowboy.

"Paxton Hall?" He stopped a few feet from her and removed his hat, showing off a mass of shaggy auburn hair.

He was fine to look at, sure, Paxton noted. But what could he possibly want?

"Ms. Hall?" he repeated, with a slight variation.

"Yes." She continued to shield her eyes. "That's me."

The hunk's smile was as brilliant as the rest of him, and that was saying something. Fine lines shot out from the corners of his eyes in honor of some years in the sun without detracting from the overall hunky look.

Paxton wished she could see the color of those eyes, hidden behind his sunglasses, and wondered if they'd be blue. Light blue eyes set in sun-darkened skin would have topped the whole thing off nicely.

"I've come to escort you to your hotel," he said in a deep voice that ran ridiculous circles around Paxton's impoverished libido. It was obvious to her that she hadn't taken enough time lately to explore the ramifications of having been without a boyfriend for several months now.

Plus...didn't every woman have cowboy fantasies?

"Your hotel," he repeated, probably wondering if she had hearing problems.

There was just something about his voice and how suggestive it was of star-filled desert nights and the almost unearthly scent of night-blooming flowers. Two sentences from him and Paxton was thrown back in time to when she had first noticed things like those strong, sweet Arizona scents.

Or maybe it was all just a side effect of the stifling heat.

"I didn't call for a taxi service," she said.

He nodded. "I thought you might like a ride."

"Because?"

"It's hot." He was still grinning, and that grin was contagious.

Paxton smiled back.

"I totally agree about the heat. But I'm pretty sure you didn't answer my question about not calling a service," she said.

"Your attorney mentioned that you might be headed this way today."

Okay. That made sense. She felt better.

"In that case, yes. Thanks. I'd like a ride to..." Paxton paused, mid-speech. "I didn't book a hotel, sure there are plenty of them."

He nodded again. "No problem. I'll take you to one. I think you'll find most of the accommodations around here acceptable."

He was staring at her, not exactly rudely, but with the kind of lingering appraisal that brought on a blush. He'd be taking in the black silk shirt, the high heels and the private plane her attorney had let her use because several well-off clients needed to hitch a ride back to Maryland. This guy would probably be thinking he'd have to book her a suite in a fancy boutique hotel.

Hell, she couldn't afford a suite. Not that she wouldn't

like one. Cash wasn't exactly tight, but it was on close watch. She didn't get paid for extra time off from her gig as a nurse in the ER, and her return trip to Maryland was on a commercial flight, in coach.

"That would be great," Paxton said. "Any hotel will do. I'm not fussy and I won't be here long."

She just needed to get out of this heat and into different clothes. Big thanks would be due to her lawyer for thinking about her enough to send a gorgeous chauffeur.

That smile he was still offering? Dazzling. Yet Paxton's instincts warned her that the guy's smile hid something. A trace of concern, maybe? Concern for what? That she'd be a prissy Easterner for whom the extremes of comfort were paramount, when that was miles from the truth?

If they spent any time together, he'd find out how unprepared she was for this trip into her past. Her black silk shirt hadn't been the greatest idea for day wear in a sun-drenched state. Cowboy would note that, too. She had worn it in honor of her father's recent passing, in spite of the fact that she hadn't really known her dad.

Briefly, Paxton closed her eyes, thinking that anyone would have assumed she'd have gotten over that kind of loss, along with old abandonment issues. But being here in Arizona again was causing a sudden emotional upheaval. Just a few steps off the plane had been all it took to bring the old days back.

"This way," the cowboy said, stepping aside, waving his hat at the terminal. "I hope you don't mind riding in a truck."

So, no real chauffeur then. Just a favor from someone her lawyer knew.

"That would be fine," she returned. "Would you mind confirming my attorney's name?"

"Daniel Dunn, Esquire."

"Do you know Dan personally?"

"As well as anyone can know a lawyer by phone."

"Great." Paxton moved forward, eager to get to the terminal. If this guy knew her lawyer, he had to be legit.

"Do you think we could get something cold to drink on the way to the hotel?" she asked.

"It would be my pleasure to make that happen," her escort congenially replied.

Though she didn't glance sideways, Paxton was aware of every move the guy made. He purposefully shortened his strides to accommodate hers. Having him beside her was both a boon and another unsettling feature of this trip. Speed hampered by the height of her heels, Paxton felt doubly foolish and out of place. She no longer belonged here. She was trespassing on the past—both its ideals and its pain.

What the hell was I thinking?

As they entered the small terminal, her companion placed a hand on her elbow to guide her toward the bags. His touch was electric, empathetic. Paxton wanted to lean into him for the kind of support she needed to get through this ordeal, when giving in to the urge to fold up like an accordion would have been the end of her.

Gently, he steered her toward her luggage, the two small bags she had seen fit to bring for a weekend in the desert. Her companion lifted the bags easily and reached to take her briefcase. She gave him a firm head shake, preferring to hold on to the paperwork she'd need for a quick sale when the reclusive Grant Wade agreed to her terms.

"There's a watering hole down the road," this guy said. "The truck is right out front."

When she glanced at him, he added, "It's a café. We can get something to drink there or take it to go."

Paxton nodded. She followed her guide through the revolving doors and onto the street where a large blue truck sat parked at the curb. Like the cowboy beside her, its lines were tall, long and sturdy. Chrome wheels and other fancy stuff were missing. The hood was covered in dust and there was a baseball-sized dent in the passenger door. This truck was a working man's transportation, not merely a vehicle meant to prove male bravado.

After tossing her bags in the back, her makeshift chauffeur came around to open her door. Getting in while wearing a short skirt took some feminine know-how when the truck's cab was so high off the ground.

Once she was inside, Paxton stuck out an arm to stop the door from closing and faced the guy helping her. "I really am grateful for the ride. And I'm sorry I seem to have lost my manners. I didn't ask your name."

"Wade," he said, the dazzling smile no longer in evidence. "Name's Grant Wade."

Chapter 3

Paxton Hall wasn't what Grant had expected, and that came as a surprise.

She looked the part of the spoiled young woman he had expected to show up, and she dressed well, but Paxton didn't really seem spoiled. She'd brought one bag and an overnight case that not too many fancy outfits would have traveled well in. She had been happy to let him choose her hotel and had allowed him to guide her along without complaint.

And she was beautiful. Incredibly beautiful. Though he'd seen a few pictures of her in Andrew Hall's file, in person, Paxton Hall was a whole new deal.

He liked all the details ringing up—the big eyes that were an unusual amber color, the porcelain skin and the kind of oval face that begged a second and third look. Dark blond hair was cut in a swingy, shoulder-length style and appeared to be natural in color. Very little makeup muddied her face, just a swipe of something dark on her eyelashes and a hint of rose on her cheeks. In his estimation, she didn't need even that.

She was antsy, her discomfort easy to read. Being beside her made his nerves buzz. Back in the terminal, when he had touched her arm, that buzz had been transmitted to a spot way down deep inside him.

The feminine perfume she wore didn't help with his initial response to her, either. Some kind of woodsy aroma trailed her, almost completely covering up a more elusive scent he couldn't yet place. Everything about Paxton Hall, all those details, were laced with a layer of subdued anxiety and anger. Because of him, in part.

He slammed her door and walked around the truck, acknowledging that Paxton was surprised by this unexpected meet up. She knew his name now, but he'd had the advantage of getting to see what she was like before she found him out and the arguments he anticipated began.

Did she consider him the enemy? A problem to be solved?

He had told the truth about her lawyer giving him a heads-up on her visit and knew Paxton would have questions. Plenty of them. Most of those were questions he wouldn't be able to answer, due to secrets he had to keep, though she deserved some kind of explanation for what was written in that will.

The reason for her visit was a no-brainer. Paxton Hall wanted to sell the land her father left her and have nothing more to do with her early Arizona upbringing. But her father had left him part of that acreage in order to make sure a sale didn't happen, so surely Andrew Hall must have foreseen that some sort of contact between his two heirs would take place.

As an ex-Ranger with connections, Grant had been tracking Paxton since her father's death a few weeks ago. And here she sat, in his truck, putting *traitor* and *Grant Wade* together in the same unspoken breath. She'd be thinking that the man she had been trusting to get her settled for the night had turned out to be more like the personification of sabotage.

Grant climbed into the cab and rested both hands on the wheel. Without looking at his guest, he said, "Would you like to talk now or wait a while?"

"Now," she said breathlessly.

Her attention on him was unforgiving. His Were senses told him Paxton's heart rate had kicked up a notch and that Paxton Hall had expected someone else attached to the name Wade. Someone different. She was trying to reconcile his image with her former ideas about who might turn up to potentially oppose her.

"If you're uncomfortable, I can call you a taxi," he said.

"I've been uncomfortable since I read my father's will, as you must already know."

Direct and to the point. Grant liked that, usually.

She turned on the seat. "You are that same guy?"

"One and the same, if you're talking about Andrew's legacy," Grant replied. "If you're talking about anything else, I probably didn't do it."

Levity wasn't going to get him anywhere. He didn't have to look at Paxton to feel the animosity creeping into her tone.

"Why?" she demanded.

Pretending to misunderstand what she was asking would have been lame, so he said, "It was important to your father and to others that the property wasn't sold."

"Why?" she repeated.

"I can't tell you about the specifics of that right now, other than to stress your father's desire for me to hold on to the town."

"You're talking about an old tourist attraction that's been closed for twenty years. I fail to see why hanging on to a defunct ghost town wins out over selling the place," she argued. "Surely you have better things to do than keep track of it."

"Not many people would understand my reasons for staying here," Grant said. "Your father did."

She zeroed in on that. "You knew my father well, then?"

"Truthfully, I didn't know him much at all."

The way she drew back told him that Andrew Hall's daughter hadn't considered that kind of an answer. Had she imagined he had goaded Andrew into handing him the town? Finessed Desperado out of a tough man like Andrew Hall?

"What you're saying doesn't make sense," she eventually remarked. "Maybe you can explain things better?"

Grant nodded. "We had a deal."

"You and my father?"

He nodded again. "Our deal was that I would inherit the town when he passed, and that I'd take care of it and never sell the land Desperado sits on or allow anyone else to sell it."

That slice of the truth would sound absurd to the woman sitting beside him. The whole truth could never be spoken, of course, though Grant could see Paxton was firm in her resolve to get to the bottom of her father's strange bequest. He just couldn't let her find that reason. Paxton Hall, along with all the other humans on the planet, had to be kept from learning Desperado's secrets—and his.

That much, at least, was clear to Grant. What wasn't immediately clear was how he was supposed to oppose her when Paxton was here, in his damn truck, with her pale face and her black clothes that reflected her consideration for a man she hadn't really known.

"Why didn't he just leave the whole thing to you?" she asked.

"I'm not sure, actually. That would have made more sense."

And it would have kept Paxton away, maybe, a fact that he had considered since meeting Andrew Hall. He had a glimmer of an idea that Paxton's father might have sent her away in the first place so she didn't learn about the werewolves in residence here, and that Andrew's ongoing silence had furthered the cause of shielding his daughter from truths too difficult to explain.

"Will you sell it to me?" she asked.

And there they were, at a standstill. Checkmate. Paxton would assume her request was reasonable, and it would have been if things had been different.

Grant started the engine. "Do you still want that drink?"

"I'd rather you answered my question."

He looked at the white-faced woman who couldn't have been more than two or three years younger than his twenty-eight. She looked even younger than that, though. Paxton truly was an eyeful, though that couldn't matter in their negotiations.

"Maybe you'll want to turn right around and go home when I reiterate that I'm not going to sell," he suggested. "Why waste money on a hotel when more time here won't get you what you want?"

"You might change your mind," she countered stubbornly.

"Not going to happen, Paxton. I made a deal."

The heat inside the car was harsh. Moisture had gathered at Paxton's temples, dampening her hair. The black silk was starting to stick to her in ways Grant shouldn't have noticed.

In any other situation, he would have liked a close-up with Paxton Hall. As things stood, the best case scenario would be for her to go away mad and never look back. She might try to file a lawsuit in order to force him to sell, but her father's attorney wasn't going to condone a move like that.

"Look," he said. "I don't want to make an enemy of the daughter of the man who left something valuable to me. So how can we resolve things before that happens?"

"Too late," she said, reaching for the door handle, "if you refuse to see my side of this argument and either buy me out or sell."

Grant reached to take hold of her briefcase, stopping Paxton from opening the door. "Stay," he said, removing his sunglasses.

She turned her head. Amber eyes lighted on him, connecting with his gaze. Earnest eyes. Wounded. Haunted. Wild.

A stunning jolt of something extraordinary hit Grant in the chest and then melted downward as a second jolt, larger than the first, hit. He had seen eyes like those before and didn't want to face what that meant. He didn't want to face *her* with what that meant.

What he saw in those eyes quite possibly changed everything—his future and hers.

Paxton Hall was a Were.

He had no doubt about it.

Still, Grant could see that she was ignorant of that fact and therefore didn't know what was in store. He believed this because he couldn't feel the thing she kept hidden inside her, in the dark. Her scent had kindled his discovery. Those big eyes of hers said it all.

Grant broke eye contact and dropped his hold on the briefcase, stung by the realization of who and what Paxton really was. Worse yet, the air in the cab suddenly seemed charged with wayward electricity that had nowhere to go due to the fact that his inner wolf had been awakened by the directness of Paxton's gaze.

"What I mean is that we can get to know each other better if you stay as planned," he said, wondering if he could let her go at all now that he knew what eventually would happen to her. "Maybe then we'll both understand where we're coming from."

Everything about this new turn of events was dangerous, he realized. Remaining close to Paxton could be bad when wolf might call to wolf, setting free what now lay curled up inside her. Letting her go without an inkling of what she was would be equally dangerous. Her wolf had to show sometime and was long overdue. For wolves, timing was everything.

She studied him frankly as she thought over his suggestion. Her eyes never left his face.

"Will you consider buying me out?" she asked.

"We can talk about that and the reasons I can't agree to doing what you ask."

Grant's mind whirled with things he wanted to say, but couldn't.

I now think your father might have been keeping Desperado for you, leaving it in my care, he wanted to tell her. *For when you...in case you needed help and a place to go for a while, among others just like you.*

No way could he tell Paxton any of that, since he was only now beginning to understand it himself.

Had her father meant to bring her here for this reason, intending for his heirs to meet? Could Hall have masterminded all of this to ensure his estranged daughter's first transition from human to Were was in safe hands? Grant Wade's hands?

"How about if we discuss it now?" she said.

Grant shook his head. "Give me a few hours to think things over."

She released the door handle and sat back, unable to mask her hopeful expression. "All right. A few hours."

He couldn't help but notice how small she looked in the truck. Although Paxton had to be at least five foot five, she was a shade too slim and as willowy as the trees along the riverbed.

She wasn't lighthearted. Hints of sadness weighed down her shoulders. Did she possess a strong Hall family backbone under all that silk?

It seemed that Andrew had also kept Grant in the dark about a few minor details concerning this legacy. And now, secrets on top of secrets had left him in the hot seat.

Grant reached for the gearshift, mulling things over.

Most likely Paxton didn't know that her father had followed her life from behind the scenes, and how much Andrew must have loved her.

Sooner or later, Paxton's wolf would make an appearance. There was no way to postpone that event forever, no matter where she lived.

And that made Andrew Hall one tricky son of a bitch.

"You believe I'm your enemy, but we're actually more alike than you know," he said, growing more uncomfortable as the minutes passed. Because, hell…

Just one long glance at those golden eyes of hers had done more than make him realize what kind of DNA she carried. It had also done him in. Captured him completely. Put him on her side. Whatever haunted her, now haunted him.

His wolf wanted to growl in protest over the burden laid upon him, because the wolf had a heads-up on what her innate sense of sadness might actually be.

Paxton Hall was a she-wolf in waiting, and her timing couldn't have been worse. With a full moon due the following night, she'd be too close to a shape-shifting pack. If she were to face another wolf up close, that meeting might bring out the secrets kept from her all this time. And it wouldn't be pretty.

It seemed like more trouble had landed in his lap, and that these next few hours were not going to be easy to get through. He had asked Paxton to stay when it now might be imperative to keep his distance from her. He wanted more than anything to take her in his arms and offer comfort, something she hadn't ever gotten from her estranged father…and that, too, could be dangerous for her.

Damned if I do. Damned if I don't.

With one more glance at Paxton, Grant said, "I think I'll need that drink."

The look she returned made his stomach tighten.

"Make mine a double," she said.

Chapter 4

As Grant Wade pulled the truck away from the curb, it dawned on Paxton that there might be a downside to remaining in his presence.

From where she sat, on the opposite side of the truck, she still felt the impression of his hand on her elbow, left over from when he helped with her bags. When she had looked at his face, searching for more hints about his character, what she'd found was a man who might not be as happy to accommodate her visit as he seemed.

They were at odds about Desperado, and Grant Wade showed signs of discomfort. Although he rested one arm casually on the window frame and the other on the wheel, those bronzed forearms were corded with tension.

Were those arms sexy? *Yes.*

Did that matter? *No.*

So, why had she even thought of questions like those? Truth was, Paxton wondered what that smooth golden skin would be like to touch and chastised herself for thinking she'd like to find out.

Her reactions to Grant Wade were as automatic as breathing. In her defense, most women liked strong, sexy men who didn't overtly try to overpower with all that testosterone. Men who could easily take control of any situation, yet sometimes knew better than to try. Handsome men at ease in their own skins who radiated self-confidence and looked exactly like Grant Wade did, from Stetson to scuffed boots.

Weren't those things tied to what constituted wet dreams for women? Because surely she was going to have a dream like that about this guy tonight, no matter how far apart they stood on her father's deal.

"Name your poison," he said to her as the truck rolled past a few strip malls and gas stations, its engine purring like a well-tuned tractor.

"Iced tea. Heavy on the ice."

He gave her a sideways glance.

"I don't think alcohol would further my cause much. Do you?" Not wanting to relax, Paxton leaned back against the leather seat, liking the masculine smell of the truck. The trip to Arizona had been taxing. She would have given anything to be able to close her eyes.

"Hotel choices," he said. "Big or small?"

"Cheap."

He nodded.

"Then you'll give in and buy me out of all that acreage. Or vice versa," she added.

"You're pretty confident one of those two things will happen?"

"Aren't you?"

Her companion didn't reply to that question and an-

gled the truck into a parking space beside a small road-
side café.

"Hungry?" he asked.

"Famished, actually."

"I hope you like burgers."

"Not unless they come with fries."

"Then you, my fine lady, are in luck," Grant Wade
said as he turned off the engine. "Though you will have
to sit across from me."

"I'll manage somehow," Paxton returned.

The café was nearly empty this time of day. A few
small tables ringed a linoleum patchwork floor and three
faded red booths hugged the windows. The only waitress
in sight, dressed in faded jeans and an apron, eyed them
curiously when she and Grant slid into a booth. After
Grant returned the glance, the waitress ambled over.

"I guess I'm conspicuously foreign," Paxton said
when their order went in.

"This is a place for regulars. Anyone new is suspicious."

"Maybe she likes you. She's staring."

"Nope. Shirleen is just curious. She has imprinted
with…" He stopped there without finishing the strange
remark.

"Does that mean she's engaged to someone?" Paxton asked.

Her cowboy nemesis took a swig of the iced tea
Shirleen had brought over. "Yep. Western slang for
people coupling up."

Paxton didn't share how much she might have liked
to couple up with Grant Wade after first laying eyes
on him, since that wasn't going to happen. She hoped
to get the paperwork signed and be back on a plane.

They ate in silence, an unspoken truce, of sorts, with

the curious waitress looking on. Grant didn't seem to notice the scrutiny, but Paxton couldn't get much of her burger down. She was relieved when Grant took care of paying the bill. By the time they headed for the truck, evening was settling in with a pink glow on the horizon.

"It's quite beautiful," she said, staring at the landscape for a few minutes before getting into the truck. "I had forgotten about that. Maybe I was too young to notice."

"You remember being here?" Grant Wade asked.

"I remember a few small things. Mostly unimportant stuff."

"Like pretty sunsets?"

She nodded. "Yes. Like that."

"There's no place better for showy horizons than this one," he said.

"Not even in Texas?" she asked, testing her new theory on Grant Wade being that former Texas Ranger.

"Similar, but not the same," he replied, opening her door and playing the gentleman card well. He added, "You know about Texas?"

Paxton shrugged.

"Know thine enemies?" he suggested.

"Hopefully you aren't one of them."

"Hopefully not," he agreed, waiting for her to climb in. "We just shared fries."

More silence ensued as they drove to the edge of town. What more was there to say without getting back into the argument over the property? Grant had asked for time to consider everything she had suggested. That was fine, if he didn't take too long.

"I'd like to go there tomorrow," she finally said when a tiny motel on the edge of a wide expanse of desert came into view.

"Back to Maryland?"

She shook her head. "Desperado."

He took a beat to reply. "I'm not sure that would be a good idea."

"You'll be driving over my property every time you go in or out of that old town. I think you owe me a look, don't you?"

His hesitation wasn't subtle.

"I can always rent a car," she persisted. "I wouldn't be trespassing if I stopped at the gate. I won't bother the ghosts."

When he offered no comment, Paxton got the impression Grant Wade might be hiding something out there in the desert that he didn't want anyone to discover. Had he found gold?

"You said *valuable*," she noted.

He glanced at her.

"You mentioned that my father left you something valuable."

"Did I?"

She waited him out, wondering what kind of actual reason there could be for keeping her away from the old town. Maybe Grant was planning on reopening Desperado as a tourist attraction and didn't want to mention that. Perhaps his deal with her father had been to make the old place live again and earn Grant Wade, former Texas Ranger, a decent living. If so, the deal was terribly shortsighted, since everyone involved had to realize that no one could reach Desperado without her permission granting the right-of-way.

Surely her father's lawyer would have pointed out to Grant that buying her out would be to his benefit? The truck had stopped without her noticing. Grant got out, took her bags from the back and again came around to open her door.

"Small and cheap," he said with a nod to the motel.

Funny, Paxton thought. That's exactly what she felt like as she watched Grant Wade enter the lobby of the two-story U-shaped building ahead of her. Small and cheap. She'd sell the land for a song if it meant getting back to her life without taking Grant Wade up on whatever emotion he hid behind those sunglasses.

Reluctantly, she followed Grant to the lobby, trying hard not to stare at the way his jeans emphasized his magnificently compact backside and how his auburn hair, badly in need of a trim, brushed his shirt collar. Taking stock of those things made her uneasy. Still, she had to assess her opponent and hope that the best person would win this argument.

As the hot wind caressed her face, Paxton felt even stranger, in a déjà-vu kind of way, as if it wasn't actually possible for a person to get over their beginnings.

She looked at her feet, then tipped her face toward the motel's neon sign. Her gaze flicked to the light of the lobby's open doorway, filled at the moment by Grant Wade. He was waiting. But what, exactly, was he waiting for—the woman to tag along behind him, or the completion of a deal in his favor?

Maybe she was just projecting her own thoughts on the matter, because, damn it, the man was messing with her sense of justice. Grant Wade, in the flesh, suddenly seemed like the perfect guy to manage a ghost town in the Old West.

And he was looking at her in that way he had, making her feel as though she was the only woman in the world on his mind.

Chapter 5

What did Paxton think he was going to do with the old ghost town?

Grant had taken to swearing under his breath and did so repeatedly in honor of the situation he found himself in now as he stood on the threshold to Paxton's room. Half the space in that room was taken up by a bed, and in a perfect world, he and Paxton might have worked through their differences on top of it. Of course, they weren't going to do any such thing. He had to get in and get out without lingering.

Cautiously placing one boot inside, then the other, Grant set Paxton's bags down on the carpet. With his hands now free, he thought seriously about reaching for her and got the feeling she might have been willing to have that happen.

Then again, maybe not.

Besides, he was needed elsewhere.

Open curtains at the window allowed the evening moonlight in. That light was a reminder that he'd need to be on guard again tonight for the return of the slippery rogue he hadn't been able to catch in the months before. His pack would already be prowling near the hills, careful to avoid ranchers doing the same thing. After four months, most of the valley was in an uproar.

Paxton stood in the doorway behind him. She hadn't followed him inside. Her watchful gaze burned a hole in the back of his shirt, and that was bringing up all sorts of wayward emotions that were never good for a werewolf to have in a closed space.

"Well, guess I'll head out." Grant brushed his hands on his jeans as if wiping away the idea of an imminent and untimely appearance of his claws. He was usually good at compartmentalizing his emotions.

"My thanks are piling up," she said when he turned to face her. "Pretty soon I'll be the one owing you a meal."

Grant nodded. "No thanks are necessary. It's an awkward situation we're confronted with. I'll be the first to agree."

She remained in the doorway, blocking his exit. Maybe Paxton was afraid of what he might do if she came inside. Maybe she could read his mind about that bed.

"I'll need a car," she said.

"You can have the truck if you need to go somewhere." He fished in his pocket and tossed her the keys.

"I'm going to Desperado in the morning," she reminded him.

"I'd advise against it, Paxton, unless I'm riding along."

Palming the keys, she said, "How will you get home if I have these?"

"Friends."

"Do you live nearby?"

"I live on the ranch near Desperado's gates, as you quite possibly already knew."

"In my old house?"

Grant noted how her voice had lowered. She'd likely be remembering the house she grew up in. *My* house, she had said. Did she think of it fondly?

He said, "It's still there. A little worse for wear, but standing. I've made some necessary repairs."

"After you sell, or I sell, will you go back to Texas?" she asked, which Grant thought was pretty cheeky for someone facing an opponent in a motel room located in a state she hadn't set her stilettos in since she was six years old. Just how far would her confidence take her, though?

He didn't glance again to the window. Didn't need to note where the moon was. He was looking at Paxton with his wolf's eyes, watching her unfasten the top button of her shirt because she was used to a more moderate climate.

Sensing his attention, she dropped her hands to her sides. "That was not an invitation."

Ignoring the comment, Grant pointed to the floor-model air conditioner. "Press the button on the left and you'll soon feel better."

Paxton's cheeks colored slightly. He noticed that, too. Now that dusk had come and gone, and darkness had arrived, moonlight flooded the motel's balcony behind her as she tossed his keys back to him.

"See you tomorrow," Grant said, with his hat in his hand like every good Texas boy under a roof. "Breakfast?"

She shook her head. Paxton's hands were shaking,

too. Why? Were her quakes a sign of pent-up anger? Maybe the moon was finally affecting her in some small way?

That was bound to happen sometime.

Moving to the window, Grant closed the curtains halfway to mute the moonlight. A random thought crossed his mind that moon children all over the world would be tuning in to that bright silver disc in the sky.

But this wasn't the time for explaining anything about that to the woman across from him. She wouldn't have believed him, anyway.

"I'm leaving. It's safe to come inside now," he announced, heading for the doorway she hadn't yet entered.

They were face-to-face, very close for a few seconds before Paxton stepped back. Close enough for Grant to feel her warm breath on his chin and to observe the tight line of her full, lush lips. There was no eye contact between them this time, which was for the best. Any further connection with those haunted amber eyes of hers, and he might have…

Well, he might have forgotten about who she was and why she was here, and also about proper decorum with strangers.

"Breakfast?" he repeated to scatter the images of what he might have done in this room with Paxton Hall if she had been anyone else.

"I'll meet you out there," she said soberly. "At Desperado. I'll find my way."

Her black silk shirt had opened just enough below her collarbones for him to get a quick view of Paxton's flawless ivory skin. It was rare to see pale people in the West, and the contrast between the black silk and the porcelain skin beneath it seemed to him a metaphor of sorts. All this time, she had assumed she was human. How could she have thought otherwise if things had never been explained to her? But the silk was only a top layer. Peel that back, and what lay beneath would reveal the real Paxton Hall.

Bathed in moonlight and the slanted glow from the motel's neon sign, Paxton seemed vulnerable and alone. Her mother had died long ago. She'd never known her father. Grant hated to leave her, but he had to.

After one quick brush of his hair with his fingers, Grant set his hat on his head, feeling the need to offer Paxton something, even if what he was about to say might sound trite.

"You're not alone. I want you to understand that," he said.

Confusion crossed her features.

"I'll take you there tomorrow," he continued. "I'll take you to Desperado first thing in the morning."

Relief softened her expression. Happy with that, Grant added, "Whatever you might be thinking, I'm not the enemy."

Another step brought him close to her. After a second quick glance toward the window, he lowered his voice. "No one here is out to hurt you. Please remember that."

Daring to touch her, Grant placed a finger against her lips, fighting an overwhelming urge to replace those fingers with his mouth. But that kind of unanticipated incursion would have ended any future dealings they might have. He got that.

Her lips were soft against his fingertips, though. And she didn't back away from his touch.

Damn those haunted eyes of yours.

Damn those lips.

He almost said those things out loud.

Hiding a shudder similar to the one he saw pass through her, Grant spoke again. "Good night. Sleep well."

It took all of his willpower—every last ounce of it—to leave her there and keep walking.

In the back of his mind, he was sure she wanted to call him back.

Fighting the impulse to shout for him to return, Paxton watched Grant go, believing the sincerity in his voice when he'd said all those things about her not being alone. Instincts seldom led her astray and were telling her now that Grant Wade would have capitulated about the property if he had been able to. Something held him back, some part of the deal he'd made with her father that hadn't been made public or available to her. Besides the mess she had found herself in, it seemed there were more secrets to uncover.

"Is it gold?" she mused. "The grand reopening of Desperado?"

If either of those things governed his deal with her dad, why hadn't Grant just come out and mentioned it? They both stood to gain from public access to the old ghost town. Land value surrounding a viable business would make her property worth more. And if that were the case, maybe Grant would make enough money to eventually buy her out—if, in fact, he was short on funds at this point.

That had to be the sticking point here, right? Money? Otherwise, owning everything would be of benefit to him. Truthfully, she didn't give a damn about his plans for the old place. Right now, she just wanted nothing more than to go home and forget about all of this.

Her cowboy stopped when he reached the truck, and

turned around. He didn't wave. He wore no smile. His only offering was a quick nod in her direction before he climbed into the truck. After that, he sat for some time before starting the engine, as if he might be reluctant to leave.

Did he have more to say?

Did she?

Paxton waited until the truck backed out of the lot, feeling caught up in the treacherous thrill of having been close to Grant Wade for a minute or two. His brief touch had contributed a lot to the current heat spell.

She was burning up, on fire and hog-tied until she got what she wanted.

Behind her, inside the room, the air conditioner waited for her to punch the button. Overhead, the small neon sign buzzed. Moonlight flowed across the desert in the distance, unbroken by barriers and buildings, having risen above the mountain range.

She remembered damp skin and unrequited longings, as if those feelings had merely been temporarily buried somewhere. Rushing back to her were more remembrances of heat, wind and moonlight, along with memories of running through the brush howling like a coyote and pretending to be one of them.

Paxton closed her eyes.

Somewhere near those distant mountains the buildings of a decrepit town nestled. The place had been legit once, a real mining hub that had fallen on hard times when the mines were tapped out. In the forties, movies had been made there with bronco-riding cowboy stars. At present, who knew what kind of shape the place was in? Twenty years had passed since she played on those dirt streets, and the buildings had been older than shit then.

The truck had disappeared. Only the hum of neon was left in a quiet night. Paxton wanted to raise her face to the night sky in search of a nonexistent breeze, and experienced a sudden feeling of abandonment that was both odd and absurd since she had just met Grant Wade.

"If you're hiding something that affects this decision, I need to know what it is," Paxton whispered. "I won't care. I swear I won't care. I just need the truth."

Her mind turned toward a darker theory.

Knowing she'd be going to see Desperado in the morning, had Grant set out tonight to clear up whatever he was hiding? There was plenty of time between now and sunrise for him to accomplish whatever he had in mind. Hide things. Keep his secrets from her.

Backing into the room, Paxton closed the door and stripped to her underwear. She pressed the button on the air conditioner and waited impatiently for the machine to kick on. Cool air felt good on her hot, bare skin. So good, she almost discarded the plan she was formulating.

Almost.

Chapter 6

Grant pulled over a block from the motel, let the truck idle and sat awhile in thought. Should he go back? Forget that last look on Paxton's face and move on?

She might not have realized how good his eyesight and hearing were. He now figured that she suspected money was a deciding factor in his holding out on a sale. She didn't trust him. Her wary expression made that obvious. But how far would she go to get what she wanted? "You won't do anything crazy?" he muttered, hoping he was right.

Though there had been a glint of wildness in her eyes when their gazes connected, Paxton didn't seem the type to blatantly ignore his warnings about a visit to Desperado being ill-advised. Still, the look she had leveled at him from the motel balcony left him unsure about how far her defiance might take her.

"Pain in the ass is right," he mumbled.

What an idiot he was, Grant decided, for worrying about the woman when there was a more important situation at hand that required his full attention. His pack would be hunting the rogue tonight, hoping to find where the bastard hung out, and he needed to be with them.

Turning the wheel, he put the truck in gear and stepped on the gas, heading for home. When the last of the city lights finally dimmed behind him, Grant breathed easier. Out here, in the open, he was more at ease. Far from the city, he and his pack were free to be what they were, and that kind of freedom was rare for his kind.

"Did you really think I'd open Desperado to the public, Paxton Hall?" he muttered, as if she still sat beside him.

Reopening the town was about as feasible as getting down and dirty with Paxton tonight in that motel room would have been. As for any other bright ideas, the only one pestering him at the moment was his desire to run his hands over Paxton's incredibly soft blond hair.

"No secret there."

Enough desert fragrances came through the open window to dislodge the scent that had taken root in his lungs. Paxton's alluring, woodsy sent. It was no joke that his thoughts kept returning to her. She also was part wolf, and he had never met anyone quite like her. Nevertheless, Paxton couldn't be allowed to see behind Desperado's walls unless she was a fully formed she-wolf in on the secrets of his kind.

"Will your first shape-shift happen here, Paxton Hall?"

What would she think about the fact that behind Desperado's facade lay cages, ropes, chains and other devices used for aiding the transition from human to Other without hurting the Were or anyone else? And that when he found creatures in need, he brought them here to help them avoid the trauma of becoming a werewolf in a human world?

This is what he did and what he was needed for.

"Somebody has to do it," he said aloud before realizing he was again speaking to the absent Paxton. Grant supposed he was, in a way, apologizing for the uniqueness of her father's will and how it had affected her.

"Like it or not, I have to watch over you now that your father sent you to me."

Maybe one of those cages would have her name on it if she sought answers so close to the full moon. Possibly Paxton was here for a reason altogether different than she assumed.

But having Paxton and a dangerous trespasser here at the same time was bad news any way he looked at it. And if, without knowing it, Paxton had arrived in time to set her wolf free, and Andrew Hall had sent her, then he owed her father another round of respect for executing that plan so perfectly.

Pushing the truck to eighty on the open road, Grant voiced one more thought before vowing to shut his mind down. He spoke a final word to Paxton through clenched teeth.

"I'll be here for you, no matter what you think of me."

And then, hearing the echoing report of gunshots, he jammed on the brakes.

Minutes had gone by since Grant had left her, and as luck would have it, the proprietor of the motel had a car to rent. It was an old station wagon, the likes of which Paxton had only seen on late-night TV.

Dressed in an old T-shirt and jeans, she plugged into her cell's GPS and drove along the highway for several miles before turning off on a smaller, unsigned road where she lost sight of other cars. Desperado wasn't in her GPS app, but the ranch next to it was. If she was careful, she might avoid Grant Wade's current residence and find Desperado on her own, though darkness might make locating the entrance to the town difficult.

Her goal, though, was to spy on Mr. Grant Wade.

The back of her neck tingled as she drove over ruts in the road. Thoughts of how many rattlesnakes existed per square yard of desert sand would have made anyone shudder, but she didn't plan to get out of the car. All she wanted was one look at the town from the front gate leading to it, to see if there were lights. She had to know if Desperado was as vacant as it was supposed to be, and if Grant had nothing to hide.

Honest to God, she hoped Grant had been straight with her. He seemed like a good guy. She got no bad vibes from him, just the odd sense that he was keeping something to himself. Some secrets were okay. She didn't need to access his life, just his plans for Desperado.

Paxton blew out the breath she'd been holding. She couldn't stop thinking about Grant. Only a fool wouldn't have envisioned what life with a man like that could be like, and she was no fool… usually…except for maybe right now, as she drove on a dark road in the middle of nowhere just to prove a point.

Men weren't always accommodating or trustworthy. She knew that firsthand. So it was important she made sure the man her father had left Desperado to had nothing to hide and therefore might be coerced into either selling his inheritance or buying her out. The key word here was *selling.*

Wondering if all these thoughts about Grant were truly rooted in business, she pounded the wheel with both hands. After meeting him, she was no longer sure. Still, plan B was to go after that sale tomorrow and then go home.

"Too damn dark," she said aloud to ease the discomfort of being alone so far from civilization. The road made the going slow at twenty miles per hour. It had to have been ten minutes since she passed another car, and so far, she saw no twinkle of distant lights.

She'd traveled fifteen miles from the motel Grant had put her in, and damn it, Desperado was out here somewhere. In the old days there had been signs leading to it and paper maps that an ancient tourist attraction might have been noted on. Current technology wasn't always so hot for things that had fallen off the radar.

Her phone, on the seat beside her, beeped, giving her a start. Paxton stopped the car and found that her battery was getting low. She sat there a couple of minutes more, trying to get her bearings and breathing in the delicious desert smells she had never really forgotten.

Reaching again for the gearshift, she hesitated, listening, hearing a noise that hadn't come from inside the car.

Rustling brush? Desert animal?

She jolted upright as a terrible thud came from the roof of the car, sounding as if something heavy had landed there.

Her muscles seized. White-hot streaks of adrenaline shot through Paxton as her pulse began to pound with a new, raw kind of fear.

She cried out when another thud came, this one from the hood of the car, and again when something dark and shapeless peered at her through the front window.

Fear froze her in place. Her frantic mind worked to dig up an explanation for what that dark thing could be, and what was going on. Hell, was it a bear?

She was shaking so hard, the keys in the ignition rattled. Her heart exploded with wild, erratic beats she felt in her throat.

Damn it. Did Arizona even have bears?

Breathing became difficult. Each new effort she made to take in air only partially sufficed. No scream would come now. Paxton thought she might pass out. The thing on the hood had its big eyes trained on her, and those eyes looked nothing like a bear's. Those eyes looked sort of...human.

And then, as if she had merely blinked this beast away, it was gone, leaving behind a loaded silence filled only by Paxton's racing heartbeats as she sat there, unable to move.

Eventually, a survival instinct nudged her to get going and hightail it out of there before that awful thing came back. Finding Desperado in the dark now seemed like a ludicrous idea. What had she been thinking?

What was that thing that had landed on the hood?

Slowly, with adrenaline continuing to push her, feeling returned to her body. Enough of her focus returned for Paxton to acknowledge that although she had been born in this desert, she'd long since become citified.

She didn't like that realization. Didn't like feeling weak or vulnerable.

Her thoughts fluttered in much the same way her heart did.

In Hollywood horror movies, she recalled, the chick

in this situation would have opened the door and stepped out of the car to see if there'd been damage to the roof and hood. That would have been a *duh* moment because, in the movies, monsters always returned to finish off their prey.

She didn't intend to become a bear's next meal. Swallowing the fear that clung to her like an unwelcome guest, Paxton shoved the car into Reverse. Backing onto the dirt lining the narrow stretch of road, she two-fisted the wheel into a U-turn without looking back.

Icy licks of fear chased away any thoughts she might have had about Desperado and Grant Wade. At the moment, she needed light. She needed people. Dents in the car were nothing when compared to the perks of civilization. She doubted that even a bear that had built up an appetite for humans could outrun an old station wagon.

At least, she hoped not.

Chapter 7

Grant drove the last stretch of road leading to the ranch like a NASCAR driver. Relief came when he turned into the driveway between two large posts still supporting the Hall sign—a reminder that this ranch was part of Paxton's legacy.

The house itself was dark, but one outdoor light illuminated a portion of the yard leading to the front porch. Another light flooded an area beside the barn, showing him that he wasn't alone. The black sedan parked there was Shirleen's.

Before he stepped out of the truck, she was beside him, utilizing the kind of speed built into most Weres. Shirleen still wore her apron, which told Grant she'd been in a hurry to get here from work.

"It's back," she said with a hand on the truck's door frame.

"Back?"

"I tried to tell you in the café, but you were busy," she said.

"Tell me what, exactly?"

"That rogue bastard's trail was found this afternoon in the hills."

Grant knew that none of his pack would have fired the shots he had heard, which meant the ranchers were already onboard tonight, just as he'd feared.

"What kind of trail was found?" he asked.

"An old campfire. I don't want to tell you what else was in that fire."

"Bones," Grant guessed, praying he was wrong.

"Yep. Bones," Shirleen replied.

"Cattle?"

Shirleen's face tensed. "Human."

Grant was out of the truck before the meaning of that word fully sank in. He didn't have to ask Shirleen to repeat what she'd said, or quiz her. She wouldn't have said it if she wasn't sure.

Part Native American, she'd been born and raised just twenty miles from Desperado, and she was their resident expert when it came to finding things in these hills. Being bitten by a werewolf in her eighteenth year had sent her Grant's way just twelve months ago. What had been bad luck for her turned out to be the welcome addition of an expert tracker to this pack.

"How old is that campfire?" he asked, heading for the house with Shirleen in his wake.

"A month at least. We had missed it because the sucker used an old mine shaft and then sealed it up afterward."

Over his shoulder, Grant said, "Those bones. Do you recall hearing about any disappearances? Has there been any mention of missing people at the café?"

Besides waitressing to pay the bills, Shirleen's job at the café was to gather information that might be important to the pack. Like a missing hiker or two, the theft of horses or more about missing cattle. Lots of conversation went on in that diner, which was a hangout for regulars and local law enforcement. Waitresses weren't usually given much notice during discussions like that.

"No disappearances were mentioned," Shirleen said.

"Hell." Grant headed for a box of battery-operated lanterns kept stored at the ranch in case Desperado's streets needed illumination after dark. "We don't have time to pursue that beast tonight. The priority is to shore up Desperado."

"Why?"

"Andrew Hall's daughter wants to see the place."

Shirleen leaned against a wall with her arms crossed over her chest. "That's the girl you were with?"

Paxton Hall is anything but a girl, Grant thought, remembering the sexy paleness of her skin. He kept that to himself.

"One and the same," he said.

"Of course, she doesn't know anything that goes on here? Right?" Shirleen pressed.

Grant gave her a wry look in response to that question.

She said, "There aren't any new Weres coming in, so the cages will be empty when the full moon rolls around tomorrow night. There haven't been any newbies for a few months now."

Grant turned from the box of lanterns. "Yes, and all of a sudden I'm wondering why there haven't been any newcomers needing our unique kind of hospitality."

Shirleen pushed off the wall. "You don't think…"

"It's a viable theory, right? That rogue might be way-laying Weres before they can reach us."

"You're suggesting this rogue might be eating a werewolf or two for supper, as well as cattle, and that's why the bones in that campfire belong to a human? Because a Were's bones would look human if it wasn't furred-up at the time of its death?" A look of utter disgust crossed Shirleen's face.

"Either that, or our elusive bastard nabbed a hiker. I guess the bones will tell us if I'm right, if the right person looks at them. Did you move those bones?"

"Ben took them."

"Good. Ben should be able confirm if my suspicions are viable. It's handy to have a vet around."

"What are you going to do, boss?"

Grant eyed Shirleen thoughtfully. "I'll have to see to it that Hall's daughter doesn't stay too long or get too nosy."

"I meant about tonight and cleaning up the town."

Grant's gaze moved to the truck, and he wished he could avoid Shirleen's question. Strange sensations ruffled inside his chest. He'd felt this same kind of sensation only once before, and that was the first time he'd seen Paxton Hall.

What did those strange sensations mean now?

Hell. Could Paxton be in trouble?

Handing the box to Shirleen, Grant strode to the door. "Take these to Desperado for me. I'll be there as soon as I can. Make sure things are closed up tight. Guard the place."

He had smelled trouble the minute his boots hit the dirt. Trouble resonated in his bones, and he knew why. Christ, yes. He knew why.

Paxton Hall's connection to him was strong enough

to enable him to almost see her. That's the way wolf to wolf communication went. Because of their attraction, a special bond had been forged. They seemed to be linked together by invisible chains that were proving to be stronger than the usual male-female kind of animal attraction. How else could he know what Paxton was feeling right that minute?

Bonds. Wolf to wolf chains binding us together...

Grant now began to fear he might have inadvertently imprinted with Paxton, settling into place an attachment that couldn't be broken by either party, no matter how hard they might try. Imprinting brought a whole new meaning to the phrase *until death do us part* and upped the degree of attraction to full-on hunger. Mental and carnal hunger.

He hungered for her that minute.

Damn it all to hell, he wanted to shout. Through that connection to her, he knew that Paxton had not stayed at the motel. Contrary to his warnings, she was out there somewhere in the dark, along with a madman, a bad wolf with a taste for cattle, humans and maybe other Weres. A beast that hunted for sport and ate its prey.

Deep in his mind, the sound of Paxton's startled cry echoed. His heart began to race, as if matching hers, beat for thrashing beat.

"Okay," Shirleen called out as Grant jumped into his truck. "We'll take care of things here."

With blood pounding in his ears and the back of his neck chilling up, Grant was beyond caring about Desperado. He had to get to her. To Paxton. That's the way imprinting worked. There was no other option. No way to avoid her call.

With his boot to the pedal and his lips moving with

a litany of unuttered curses, Grant headed at breakneck speed back toward the city.

Paxton hit the highway with relief and with her heart hammering. Her knuckles were white from her grip on the steering wheel, and she kept repeating out loud how sorry she was that she had left the motel.

Though the highway was pretty much deserted, two cars heading in the opposite direction passed, and Paxton was finally able to take a deep breath. Cars meant the city wasn't far off. But as their headlight beams bounced off the sizable dent in the hood of the station wagon, she rang up the cost of the repairs she was going to have to pay for. Worse yet, she'd have to try to explain what had caused it.

She had to be right about the bear.

Skin tingling with remnants of leftover adrenaline, Paxton kept her attention glued to the road as the speedometer inched upward. Lightheaded from lack of sleep and from being scared half out of her wits, she spoke again out loud to cover the sound of her heartbeats.

"If I didn't actually want to think more of you, I might start to believe you set this up on purpose, *Dad*. So, what's this deal you made with Grant Wade going to turn out to be?"

When a voice replied to her question, she nearly spun the car off the road. But the voice was inside her mind, and likely a remembered thought in one word. *Stay.*

Grant Wade had asked her to stay. Given that he might be hiding something from her, why would he have then issued an invitation to go there tomorrow and then advised her not to visit Desperado?

"Which is it, Wade? Stay or go?"

Her fear was just beginning to evaporate when she

noticed a set of headlights behind her, closing in fast. Turning the wheel, Paxton hugged the right side of the road to allow the car to pass. Instead of doing so, it pulled up alongside and stayed there long enough for her to get a clear picture of the man inside that blue truck.

Grant.

Satisfied that she'd seen him, he backed off the pedal. The truck pulled in behind her, as if the man driving it knew what she had been through and was extending his job description to encompass the term *bodyguard*.

Swear to God though, Paxton was glad to see him.

The café where they'd shared their late-afternoon meal was the first building she saw. She pulled into the lot and turned off the engine. Grant was beside her in a flash and opening the door. Concern darkened his handsome face as he leaned in.

"What happened?"

"Bear. I think a bear jumped on the car."

He hadn't looked at the dent in the hood or the one that had to be on the roof. Grant Wade's focus was on her.

"Are you okay?" he asked.

Paxton heaved a sigh. Having this man here with her made her feel safe. She didn't recall ever having felt completely safe before.

"I'm fine," she lied, not quite sure her legs would hold her up if she got out of the car. "Just scared."

"Coffee?" he suggested.

"So you can scold me in public for driving into the desert?"

"You're not a kid, Paxton. You could have been hurt."

She nodded, in full agreement with that last part.

"Coffee?" Grant repeated. "Or something stronger?"

She offered him a weak smile, still gripping the

wheel. Seeming to read her tension, Grant reached in to unlock her grip. He helped her out of the car and to her feet, his touch providing the same kind of charge she had experienced earlier.

She supposed she was a sucker for feeling anything at all for this tall stranger, and countered those thoughts by telling herself he merely made her feel silly about going out there.

"Come on." His tone was gentle but firm.

When Paxton didn't immediately start walking, he pulled her closer to him with a snap of one arm. Their chests met. Their hips met. Grant didn't appear to think this was awkward, when, for her, their two bodies meeting in a parking lot where other people might be around seemed almost obscene.

Truly, Grant Wade—solid, somber and handsome in the extreme—was likely every bit as dangerous as that damn bear. His hold on her was light, yet supportive. His pulse was pounding as hard as hers. And he was every bit the solid he-man male she'd imagined he would be.

Was he going to kiss her? She knew he was thinking about it.

Would she allow such a thing?

With cars coming and going from the parking lot around them, Grant acted like they were the only two people here. She was in his arms and couldn't shake herself free. Hell, she didn't even try.

Her cowboy's eyes didn't meet her questioning gaze. Nor did his mouth come anywhere close to hers. He continued to steady her quaking limbs...and she was a sap for thinking he might have had other plans.

"You think you saw a bear?" he asked, reminding her of what she'd said.

She nodded. "Yes. Big, dark and like nothing I've ever seen."

"It got that close?"

There was no way to miss the trepidation and concern in his voice. Each word he spoke made his chest rumble. However, Paxton couldn't figure out why he was so concerned about her when her father's will stated that if anything were to happen to her, the land she'd been left would go to guess who, along with Desperado.

"It looked at me through the windshield before taking off, and nearly wrecked the car," she explained.

Grant's hold on her loosened. She didn't ask him to wait another minute before letting her go. Didn't confess to needing his strength a while longer. What right did she have to expect anyone to save her from her own stupidity?

"I shouldn't have tried to follow you," she admitted.

His voice lowered. "It was a regrettable move, but not entirely unanticipated."

Had he read her so easily, then?

Maybe that's why he had found her out there on the road. He had expected her to act like an idiot. Expected her to spy on him.

"Do you know about the bear?" she asked.

"I haven't heard of one, but we'll be on the lookout after this."

"Then why did you advise me not to go out to Desperado on my own, if not because of that bear?"

"The desert can be a dangerous place for other reasons."

"Such as?"

"Snakes." He hesitated before adding, "Wolves."

"The threat of snakes and wolves is what made you warn me off?"

"In part."

"There are more parts?" Paxton got the fact that Grant Wade didn't appreciate being questioned when she was the one who had been caught in an unfortunate act of defiance.

Just one more question, she told herself.

"Were you driving back to town? That's why you saw me?"

He returned a question for a question. "You're sure it was a bear you saw?"

She pointed at the car. "What else could it have been? No wolf or coyote I've ever heard of is that big."

Paxton was sure that having coffee while sitting across from Grant in a lighted café was not going to make her feel better about that dent in the hood. In fact, she felt foolish any way she looked at tonight's events... and that made her angry.

"I'm all right," she repeated. "I should probably get back to the motel and face the fire about this accident."

"I'll follow you," he suggested. "I can talk to Dev, the manager of the motel, about the car."

"My insurance might cover the damage, if anyone were to believe how it happened."

Her self-appointed cowboy bodyguard smiled weakly and said, "I'll take care of it."

He hadn't let her go and seemed as reluctant as she was for him to do so. And, okay, she had to admit that having his arms around her was nice. But she also got the feeling Grant was waiting for something. What? An invitation for that kiss?

Stupid girl. How inappropriate would that have been? How absurd was it to wait for a kiss that was not going to happen, in light of them still being strangers on the opposing sides of an upcoming round of litigation?

The thought had barely receded when Grant Wade rested his mouth on hers.

Chapter 8

It wasn't the smartest move, Grant knew. In fact, kissing Paxton was the polar opposite of smart. He just could not help himself.

The kiss was meant to be a further comfort for her, but didn't turn out that way. Desire to devour the woman in his arms filled him the second his lips touched hers.

She was soft, and tasted good. He held her lithe body to his, thinking it might have been a fluke that she kissed him back. A kind of stunned reaction. Whatever the reason, Paxton, at least for the moment, accepted the pressure of his mouth as if she also had been waiting for this moment to arrive. As if it had been merely a matter of time before this happened, given their attraction to each other.

Possibly she needed an outlet for getting rid of her recent fear. Maybe he kissed her for the same reason, or because of the growing suspicion that his desire for her wasn't normal. This wasn't how strangers behaved. Something else had to be driving them together.

The kiss deepened. He couldn't seem to get enough of her and didn't want to stop. Distant thoughts nagged about being needed elsewhere, but Grant shook those warnings off in favor of exploring his ardent desire to possess Paxton Hall.

In that moment, he felt exactly like the animal he was. As his lips moved over Paxton's, his sense of connection to her doubled. Flames of greed licked at his insides, piling higher and higher with each passing stroke of his palms over the fine bones of her spine. She didn't struggle to be free or pound him with her fists. Her mouth was pliable, plush and accepting. If she had offered any hint of wanting to get away, he would have backed off.

That's what he told himself, anyway.

Enough, his mind cautioned after more seconds slipped by. But he didn't want to listen. He took hold of her shirt, intending to tear it from her body without giving a damn about who might be looking. The sheer force of that thought made him draw back.

Paxton's breath came in rasps. Her face was extremely pale beneath the glare of the café's lights. As their gazes locked and his body continued to harden in all the wrong places, Grant knew for certain he was in real trouble where Paxton Hall was concerned, and that his wolfish impulses were the instigators of those feelings.

She stood there, looking at him.

He wasn't sure what to say.

The quick fix for this problem was to drive away and leave her there, as he should have done in order to regain his wits. But he did have to get her back to the motel. See her safely there.

Taking her hand in his, Grant led her to his truck in what amounted to a race against time. Sooner or later they would come to their senses about this connection and be able to manage the passions accompanying it. He preferred that to be later, because what he intended to do to and with Paxton was going to take some time.

Paxton's curious expression told him she wasn't going to stop this madness, either. Not yet, anyway. Whatever was taking place between them was seriously spiraling out of control. Not just for him, but for both of them.

She climbed into the truck when he opened the door. Grant was already mulling over the added difficulty of getting her out of the jeans she now wore.

All women should wear skirts, he thought. *Black silk, preferably.*

His passenger sat silently as he drove, her focus glued to the windshield. She was all legs—long, slim legs encased in dark blue denim. Her shirt was tight enough to show off curves he wouldn't have anticipated, given the leanness of her overall silhouette.

She didn't know what do with her hands, so they fluttered in much the same way his insides were fluttering, as she tried to rest them in her lap.

Are you pondering what might happen when we reach the motel?

Why didn't she look at him?

Grant's body and mind were at war with each other over those rampant desires. Emotions usually reserved for after a shape-shift were hitting him hard. Each of his fingertips stung as if his claws were going to make an unexpected appearance…all because of his sudden need for the woman across from him.

Back off, Grant said to his inner wolf.

Keep cool.

Neither he nor Paxton said anything, because what was there to say when she was in the dark about so many things? Strangers had a certain level of anonymity where one-night stands were concerned, she might have been thinking. But they'd have to deal with each other tomorrow.

Will you pack up and go away if we hit that bed together, Paxton? Will shame taint our business dealings after a night in the sack?

She might give up, he supposed, and give in, if shame played a part in a day-after scenario.

He had vowed to stay away from her for so many reasons, and look how that had turned out. The last of his willpower was fleeing because of a woman he'd just met.

All right, he wanted to say to Paxton. *You can have it all, and to hell with your dad.*

Of course, there was no way he could let Desperado go. Not now. Not ever. As alpha, he had responsibilities that lay beyond Paxton Hall, responsibilities to his pack and any other werewolf looking for help and direction.

How could he tell Paxton how easy it was for him to read her, or how much he shared her discomfort over this whole ordeal?

Pulling into the motel's parking lot, Grant figured he could change the outcome here. He could drop Paxton off and say good-night. He was close to promising himself to do exactly that, in spite of his urges. Maybe, though, he should walk her to the door. Make sure she got safely inside.

She was out of the truck before he could get around it and coming straight at him. Grant thought she might finally raise a hand and slap him for that kiss. But she didn't.

Stopping a few feet away from him, she stared. Seconds later, as though pulled by forces beyond her control, her body impacted with his.

So much for vows...

She was in his arms and looking up at him. There was only one thing to do in reaction to that.

Their mouths joined in a kiss that was hungry, angry, deep, and a heady surprise in a growing list of surprises. Touching Paxton's hot, damp tongue with his was a torment. She nipped at him like an animal with its desire unleashed, as though her wolf was already partially in control of her actions. As if the longings of man and woman, wolf and she-wolf, had joined up, making lust a priority that could not be ignored.

Her breath, in his mouth, was hot. Her skin felt hotter. Was he supposed to brush this off and leave? Put a stop to it?

Was there actually a way to do that?

They wouldn't get anywhere in the parking lot. Pulling back to catch a breath, Grant again took Paxton's hand and made for the stairs, still vowing not to let the strength of his insatiable ardor take the lead. He didn't kick in the door to her room but waited for her to open it with the key she had taken from a pocket.

Then they were inside. Two consenting adults who weren't quite human, although one of them hadn't realized that yet.

Maybe he could do this. Possibly Paxton's wolf wouldn't respond to his wolf, and it would be all right to indulge in some mind-blowing sex. She'd go away tomorrow and the chains he feared would go with her.

Telling himself that was a lie, of course, and Grant knew it.

He unbuttoned his shirt quickly, studying Paxton for any sign that she was going to change her mind. When she removed her T-shirt, silky blond hair brushed the tops of her shoulders, sending him a drift of that fragrant, woodsy perfume.

She stood by the window in her jeans and a filmy lace bra that would be no barrier whatsoever to the deliciousness beneath it. He could have looked at her like this forever, staring, thankful, ravenous. His body pulsed with longing. His temperature spiked dramatically. His inner wolf, caught up in these new emotions, wanted to get in on the fun.

Without knowing how he got there, he had Paxton on the bed, on her back, and was leaning over her with his hands on the mattress. Her face was serious, sober. She was quiet.

Kissing her again, briefly, teasingly, he drew in her breath and played with her lower lip, backing off seconds later to look into her eyes. The corners of her lips quirked to show him she was on board. Her scent already saturated his face and his skin with she-wolf pheromones that were exotic and intoxicating.

Paxton was gloriously beautiful, and also so very small when pitted against the sheer force of his desire for her. Having her for himself had become necessary. Grant felt truly possessive as he got down to the business of removing her shoes. He then rested a hand on her zipper, testing his willpower by waiting out several harsh breaths, counting each tick of passing time through the strong pulses in his neck.

The zipper hummed a siren's tune as it slid downward. There was still time for Paxton to stop this. Once her jeans came off, it would be too late.

All you have to do is whisper one word, Paxton, and I'll be gone.

That word didn't come.

Fragile lace underwear, a deep midnight black, peeked out from behind the zipper, barely covering a taut belly that stretched between sharp-bladed hip bones. Grant stared at those things as if temporarily transfixed until Paxton made an impatient sound that made him glance up.

"What are you?" she asked when their eyes met.

"Hungry," he replied.

Paxton's amber eyes were bright. She wasn't smiling now. He knew she couldn't possibly have seen the wolf lurking behind the man's facade, because she wasn't yet in a position to recognize it. So he waited for her to back up her question.

"I'm not sure what this means," she said.

She was confessing to being as confused as he was about ending up on this bed with a stranger. Grant supposed she thought men were often more lax about casual sex than women were.

"Does it have to mean anything?" he asked.

"I have a feeling it does."

"Yes," he admitted, while knowing Paxton couldn't possibly understand the intricacies of wolf needs, even though her comment showed that she was trying to find a reason for putting herself in this situation. "I have that same feeling."

Her face was smooth and expressionless. "If I think about it, I won't want this to happen," she confessed.

"Should I go?"

She shook her head. "Don't you dare."

Those were the words Grant wanted to hear. Two tugs over Paxton's sleek thighs, and her jeans hit the floor. The next question Grant faced was whether he would take the time to fully undress, or if his rush to have her would win out. He was hard, aching and barely able to suppress a groan. In spite of the things she'd noted, Paxton was willing.

She sat up gracefully, bare except for the insignificant lingerie. Pushing him away, she got to her feet and backed him toward the wall by the door. With shaky fingers, she unbuckled his belt and slid his zipper downward without taking her gaze from his. In those amber eyes, Grant watched a flicker of wildness grow.

Deep inside him, his wolf moved, stirred by his racing pulse. He'd never felt so large, so strong, raw and powerful as he did right that moment. Hell, yes, he wanted this. Wanted her. What he felt for Paxton Hall, the sheer depth of emotion, was a first for him. He'd been with plenty of women. Hell, he was no saint. But he hadn't felt the need to devour or possess any of them.

As much as he hated to believe it, signs all pointed to that damn word he had managed to avoid for all of his life so far. *Imprint.* Because if that were true, and that's what was happening to the two of them, there really would be no escape clause if and when Paxton's wolf finally emerged.

It was far too late to worry about that now. Paxton's hands were on his zipper. Her fair hair curtained the sides of her face, contributing to that hint of wildness. Contained in the gleam of her golden eyes were flames that might have set his soul on fire.

"To hell with it," he whispered, wrapping his arms around her. "Question time is over."

Paxton's breath whooshed out as he took her back to the bed with the kind of speed she should have questioned. As he stretched out beside her, Grant bristled with pleasure. His wolf silently called to hers, but the moon wasn't full tonight, and that fact was in Grant's favor. Man to woman was how this was going down. Paxton couldn't shift without that moon, given that now was the time for her first transformation to happen. He didn't have to worry about intimacy tonight, though tomorrow would be another matter.

Slipping his hand between her thighs, he skimmed the black lace, seeking the soft feminine folds that lay beneath the filmy scrap of fabric. Paxton made another sound…a surprised, breathy, totally sexy sigh.

He stroked her gently with his fingers, studying each reaction she made. Paxton clutched at the covers and arched her back. The light pressure of his fingers on her sex made her reach for him. In an attempt to hold on to whatever pleasure she was experiencing, she dug into him with her nails.

"Go ahead," Grant whispered to her, his voice hoarse with expectation. "Enjoy this. Hell, your father might have planned for things to happen this way."

Paxton's lips parted as if she might challenge his remark. Grant's mouth again found hers, sealing off any argument she might care to make.

Her hands moved, sliding up his neck and into his hair to tug him closer. He didn't need the extra invitation. His hardness, at the moment still tucked inside his jeans, pressed against her hips. She, in turn, writhed on the bed enticingly, seductively, as if she couldn't wait much longer to accept everything he held back.

But sliding his fingers over her arms made him hesitate. What he found there made him balk. Paxton had a birthmark on her left upper arm, a few inches down from her shoulder. Without having to see it up close, Grant knew exactly what that mark meant. Christ, he had one just like it.

Paxton Hall had a moon mark—a special kind of birthmark that would look exactly like an old bite from a full set of wolf teeth. And moon marks were proof of Were heritage that went way back.

What did she assume that mark was? Wouldn't anyone question something like that?

"Do you know?" he asked her with his lips moving over hers, hoping she was too caught up in the same sensations moving through him to understand what he was getting at. "Do you understand what this is, between us?"

Realizing there was no way for Paxton to make sense of those words, and feeling way too wolfish all of a sudden, Grant took the fragile ivory skin beneath her right ear between his teeth and bit down lightly, as if teeth were part of the mating game.

He brought his lips back to hers for more kisses, more connection, more fire, tasting Paxton's heat and allowing the flames she gave off to sink in. Her body moved like liquid sin beneath his. Her mouth was a monstrous delight.

The time had gone for adhering to rules governing wolf behavior. These moments were full and incredibly rich. Here she was. Paxton Hall. A she-wolf in human form. And she was waiting for the very thing he wanted most without realizing it could mean they would never again accept any other partners.

The sting of her nails on his back kept Grant's wolf tethered, so the man could have his fill of the woman beneath him without interference. Faint traces of the scent of blood filled the air. Her nails were going to leave welts.

With his hands on her hips, Grant pressed his body against Paxton's, tight to the spot that would soon open and accept him.

She was ready.

He was ready.

To hell, he wanted to shout, *with everything else.*

As he pressed her into the pillows, Paxton made another sound, one that abruptly brought Grant up from the world of dreams and rapidly fading willpower. It came from deep in her throat. Not a moan, a sigh or an argument against what they were about to do.

No.

Not this time.

Paxton growled.

Chapter 9

Her cowboy drew back as if he'd been slapped. Paxton's eyes flew open. What had happened? What was wrong?

Grant had stopped moving. His eyes bored into hers as if searching out a reason for his sudden reluctance to go through with what they both wanted. His hand was wedged between her legs with his fingers splayed. He was hard as a rock inside those jeans he wore.

The suddenness of his restraint was a shock to her searing, blistered senses. The room seemed to whirl.

"What?" she demanded, her tone rough with leftover anticipation.

"It's nothing," he replied in what was obviously a lie, since his body was still and only his gaze continued to probe.

The interruption in whatever raw passion had brought them together was accompanied by a swift return of Paxton's common sense. In that moment, she began to feel foolish and way too exposed. She was on a bed in a motel room, almost completely naked, with Grant Wade's muscled body hovering over hers.

Had she been hypnotized? Mesmerized? She didn't know this man. Grant Wade was nothing more than a hiccup in her plans, and she had almost lost whatever dignity she'd had in their standoff by being caught like this, with his hand between her legs.

Closing her eyes, she considered how she was going to get out of this situation gracefully and quickly realized there wasn't any way to accomplish that. She pondered how to salvage what was left of her rapidly dissipating self-control. Clearly, something had caused the interruption in their plans to tear into each other, so wishing they hadn't been on this bed in the first place was a total waste of time.

Grant had merely come to his senses before she had. Did he expect a medal for that? Would he hold this little slipup over her tomorrow when paperwork crossed his desk? Embarrassment didn't begin to describe what she was feeling as the man she'd been about to get down and dirty with sat back on his heels. She couldn't meet his eyes, so she concentrated instead on the way his pulse beat softly beneath his right ear.

Cool air flowed over her without Grant's incredible body heat to block it. Swallowing the lump in her throat, Paxton finally glared at him.

"You're right," she said. "This was a bad idea. I applaud your self-control."

Grant shook his head. "I wanted this. Wanted you."

Wanted. Past tense.

"I'm flattered. Really. You're..." Paxton let that remark dangle for several seconds. "Well, you are very strong, and I had a scare out there tonight."

She hated how that statement made it sound as though she had been about to use her body to thank him for being there when she needed somebody. Bodyguard sex.

"Fact is, I'm no good for you right now," Grant said in a low-toned, gravelly voice.

Hardly able to speak after a remark like that, she said, "Thanks for the heads-up," and shoved him away.

Rolling sideways, she edged off the bed and stood. Any attempt to cover herself would have been absurd, so she planted her feet near the air conditioner wearing nothing but her fancy lingerie.

Grant Wade stared at her for a long time before reaching for his shirt. There were, Paxton noticed, only a few buttons left.

Having him stand there with his chest exposed and his six-pack visible made her uneasy all over again. This guy was one of the finest specimens of manhood she had ever seen. She had let that go to her head, and promised herself not to let that kind of lapse happen again.

Seeing him tomorrow was going to be a bitch.

Her cowboy turned from her to retrieve his hat, but didn't leave the room. Did he have more to say? Anything to explain the awkwardness of the situation? Because that might have made her feel better.

"That thing you assumed was a bear. How did you happen to see it?" he asked, foregoing any mention of what had nearly transpired here, just several moments ago.

"That's it? All you want to say to me?" she fired back, sure this was strange timing for a complete switch in subject matter. Yet, because Grant seemed serious, she answered his question.

"I was driving along the dirt road I assumed led to Desperado, and the thing came out of nowhere."

"You thought it was a bear—why?"

"You saw the dents it made in the car."

He nodded. "You mentioned that the animal looked at you."

"Through the windshield."

"Then what did it do?"

"It went away."

"You didn't do anything? It just went away?" he asked.

"The thing was there and gone in several very frightening seconds. I'll admit to panicking and maybe forgetting a few details."

"Did it have a shape?" Grant asked.

Paxton shook her head. "The whole thing happened very fast. Seconds. All I saw was a dark blur."

"So you didn't actually see what this thing was?" he pressed.

"I'm not Sherlock Holmes. I had no desire to stick around and find out exactly what that thing might be. Are you suggesting it might not have been a bear?"

"No. Nothing like that. I'd just like to get the word out for folks out that way to be on the lookout."

Again, she found this conversation odd in terms of timing. On the plus side, however, Grant hadn't chastised her for the spying business or alluded to the fact that she might have gotten what she deserved for flaunting his warnings about going to Desperado on her own after dark.

"Look," she said, glancing to the bed. "We made a mistake, like people do from time to time. Hopefully what happened in this room tonight won't hinder our negotiations."

Grant Wade went to the door and paused with his hand on the knob. Over one broad shoulder, he said, "Are you feeling okay, Paxton?"

She considered shouting, *No. Actually, I'm standing here in my underwear, feeling like an idiot. What do you expect?*

She said with effort, "You've helped to ease the fright that thing gave me. So, thanks."

He waited, as if unsure about how to respond to her remark. Then he nodded and left the room, closing the door softly behind him as though nothing had happened, or almost happened, between them that deserved any kind of explanation.

Paxton's legs gave out the second she heard the door snap shut. Holding on to the air conditioner for support, she parted the curtains and looked out.

When Grant reached the parking lot, he looked up at her with a somber expression on his handsome face that caused a reactionary ripple between the thighs the man had nearly been on intimate terms with. Grant Wade was gorgeous, for sure, and had almost made her forget herself. Throughout history, good-looking guys like this one had ruled what happened on motel mattresses.

It just happened that Grant's willpower had won out tonight in the absurd onset of lust between a couple of strangers destined to oppose each other over her father's will.

"Let that be a lesson about future negotiations," she muttered, feeling slightly unnerved.

Stumbling sideways, she face-planted on the bed, listening to her skyrocketing heartbeat begin to slow down before bouncing back up to make sure the door was locked. After that, she was back at the window, expecting to find Grant still out there, perhaps feeling as foolish as she did. She was unable to explain why the fact that he wasn't in that parking lot left her feeling disappointed.

The truck was gone. He had gone. Only his scent lingered in the room, and Paxton closed her eyes as she breathed it in.

"All right. Okay," she said with finality. "What's done is done."

That truck wasn't going to magically reappear because she wished it would. Nor could she replay what had happened and give it a better outcome. So with her dad's will in mind, Paxton turned her thoughts to more serious possibilities for Grant Wade's behavior and his sudden disappearance.

What if it hadn't been willpower that ended their near-miss lust fest? What if he had been messing with her?

Maybe Grant supposed he could chase her away by combining the fine arts of shame and seduction. Maybe he planned to have sex with her and then talk her into caving on her requests. Kiss her into giving him what he wanted. Corner her into pursuing new negotiations by proving himself the better negotiator.

What if he had somehow planted that bear on the road to Desperado, hoping she would turn around and head back to town?

He had, after all, been out there. He had found her on the road.

Then what? He planned to take advantage of the situation and play at being a white knight for a damsel in distress?

Paxton sagged against the wall. If any of those things

proved to be true, Grant Wade would be a devil in disguise. A monster.

"Unfair tactics hidden behind such a pretty face?" Paxton grumbled as she stared at the empty space where the blue truck had been parked.

"So you know, Mr. Cowboy, I've always been stubborn, so I will take up this challenge and be here in the morning. Just you wait and see. You can't get rid of me that easily."

If Grant had somehow manipulated the whole second half of this long day for his own benefit—the ride in his truck, the meal at the café, chasing her in the desert in the dark, the kiss and what else had almost happened in this room…

"If that's what you think, then you have another thing coming," she declared. "I might not have known my father well, but I carry something of his strength inside me. Enough to get what I want in the end."

Putting a finger to her mouth, to the residual imprint of Grant's talented lips, Paxton was even fairly sure most of that last statement was true.

Chapter 10

Would she stay? Grant wondered as he drove out of the city for a second time that night.

The story about her encounter with a bear bothered him, since there hadn't been bears in the area for as long as he could remember.

No. Paxton had not seen a bear. And she had been extremely lucky to have survived a run-in with whatever kind of creature she had encountered. He knew it had been a beast scary enough for Paxton to have telepathically broadcast her fear.

As far as clues to Paxton's hidden possibilities went, that kind of broadcasting was a big one and more proof of what lay nestled inside her. The fact that he had heard her without her having transitioned was disconcerting, though, as was the growl she had let escape in the damn motel room.

Had he caused that?

He wanted to flat-out refuse to believe those imprinting chains were being fastened to his own ankle by a stranger. Grant thanked his lucky stars he had left Paxton in the nick of time. The growl had to mean that she was responding to his wolf when she wasn't supposed to. Going to bed with her might have made things worse. He'd had to let her go, had to escape from the exotic feel of the heat in that motel room.

Paxton was...

Well, she was...

Hot. In more ways than one.

"A fine mess," he muttered, slinging his hat on the seat so he could rub his forehead. An ache was building there. Each mile he traveled made that ache worse and took him farther from Paxton. Grant slowed the truck.

He turned his head.

Through the open window came a peculiar scent that raised the hair on his arms. Almost instantly, a different, more familiar scent piggybacked on the first one.

He stopped the truck and got out, leaving the engine running and the headlights on as he scanned the surrounding darkness.

"Ben?" he called to the familiar presence.

"I thought you might come this way." His lanky, thirtysomething packmate stepped into the headlights. "I've been waiting."

Grant looked beyond him. "Our rogue is nearby. I can smell him."

Ben nodded. "I tracked him to this point and then the sucker disappeared as if he'd been swallowed by a black hole. The creep isn't afraid of cars, which speaks to the point that he must either be used to them or he's human at least some of the time."

"Where are the others?" Grant asked.

"Half the pack is at Desperado doing the cleanup you requested. The rest of us are taking a look around out here. Our freak should be in human form tonight, right? If it's a shifter we're after?"

"Paxton said he looked like a bear."

"Paxton?"

Grant explained about Andrew Hall's daughter, leaving out the part about Paxton's wolf and the bed in the motel room. He added, "You assessed the bones found near that campfire, Ben?"

"Yes. They're human, as far as I could tell. Male. Young. No sign of that human being a wolf."

"Hell."

"Probably was hell for whoever that poor guy was," Ben agreed. "The bastard we're chasing gnawed on some of those bones."

Disgusted by that news, Grant swore under his breath. "You found bite marks? Teeth imprints can tell a lot about the animal doing the biting, if I'm not mistaken."

"That's the odd thing," Ben replied. "I couldn't tell anything about what kind of creature made those marks. They were more like scrapes of teeth. Long vertical drag lines."

Grant looked up. "Christ, could it have been a bear?"

Ben shrugged. "Have you ever come across one out here?"

"Not personally."

"Me, either. But I tend to think it couldn't have been a bear because of the width of the drag lines. I'm thinking a bear's teeth would have made larger grooves in the bone or ground up those bones."

Grant sidestepped the headlights. "I wonder what we have, then? What that leaves?"

"The Paxton woman said the thing that jumped on her car was big?" Ben asked.

"I saw the dents it made. Not much exaggeration there."

"Wolf?" Ben suggested, steeping closer to Grant.

"Not possible tonight, since our rogue couldn't have been furred-up."

Ben was serious. "Unless this guy is more like you than like the rest of us?"

That suggestion made Grant uneasy. Ben meant it could have been a Were able to shift without a full moon present, making the rogue not just any werewolf, but a full-blooded Lycan version with a long Were lineage. So far, Grant had never heard of another Were this side of the Mississippi, other than himself, able to perform that trick. The possibility couldn't be ruled out, though. And if that was possible, things would be twice as hazardous for everyone involved, including the neighboring ranchers.

"Bad scene, if true?" Ben noted.

"If this guy is a full-blooded Lycan, he would be far stronger than most of our Weres chasing him, and deadly in a showdown with the neighbors."

However, Grant thought, it also might explain what Paxton had encountered out here. Werewolf. Not just any Were, but one with fancy DNA.

"That kind of ability might explain a lot," Ben went on. "Like how it's able to outrun us and why its scent is hard to define. Also of note is that a Lycan can probably hear everything we're saying, even if we whisper. Am I right?"

"Partially right," Grant had to admit. "If he is within close range, yes, he might hear us talking. Otherwise we'd have to channel our thoughts the way we do when we're furred-up and on the move."

"But perhaps," Ben countered, "if this is a special type of Lycan, he can tune into you, Grant, easily avoiding us each time we make a plan to catch him."

Grant didn't utter the oath that came to mind regarding that possibility. He didn't like the sound of this at all. Worse yet, if the rogue they sought could shift without the moon and tune into Grant's thoughts, that beast might know about Paxton being a she-wolf and about Grant's budding feelings for her. Would that mean something to a rogue Lycan? Could hunger be passed along from one Lycan to another over the same silent channels?

Was a she-wolf fair game to all males of the Were species?

"Grant?" Ben said.

Grant turned his head.

Ben said, "I'll follow this road and see what I can find. You do whatever you have to do."

But could he, Grant wondered, in all good conscience, continue to send the pack out if this intruder turned out to be what they now suspected—an unconscionably strong beast with a taste for blood?

"I'll take care," Ben said, reading the worried look on Grant's face.

Grant couldn't demean Ben by mentioning again his doubts about Ben or the others facing off with a monster like that. He threw up a mental block so he wouldn't communicate his sudden fear about Ben potentially being right about what kind of beast they were chasing.

"Okay," he said. "Connect with the others now that we have a good guess as to what might be out here. Let them know."

He wondered again about how Paxton had escaped with her life. Supposing that her encounter had been with such a monster, why weren't they looking for her bones?

The thought made him sick. He wondered if her eyes and the beast's eyes had connected through that thin sheet of glass, and if the beast, a possible rogue Lycan, had let her go for some other ungodly reason, such as the recognition of another wolf.

Grant glanced warily to the west. Across the distance, he felt Paxton thinking about him. She wasn't scared at the moment. For the time being, she was safe in that motel. He found that something of a comfort.

There had to be a new plan. Given that this beast might indeed be a Lycan with special abilities, Paxton would either have to leave Arizona or be taken to Desperado, where she'd be safely surrounded by his pack. No human in this world could stand against such a beast, especially one with a nose for female pheromones.

"Dangerous rogues, whether of special lineage or not, have never dared to set foot or claw in a place governed by other wolves," he said. "There are strict rules about marked pack territories."

Another thought occurred to Grant. He spoke out loud to hear the idea voiced.

"Since Desperado is notorious among many Were communities, possibly that's the reason this werewolf has come, if it is a Were. So why then hasn't he shown himself?"

"I can't even make an educated guess about that," Ben returned, moving into the darkness before calling back, "See you in a few."

"I'm headed to Desperado now," Grant said.

Yes, he had to get going, but he was still torn. Ahead lay the hideout he had created for werewolves, which was also the home of his pack. Behind him was Paxton, who might be in significant danger if that beast on the loose sought a further connection to her. Paxton's moon mark, that white ring on her arm, could mean she was Lycan bait for more Weres than just Grant.

"Damn it. You shouldn't have come here," he said to the woman who was miles away at the moment, feeling right then as though he might be the only thing standing between Paxton and an unforeseeable doom.

Pack.

His pack came first. Had to come first. Paxton Hall wasn't his responsibility. Others depended on him.

Back in the truck, Grant drove, wishing he could join Ben and the others in their search. For now, though, he needed more than ever to make sure Paxton found nothing out of the ordinary at Desperado in the morning.

As for sending her away for her own safety and away from a raging beast…well, that wasn't a viable option. Even if imprinting chains could be stretched, Paxton might have an unexpected surprise the next night. An agonizing surprise that often killed some Weres going through their first transition. There was a slim possibility that since Paxton hadn't shape-shifted in all this time, when that was long overdue, distance from other wolves might postpone her wolf's appearance for a few more years.

Then what?

Who, in her fancy East Coast cities, would help her?

Hell, she couldn't leave here, especially on the day of a full moon, after showing the first sign of her wolf's awareness by issuing that growl. He had to see that she stayed.

"Holy mother of…" he sputtered, wincing as he glanced out the window at the dark desert tableau.

Instinct promised him that postponing Paxton's fate wasn't going to happen. Somehow he sensed that her wolf was about make its debut. Now. Here.

Tomorrow night.

The truth was that both he and Paxton owed Andrew Hall's ghost a swift kick for keeping some secrets too damn well.

Paxton paced back and forth across the worn carpet. Sleep was a nonissue. She felt antsy, like she had downed too many cups of coffee when she hadn't had one. She kept looking out the window at the parking lot.

At ten in the evening the motel was quiet. There were only two cars in that lot. She supposed the lobby lights would be on all night. With her curtains open, those lights vied with the moon's opalescent glow.

She wanted to go out and also wanted to stay where she was. She thought about telling Grant all of the excuses she had come up with for not staying here after their negotiations were over. Closure was what she needed, damn it. Couldn't Grant empathize with how necessary it was for her to end her association with Arizona? It was just like her father to stick it to her again, this time from the grave.

She'd have to wait for Grant to pick her up in order to get to Desperado, since she had ruined the rented car. It was either that or go back on her pledge to remain here and ask her dad's lawyer to turn everything over to the cowboy without having to see him again. Closure, the easy way, seemed an attractive option for about five seconds before the rapid beating in her chest returned at the mere thought of Grant Wade.

Maybe part of her didn't want to put Arizona behind her.

Possibly a cowboy named Grant was the new sticking point.

But he had not believed her about the bear.

So, okay. She had never been weak, and going home was not going to reinforce that. ER nurses couldn't afford to get weak-kneed when it came to facing trouble, and she'd seen her share in three long years in the ER.

Swear to God, she wanted to shout. *Although I don't live in or anywhere near the Wild West, I'm pretty sure I'd know a bear when I saw one.*

Leaning back again, against the wall by the window, fatigue was a real physical strain. Even that couldn't keep her from glancing out the window again.

Everything beneath the balcony was illuminated by moonbeams so bright it was like a searchlight had been centered on this motel. She had never thought much about the moon, and this one made her uneasy. The thing was too big. Too something.

The glass was cool to her touch, due to the humming air conditioner beneath it. The rest of her felt feverish. She blamed the fever on Grant. His kiss had kindled inner fires that his hasty departure hadn't doused.

"Damn cowboys."

Her forehead hit the glass. Nerves jangled. Out of the corner of her eye, she saw movement in the parking lot. The fact that someone was between the two parked cars shouldn't have been of concern since people were free to come and go as they pleased in motels. Yet the blur of movement down there caused a nerve spike that made her want to hide.

Paxton purposefully regulated her breathing. She

was being far too dramatic and allowing her brief encounter with the bear to upset her equilibrium.

I'm better than this. Tougher than this.

Inching sideways, determined to put a stop to her
anxiousness, she peered out again. Finding nothing out
there didn't make her feel any better. Nerves kept firing. Her fingers were clenched. That damn bear and
the fright it had given her had strung out her nervous
system.

A sudden crashing sound made her stiffen, though
everything in the lot looked the same as it had minutes
before. Had someone tried to break into a car? If that
were the case, she expected the motel's manager to take
a closer look. Those cars weren't parked far from the
open lobby door.

Paxton picked up the room phone and hit the key
for the main desk. After several unanswered rings, a
machine picked up. Without listening to the canned information about the motel, Paxton slammed down the
phone and reached for her jeans. She tugged on her shirt
and opened the door, hearing nothing now but normal
distant traffic sounds. No one was in the lot to investigate the noise she'd heard. She noticed no glint of broken glass on the asphalt from a shattered car window.

She cautiously moved across the balcony, looking,
listening, waiting to see if other motel guests had heard
anything. As far as she could tell, no one had.

Taking the stairs slowly, Paxton headed across the
parking lot and toward the lobby, careful to scan for
further signs of trouble. In the doorway, she stopped
abruptly with her hands covering her mouth. The place
looked like it had been ransacked. Like a storm had
blown through. Tables were upturned. Papers littered

the floor. The registration desk had been upended and no motel personnel were present.

When she called out, there was no response. She picked up the desk phone and hit the posted three-digit code for Arizona emergencies.

"Need help," she said breathlessly to whoever had picked up.

Chapter 11

Special lanterns burned along the dirt road leading into Desperado, with small flickering lights that would be invisible to anyone not passing over in a low-flying plane.

Dots of lights in some of the windows of a supposedly abandoned ghost town always produced feelings of wariness in Grant, given that the neighbors had no idea anyone was living there, let alone fourteen werewolves. However, a bit of cleanup was necessary, and that called for light in places the moon couldn't reach.

There hadn't been much to do here these past few months. Shirleen had been right about that. It was damn lucky that no newbies had shown up needing to be locked in.

A few more nails on the doors would make Desperado look the way it had when its gates had closed to tourists twenty years before, and Grant saw that things were already well in hand on that score. He also saw the flaw in all of this, as far as Paxton's thinking would be concerned. What good was an abandoned ghost town that brought in no cash? She'd be wondering why he would be stubborn about either selling or buying her out.

"If you only knew," Grant muttered, parking near the old saloon, where he was greeted by Shirleen and two other packmates holding hammers.

"Nearly done," Shirleen announced. "If no one pokes their noses too far into where they don't belong, we should be fine."

Grant nodded, but his mind was distant. The hairs were rising on his arms again. His cell phone was ringing.

"Yeah, Steffan?" he said, answering.

After listening to the local sheriff's brief message, he stared at the truck, already fishing in his pocket for his keys.

"Break-in at the motel. The manager was missing," he explained to the others.

And this, he realized, was too damn close to being a complete farce when it came to the theory of coincidences. He had to get Paxton out of there.

When he looked up from inside the truck, Shirleen was at the window. "I'll come along," she said.

Grant didn't have time to mull over the benefit of having company. The local sheriff had given him a heads-up and was on his way to the motel. Steffan was a loyal pack member and had sensed the possibility of trouble that lay beyond the scope of other law enforcement officials, given the strange events that had been going on recently in this desert. The pack knew it took a werewolf to deal with a werewolf. In this case, however, if that bastard was as big as the dents on Paxton's car, it might take four or five.

Before he could reply to Shirleen, she was in the passenger seat and speaking. "My talents don't include hammers, so I'm not much use here."

He didn't argue. Chances were that Paxton might respond better to the presence of another female if the motel was no longer safe and they had to relocate her.

Was that the case?

He had to wonder how comfortable Paxton would be as his guest for the night at the ranch where she grew up. Just the two of them under one roof, with the added bonus of a couple of Weres coming and going.

"I'm pretty sure Paxton is going to argue her way out of an invitation after what almost happened in that motel room," he said, not stopping to explain to Shirleen about that motel room. "Steffan said she made the call," he added. Which meant she was all right, for now, and that Steffan would be there in minutes after a call like that.

Tires spun in the dirt as he backed the truck up and turned toward the road. Chills were climbing his spine with a sensation similar to the prelude to shapeshifting. One lone claw popped on the steering wheel, which he quickly reabsorbed as he fixed his attention on the dark stretch of road between Desperado and the highway. He couldn't seem to shake off his nervousness and was stuck in a dangerous loop of thoughts.

"She can stay with me," Shirleen said, eyeing his hands.

"With you and Ben getting down and dirty in the next room?"

That was as close as Grant could get in an attempt to

somewhat lighten the mood and ease his own tension, but no one was fooled.

"I see your point," Shirleen said.

Miles flew by. With Steffan the only lawman on duty tonight, there was no one to slow this truck's speed. Still, it took ten minutes of pushing ninety to reach the motel.

He saw Paxton before getting out of the truck. She was standing beside Steffan, looking wan. Other motel guests were there, too. Families. Maybe six people, in all.

Paxton's gaze found him immediately. Her expression made Grant's previous chills seem like child's play. She wasn't swaying or shaking. Two scares in one night, and Paxton Hall stood her ground, showing grit.

"I like her," Shirleen announced as she got out of the truck. "Don't ask me why."

"So do I," Grant muttered, striding toward the lobby. "So the hell do I."

Paxton didn't rush to meet him. She didn't take a single step. All the same, Grant felt the extent of her relief to see him. She was glad he had come back. Her beautiful face lost some of its tightness as he got closer to her. Lips he had kissed parted slightly, as if she was about to speak.

He stared at her mouth, recalling how those kisses had sent them both over the top in terms of temporarily forgetting their differences. He thought about taking her into his arms now.

When their gazes connected, the same thing happened to him that had happened in the café parking lot. Time seemed to stop. They seemed to be the only two beings at this scene. The only two who mattered.

Surprised by the sensations slamming into him,

Grant hesitated. Paxton was assessing him. Her long lashes hid her eyes only briefly before her amber gaze again met his. Heat replaced his chills. He felt his face grew hot, and also his groin. Although the air he breathed in was fiery with expectation, he could not reach for Paxton. He had to maintain a surface calm so that he wouldn't frighten her further or appear to be taking more liberties.

"Steffan." He greeted the sheriff near the doorway to the lobby, running a hand through his hair to keep from touching the woman who didn't really belong to him.

"Grant," the sheriff returned, holding a pad and a pen he'd been using to take notes.

"Do we need to worry about this?" Grant asked, his eyes still leveled on Paxton.

"The lady heard a noise and came down to find the place in disarray," Steffan said. "Looks like a burglary, except for one thing."

"The manager's missing," Paxton said.

Grant shifted his attention to Steffan. "He's still gone?"

Steffan waved the notepad. "AWOL, as far as anyone can tell."

"That's unusual," Grant noted.

"Highly," Steffan agreed. "I can't let you in there until we determine the extent of the damage."

Grant nodded. "Others are on the way?"

"Yep. Had to call them in."

"Can the lady go, or do you need her?"

"There might be more questions, but Ms. Hall is free to leave, as long as she stays in the area," Steffan said with an unspoken warning about what might have been the cause of this latest disruption.

For show, Steffan added, "I believe Ms. Hall is new

in town and on her own. Do you suppose you can help
with that? Put her in touch with another place to stay,
maybe?"

"I can and will, if Ms. Hall agrees to accept my
help," Grant said.

Paxton was looking at Shirleen now. Grant read the
tinge of jealousy that crossed her mind, and that made
him feel hotter. She had asked about Shirleen in the
café and he'd told her there was no liaison, but here
Shirleen was. It would have been hard to explain to
Paxton about that.

He said, "You remember Shirleen?"

"Yes," Paxton replied. "Help would be appreciated."

"I needed a ride," Shirleen said, explaining to Paxton
about her presence. "Still do. We all can fit in the cab
of Grant's truck, and he can run me home."

Paxton's amber gaze slid back to Grant.

"Might as well come out to the ranch," he suggested.
"It's yours, anyway, according to your father's will. And
it's a long way from motel robberies."

"And bears?" she asked.

"I can't promise anything in regards to the intentions of any bear that might be roaming around these
parts. What I can promise is that you won't see one at
the ranch."

Paxton was quiet before nodding her head. "Will we
be alone there?"

"If that's a problem, I can sleep in the bunkhouse,"
Grant said.

"It's no problem."

"Good."

Shirleen broke in. "I'll go with Miss Hall to her room
to get her things."

Paxton nodded again without moving toward the

stairs. Grant got the impression her legs might not be working properly after everything that had happened to her in a single day. She'd hate it if he tried to carry her, so he took her arm and tugged her away from the door she'd been leaning against. He steadied her when she swayed on her feet.

"Shirleen, can you pack up her things?" he asked.

"Done," Shirleen replied.

"Twenty-two. Second floor." Grant glanced at the balcony. "The door is open."

Paxton didn't protest this arrangement. She didn't try to evade his touch. Although she appeared fairly calm, the fact that her arm shook beneath his fingers told Grant a lot.

The sheriff was inside. The motel's other occupants were heading back to their rooms after assurances that the motel would be watched tonight, and safe. That left Grant alone with Paxton in the small space near the lobby door.

"I'm sorry this happened," he said to her.

"It's not your fault." She was looking at his hand on her arm.

"You'll be safe at the ranch."

"I know."

Grant quirked an eyebrow in question.

"I know you mean well," she elaborated. "And I know you have your reasons for holding out on any deal I might want to make."

"We don't need to talk about that tonight. Let's get you to bed."

She looked up at him.

"All by yourself," he clarified. But the thought of Paxton in bed, in a room at the ranch, made him question the interior quakes that came each time he thought anything about her. Just thinking her name increased his core temperature by several degrees.

Yes, at the ranch, she would be safe from anything outside. He just wasn't sure if she would be safe from him.

The hand on her arm was warm. Grant Wade's grip was firm, supportive and distressing. If she jumped into his arms, only the two of them would see it or care. She could ditch all the reasons for her concerns regarding Grant and the transactions facing them, and get on with a night that promised pure tactile bliss.

Why not?

What was stopping them?

With a glance to the motel, she said, "I'm fairly sure no bear did this."

Grant's expression changed when he heard those words. She had let the world back in when they had somehow been temporarily removed from it.

"Seems likely that you're right," he agreed.

His grip on her didn't ease. He didn't do her the courtesy of looking away or allowing her some breathing room. Paxton felt heat rising to her cheeks.

"I've been nothing but trouble for you since I arrived," she said.

He didn't argue with that statement.

"And you have been kind," she added.

His penetrating gaze made Paxton want to look down to make sure she was fully dressed. He had the ability to strip her emotions and her body down to bareness.

"You have returned twice, believing I need help," she said.

"Don't you?" he countered.

"The truth is that I'm not sure. Weird things seem to

be piling up. Is this city usually so creepy? It feels like I've become a magnet for trouble."

"You'll be protected at the ranch," Grant reiterated, his voice filled with an emotion Paxton thought she could almost read. Further truths had to be examined here, she supposed, and part of that was the fact that Grant was far too sexy for her own good. The other part was about her being a fool for not getting a grip on herself.

"Come on." He turned her toward the truck. "Maybe a good night's rest will help."

Paxton could have ignored the sound of Shirleen's little burp of laughter over that last statement if it hadn't been for Paxton's notation of how quickly the woman had returned from packing up her things.

Startled, feeling slightly sick from mounting fatigue, Paxton checked out Grant's face, thinking he also looked concerned.

"I know how you feel," he said seriously. "Let's get you home."

That was the second to last thing Paxton remembered as she felt consciousness slipping away.

The other thing she remembered was a brief final glimpse of Grant's hand, where, in her disappearing awareness, every one of his fingers sported something that resembled a claw.

Chapter 12

Other images came and went as if Paxton were trapped in a dream sequence. In the dream, she was in the truck, stuffed between two warm bodies, and those people were talking about things Paxton didn't fully understand in a language that seemed foreign to her.

The truck jostled and bumped its way over a rough road. She wondered vaguely if her bear would appear in the headlights or if they were driving in the wrong direction to find it.

Then she was out of the truck and being carried up a short set of stairs. Each breath she took was filled with scents that brought back bits of memory. Wood. Leather. Paint. Dust. Sagebrush. Smells belonging to the West she remembered and that existed nowhere else. Was she a kid again, being carted to bed after a long day? Had a hole in time sent her that far backward?

There was a sudden softness beneath her and the

squeak of bedsprings. Her head fell back against a pillow. Whoever had carried her had laid her down on a bed, and that person hadn't gone away.

Grant Wade.

Reaching up, Paxton took hold of his shirt and held on until his two hands covered hers. The heat in those hands was a further jolt to her senses and served to wake her up.

"You're at the ranch after a rough day," he said, looking down at her. "I'll find you something to eat and then you'll feel better."

"The ranch?" Paxton's mind filled in some of the blanks, but not all of them. "What happened?"

"You lost consciousness," Grant said.

"For the whole drive out here?"

Paxton glanced at the hands covering hers. No claws were in sight. This was Grant, not the bear.

"I'm pretty sure you'll be okay," he said.

"You know that? Because I'm not so sure."

Paxton studied the excruciatingly handsome features of the cowboy she'd nearly been on intimate terms with not all that long ago—the perfect chiseled features, wide brow, intelligent eyes and shiny hair. For once, embarrassment about allowing her gaze to linger didn't enter the picture.

This guy was a freaking white knight, willing to come to her rescue over and over. And though she never would have imagined it, and had been independent all her life, Paxton knew she temporarily needed his kind of help. Then again, maybe she just wanted to believe Grant had her best interests at heart in spite of their business dealings. One human being to another.

"I take care of people for a living," she said. "That's my day job. You're good at the same kind of thing."

He nodded, accepting her compliment.

"A blackout like the one I've just had isn't normal," she said.

"It is for some of us," he returned.

"I have never fainted," Paxton insisted.

Her host, who had been sitting on the edge of the bed, got up. "Let's have a drink before I search for food. I know I could use one."

He looked around the space, then spoke again. "I hope you'll be comfortable here. I believe this might have been your old room."

Paxton followed his gaze to a tall dresser beside the open door. On top of that dresser stood several plastic horses in prancing postures. Her horses. The ones she had placed there over twenty years ago. Surprised, Paxton sat up. Her stomach turned over.

"I guess your father kept some of your things," Grant said.

Was he talking about the same man who hadn't spoken to her in all that time? Never once showed his face or the least bit of concern for her well-being? That was the person Grant was referring to?

"There are other things in the closet," he said. "You might want to have a look tomorrow."

Paxton shook her head, ready to deny that her father could have been sentimental in any way and thinking that it was more likely her father hadn't bothered to clear things out.

"He stayed here? Lived here for years?" she asked.

"Your father? Yes, he resided here until a year before his death."

"How long have you been here?" she asked.

"Five years, mostly in the bunkhouse."

"Why did you come? You were a Ranger."

"Somebody had to watch over things around here. Your father was ill and needed help."

That news was yet another surprise. She hadn't known about an illness.

"How did you meet him?" she asked.

"Andrew reached out to my family for help with this place. Our fathers were old friends."

Paxton said, "I didn't realize he was sick."

"Not many people did. Your father was tough and very private."

"I'm well aware of that last part."

Grant's smile made her chest tighten. Though it wasn't a completely light expression, the smile made his eyes seem even brighter.

"This was an opportunity to give back, to help others. I couldn't refuse. That's why I came," he said.

"You're talking about helping the town's ghosts?"

"No. Not the ghosts."

He left her with that, walking away with calm, easy strides. Paxton wanted to call after him that he was wrong if he meant there were no ghosts around here, because she felt like they were lining up to welcome her back.

But what good would taunting Grant do at this point?

Warily, she stood up, tired beyond what was left of her endurance. Her legs wobbled slightly. She felt light-headed. But she didn't want to be in this bedroom. And she wasn't an invalid.

Walking cautiously into the tile-floored hallway, running her fingertips over the stucco walls, brought more memories of this place back. She knew each dent and ding in those walls, as though she had lived here long past her early years.

The big front room of the house was decorated in a

Western theme. Brown leather couches and chairs sat in a cozy pattern beside the fireplace. Moose antler lamps lit the tables. A thirty-foot ceiling was shored up by rough-hewn log beams. All of this was familiar, too, minus the fact that no artwork hung above the stone fireplace now, and the mantel that had once displayed pricey bronze statues was bare.

Moving toward the front door, Paxton thought briefly about what might have happened to those things and why Grant had kept the same furniture configuration when he could have made the place seem more like his own.

On the porch, she breathed a sigh of relief to be in the open. She welcomed the night's hot, dry breeze and the darkness intensified by the lights at her back. But those same things also brought on more feelings of unease. She no longer belonged here, in this place, on this porch. Her life had taken a different turn.

Grant's blue truck was parked near the steps. In the distance, outbuildings that had once held ranch equipment looked skeletal in the moonlight. She remembered a lot, but not everything. Dark, vague images of the past crowded the outer edges of her memories like the shadows cast by half-forgotten nightmares.

Had problems been highlighted in the moonlight back when she was a kid? She never had figured out what those dark shapes might have been, and trying to pinpoint something so far back in memory was useless.

Another puzzle was the question of how her mother had died and where she was buried. The subject wasn't broached with the couple she had lived with in the East, and had always been taboo.

The top question at this moment, though, was what had trampled the hood of her car.

Her mind was moving too fast for her to catch up, but the ranch did seem darker than she remembered. Probably she was allowing what had happened tonight between her and that damn bear to taint her perceptions. Darkness didn't have to be full of surprises. And although she had assumed her childhood was good while she was experiencing it, running and riding and playing with plastic horses obviously wasn't always indicative of what went on between the people living here.

Grant returned and handed her a glass. "Whiskey," he said. "It could be argued that everyone deserves a drink now and then," he added.

The liquid in the glass sparkled in the light spilling from the windows. Paxton took a sip, relishing the unfamiliar burn as she swallowed.

"Is it as you remembered?" Grant asked, waving at the area beyond the porch.

"Almost, though not entirely," she replied truthfully.

He was waiting for her to explain her remark. Maybe she owed him that for acting as her protector.

"On the surface, things are the same," she elaborated, observing how Grant's lips touched his glass and the way he showed off more bronze skin when he tilted his head back to take a drink.

"How much time did you spend at Desperado as a kid?" he asked.

"Most of my time. When the place was closed to tourists, I imagined it was my town."

He nodded. "Were you ever there after dark?"

"I wasn't allowed out past the barn after dark. Too dangerous for a kid, I suppose."

Grant lifted his glass as if toasting the rightness of that remark.

"Are there horses here?" Paxton turned to look at the barn she had just mentioned.

"No. Not anymore."

"You don't ride?"

"I prefer the speed and comfort of the truck."

Paxton was aware of Grant's attention veering from her. Without his scrutiny, her skin began to cool a few degrees. She was sure she detected a new tenseness in Grant's stance as he checked out something in the distance that she couldn't see. It was obvious he didn't like what he thought he had found.

Call her nuts, but she imagined there was a change in the air. The breeze had grown thicker, cooler. The night, usually filled with the lulling sound of insects, had gone quiet. Listening, staring into the dark, slivers of old nightmares returned to haunt her. Old shapes and shadows. Unusual smells. Warnings by others in the household to stay inside the house after the sun set.

"Maybe you should go inside now," Grant said, as if he had read her mind about those past warnings.

Whatever Grant perceived out there beyond the lights made his voice rumble. Suddenly he was all business and again taking a stance as her protector.

"What is it?" she asked. "What do you see? Could it be the bear?"

Grant stepped in front of her and set his glass on the railing. "I'd really like to keep my promise to you about safety. I can only do that if you're willing to listen."

"What's out there?" Paxton repeated.

"An animal, I think."

All she could think of was the word *bear*.

"Do you have a gun, Grant?"

"I do."

"Is it close by?"

"Close enough," he said.

"If it is the bear, you'll see I was right."

"It can't be allowed to come closer, whatever it is," Grant said to her. Without turning around, he called for Shirleen.

Before Paxton looked over her shoulder, Shirleen was at Grant's side, appearing as suddenly as if the slender young woman had just materialized out of thin air.

"Call Ben," he said. And the woman was gone again.

Paxton blinked slowly, needing to understand what was going on. "You'll go after whatever is out there?"

"Yes, if you'll promise to remain here and stay inside."

"There's no way I'm staying here if you all go after that thing," she protested.

"This is no time to be stubborn, Paxton. An animal like you described could be dangerous."

"Fine. Then you be the one to relent on the issue of me staying put. This is my place, remember? My ranch."

"Are you always this stubborn?" His frustration with her was evident.

"You have no idea," she said soberly.

Grant swore under his breath.

"Ben's on his way," Shirleen announced from the doorway, her cell phone resting on her palm.

"You'll stay with Paxton?" Grant asked, and Shirleen nodded.

So, if Grant had his way, she was to be quarantined on her own ranch with a babysitter. Needless to say, that idea didn't sit so well.

"Maybe you're hard of hearing," she said to Grant.

"And maybe you have a death wish," he returned. "But even if that were the case, I wouldn't want to be responsible."

He backed up, pushing her into the doorway where Shirleen laid a hand on her shoulder. Damn it, she wasn't a kid. If a bear was roaming these parts and scaring the pants off people, she wanted to help find it. She would give that asshole a swift kick for scaring her.

The night sounds had returned, filling her ears with a whoosh and a whisper. Grant's attention hadn't strayed from the barn.

The whisper came again. Paxton heard a voice. But Grant hadn't spoken and neither had Shirleen.

Paxton turned toward the distant hills, struggling to hear past the irregular uptick in her heartbeats. When the voice came again, she heard every word.

"You have returned," said someone who wasn't on the porch with this small group.

Paxton pressed on her ears, trying to discern if she'd made that voice up and if her mind was up to its old tricks.

"Who are you?" she said before realizing that Grant and Shirleen had heard her.

They were both looking at her as if she were one of Desperado's ghosts.

Chapter 13

"Who are you talking to?" Grant asked, confused by Paxton's question.

"No one," she replied soberly. "I sometimes talk to myself."

He didn't press her, but did notice that Paxton had gone a shade or two paler.

"Okay, then." Taking the cell phone from Shirleen, he went to the truck, swung his legs in and slammed the door. Ben was on the line, and Grant didn't want Paxton anywhere near the conversation he anticipated. She was too much of a rebel already.

"Trouble?" he said into the phone before Ben could get in a first word.

"That's a benign way to describe it," Ben said on the other end of the line.

"Where are you?"

"At the gates to the ranch."

"And?"

"That sucker is here somewhere. I'll swear to it," Ben said.

"Yes," Grant agreed. "The wind has changed."

There was, he told himself, no way Paxton could have perceived that subtle change without her wolf in residence. She hadn't yet been able to explore the extra senses that came with being a Were. Hell, she didn't know she was a wolf, so her ashen pallor had nothing to do with sensing the stealthy approach of a rogue.

Ben was quick to respond. "So, maybe you can tell me how it could be here right now, even if this were to be a Lycan we're after? Assuming it's the same creature that hit the motel, miles from here."

"We're only assuming it's Lycan," Grant reminded him.

"And we can also assume it's driving a car?"

Grant didn't like this. If the creature they were chasing was looking for Desperado, why would it have gone to the motel? And why would it have followed them back here to the ranch?

"Doesn't make a whole hell of a lot of sense," Ben said.

Not unless that beast was after another look at Paxton, Grant thought.

"Paxton Hall is here. Shirleen is with her," he said.

Ben's voice lowered. "I can read between the lines of your reasoning, Grant. You're formulating an idea that Paxton has something to do with tonight's revelries?"

Grant tightened his hold on the cell phone and glanced up to make sure Paxton was out of hearing range. She stood on the porch as if anxiously waiting for something. *And when it does appear, you'll get a hell of a surprise*, was what he didn't tell her.

"I can't come up with any other excuse for the sightings," he said into the phone, to Ben. "And I can't let this thing come here. I'm on my way." He tossed the phone onto the seat and started the engine.

Paxton watched him leave. His eyes remained glued to the rearview mirror until the house was out of sight.

Cursing every single rut in the road from the ranch house to the distant gates, Grant half expected the nebulous creature to jump out at him. He actually hoped it would.

Things were in a tangle. Paxton might not be central to this latest round of hide-and-seek with the beast they were after. Cattle had been disappearing for months before she arrived.

It was possible that she had met that creature on the road tonight by accident. Possibly the break-in at the motel had nothing to do with her or anything else monsterish by nature, and was merely coincidence.

When he reached the gate, he saw that Ben stood in the center of the road in a wide stance, a flashlight in his hand. Two other members of the desert pack were with him. All these guys were big, serious and intimidating. No one would have wanted to meet these Weres on a dark road, whether in their human forms or not.

Grant got out of the truck.

"Nothing," Ben said, reporting what the others had told him. "A further search has turned up a big fat nothing."

"Which is, in itself, suspicious," Grant acknowledged, looking from Ben to the other two Weres. "It's here somewhere. I felt the bastard's presence from the front porch."

"Slippery as an eel, is how the saying goes," Ben agreed. "I'm not sure how any Were, if this turns out to be one, could make itself known and then immediately disappear without a trace."

"Not without a trace," Grant corrected, raising his face to sniff the breeze. "He's here, nearby. I can feel it."

"That's just it. We all can," Ben agreed, to nods from the others. "So, do we have a plan to lure that thing into the open?"

Grant didn't like what Ben might have been thinking. That, unknowingly, Paxton could indeed be a key figure in this wicked game of show-and-tell. The image of Paxton, white-faced, in the rearview mirror had stayed with him.

"Not going to involve her," Grant said, putting an end to the unvoiced idea. "She doesn't know what she is and is about to find out the hard way. Piling another shock on top of that could throw her over the edge."

Ben nodded. Every werewolf remembered with horror their first transition to man-wolf.

"Let's call the others and circle the main fence," Grant said. "Leave two or three of the pack at Desperado."

Ben nodded again. Grant was alpha and to be obeyed. As Grant's lieutenant, Ben was already on his phone.

"We circle, then gather to protect the town tonight if the ranch fence is breached," Grant continued. "The ranch house is our priority while Andrew Hall's daughter is in residence."

The other Weres scattered, save for Ben, who closed his phone and had more to say. "You'll stay with her? The Hall girl?"

"Just in case," Grant confirmed.

Ben melted into the night. Alone again, Grant searched the darkness. *"I know you're here,"* he silently sent to the elusive beast. *"We have a good idea about what you are."*

Surprisingly, he got a reply in the form of a thought carried in the now almost nonexistent breeze. Fleeting, distant, but there.

"No," the deep, resonant voice returned. *"You know nothing."*

Grant leaned back against the truck, blown away by the suddenness of the communication, but not much more enlightened than he had been before the bastard decided to speak up. Due to that voice in his mind, however, Grant did know one thing for sure.

That sucker was one of them.

They were chasing a werewolf.

Paxton was rooted to the porch, sensing how much Grant had been worrying about her. She didn't know why, exactly. Grant had told her he had a gun, which would take down a bear if the bear posed a threat to other people in the area. Did he keep the weapon in the truck? He hadn't gone into the house to get it.

"Do you want to go inside?" Shirleen asked.

"No," Paxton replied. "Do you?"

"No," Shirleen admitted.

Turning her head, Paxton took her first good look at the woman standing beside her. Shirleen was exotic. Black hair, long and loose, reached to her waist. She was slender, yet solid, and medium tall. Light brown skin, big brown eyes and the sharp features of some Native Americans made Shirleen a beauty.

Paxton fought off another pesky pang of jealousy. Shirleen was comfortable here, both in and around this ranch, which meant she had known Grant for some time.

"Ben and I live a little farther to the east," Shirleen said. "Ben inherited his father's place."

Paxton nodded, believing she might get a straighter answer from Shirleen than from anyone else.

"Do they think it's a bear out there, Shirleen?"

"Unlikely," Shirleen replied. "Though not entirely out of the realm of reality, I suppose."

"If not a bear, what could it be?"

Shirleen shrugged. "Another kind of animal. Or a man in a bear suit."

Shirleen wasn't smiling when Paxton looked to her again. Paxton considered whether Native American traditions and superstitions might actually make a man dress up in a bear suit. However, she didn't think it prudent to ask questions about Native American religious practices with so much going on.

"He's coming back." After making that announcement, Shirleen focused on a spot in the dark distance.

Paxton moved down one granite step. "How do you know?"

"If you listen carefully, you can hear the truck coming up the road."

Paxton closed her eyes and listened, hoping she wouldn't hear another imaginary voice. Hoping Shirleen was right about the truck.

"Out here, sound carries. There's not much to get in the way," Shirleen explained.

Paxton moved down another step, gazing out with her heart in her throat and realizing that she was anticipating Grant's return far too much. Her anxiousness to see him wasn't merely about information and learning what he might have found out there in the desert. Her need to see him was more than that.

Though she had jokingly called him her bodyguard,

the truth, if she dared to acknowledge it, was that he truly did make her feel safe. She couldn't see anyone besting Grant Wade in a physical fight.

As she waited for him to arrive, she began to sense Shirleen's tension and had to wonder why everyone was on guard.

She had a feeling this ranch and all the people involved with it were embroiled in a mystery that she, as an outsider, wasn't privy to. Years in the ER had sharpened her awareness for puzzling out potential problems, yet she was out of her element here. Did this mystery have to do with her father's will, or Desperado itself? It seemed to her that she wasn't to be trusted with what might be going on.

Grant's truck rumbled into sight at a slower pace than when he had left. Only Paxton's heart sped as Grant parked and got out.

Sober-faced, he spoke first to Shirleen. "Thanks for staying awhile. Ben's expecting you, so I told him I'd send you along."

Only then did Paxton realize how tight her grip on the railing was, and that she had descended all of the steps without noticing.

"No bear?" she heard herself ask.

When Grant's gaze lit on her, the same sense of connection to him she'd experienced before snapped into place. His looks didn't help her ignore the return of the flutter deep inside. Neither did noticing that he moved with the grace of a panther or how corded his tanned forearms were. His shaggy hair was in need of a trim, but somehow suited him. Fact was, she couldn't picture him looking any other way than exactly as he did in that moment.

His expression was one of anger and regret. Though

he hadn't been gone long, he hadn't found the animal he'd gone in search of.

Her heart skipped several beats when his worried state registered. He was avoiding her eyes. Was that because his concern had something to do with her?

She was so tuned in to Grant, and so glad to have him back, she could have sworn she heard him say to the woman beside her, *"Go ahead. You're needed else-where,"* though his lips hadn't moved. But that was just her imagination working overtime. She wasn't psychic; she had no special talent for reading things outside of patient symptoms in the hospital where she worked.

When Grant finally turned his attention to her, she almost took a telling step toward him. Shirleen's depar-ture was silent and Paxton barely noticed it. The night had again gone quiet, as if for the second time in a small span of time, someone had punched the mute button.

Grant stood a few feet away from her. The space between them was alive with a kind of palpable fric-tion, each of them wanting to move toward the other without doing so.

To break the silence, Paxton asked, "What hap-pened?"

Grant's eyes were waiting for hers to find them now. His serious expression projected a fierceness that left her pulse pounding.

"Friends are watching for your bear," he replied.

That information would have been mildly pacifying if she hadn't known he was lying. Either lying or not telling her something vital to her peace of mind. After her brief conversation with Shirleen, the word *bear* had lost its shine as the monstrous opponent she'd met on the dark road to Desperado. So, what kind of animal was as large and as heavy as a bear? That question, posed moments ago to Shirleen, still awaited an answer.

"What's really going on?" she managed to ask, feeling a flush heat her cheeks due to the intensity of Grant's blue-eyed observation.

Grant didn't answer her question. Instead, he closed the distance with three long strides to stand close enough to her to make her look up to see his face.

"We've been hearing things about a trespasser for a few months now," he said. "This might be the same one."

"Man or animal?"

"We're not entirely sure," he replied.

"If it turns out to be a person and not an animal that you're searching for, would that person be dangerous?"

"He's already a danger to livestock in the area. By default, and because we're trying to stop the thievery, we can't rule out the possibility of drawing that freak's anger. That's why it's safe to be on the lookout."

She felt better, knowing this. Felt better thinking that it might be a man, rather than a giant animal. Still, having a human trespasser didn't explain why the man standing in front of her right now believed she might be in danger, personally.

"You're not telling me everything," she asserted.

"No. Not everything," he admitted after taking time to think about his response.

"You believe I might be in danger and won't tell me why? Is that fair? What good can come from keeping me in the dark?"

"I don't want to frighten you," Grant said, and his remark rang true.

"It would only upset me if I had something major to fear. Since I don't know anyone here, except for you and Shirleen, what is there to link me to the danger you seem to be expecting?"

"Nothing concrete. And not just you. This concerns everyone around here. My neighbors aren't happy about the missing livestock and are out there with guns."

Paxton tried to break eye contact. Grant's smile, weak, though still dazzling, kept her from turning away. Even with all the mystery and secrets, she wanted him around. She wanted him, period. She couldn't imagine him being hurt by a livestock rustler and didn't want him to leave her again, for any reason.

Who the hell cared about any outside event when Grant was looking at her the way he was? When her first instinct each time she saw him was to jump his bones?

They were adults. There was no danger in this yard that she could see. So it truly seemed as though they had some unfinished business to attend to and get out of the way, so that she could again think clearly and pave a new path for herself in the days ahead.

Sex was the obstacle to more negotiations. Sex had to be taken off the table so they could get on with things. She had to stop thinking about how much pleasure she'd derive from running her tongue over every inch of his unbelievably honed body. And vice versa.

Paxton looked away.

"What now?" she asked breathlessly.

"This." He placed a finger under her chin to tilt her head back.

Holding her captive with no more than one single finger, and proving himself a talented master in the art of seduction, his mouth did exactly what Paxton wanted it to.

Chapter 14

It didn't matter that she had questions Grant couldn't answer or that now wasn't the time to give in to the impulses overwhelming him. Insatiable hunger ruled the moment, and Grant was all for that.

The woman in his arms kissed him back with the fervor of a female with her wild side taking over. She might be demanding on the outside, but her mind no longer seemed to be revolving around the concept of reason.

Unlike him, she had no idea why she was feeling this way—so hot and so very bothered. She could no more have resisted him than he could have stayed away from her. Their attraction was supernatural in scale. Preternatural. Inescapable.

He kissed her long and deeply, curving her spine backward, holding her tightly. Warnings about voices at the gates and monsters on the loose scattered, burned away by the incredible heat of their embrace.

Paxton's lips were pliant. She was desperate for feeling and had come to the right place. Through the deep, drowning kiss, Grant willed her to believe he had her best interests at heart and that he would be there to help when the moon came for its newest Were acquisition.

Then even those thoughts left him.

The kiss was unending, a true devouring and an example of experiencing the sublime. Ruthlessly, they explored with moving hands, their hips rubbing in all the right places. Mindfulness became a thing of the past, overruled by the blistering heat of Paxton's body pressed to his.

But they were in the open and nowhere near a bed. The ground beside them was hard.

Paxton's eyes held a golden glint when he pulled back far enough to meet them. Her cheeks were flushed a becoming shade of pink.

Grant waited for her to argue that this behavior was one of his tactics for avoiding more of her questions, but in truth, she had asked for the kiss.

Smiling, Grant stroked her right cheek with his fingertips. Without returning the smile, she said simply, "Not my room," and turned toward the steps leading to the house.

Grant stared after her, earlier dilemmas returning to haunt him. In order to protect Paxton, he had to rely on an acute awareness of his surroundings and tune in to the Weres guarding the ranch. In spite of that and the possibility of her future anger, Paxton was expecting him to follow through on the invitation she'd just issued.

Not my room...

Grant's gut twisted. He desperately wanted to follow her up those steps. If he did, the damn beast roaming out there somewhere might tune in and take advantage of the situation.

What the hell had that monster said to taunt him?

"You know nothing."

Paxton walked slowly, using the railing to haul herself to the porch. Her jeans molded to her legs, showing off each luscious curve he'd glimpsed once before.

Her spine flexed fluidly as she climbed. Her shiny blond hair fell to her shoulders in tangles. When she reached the porch, she paused to glance at him over her shoulder. *Are you coming?* her eyes seemed to ask.

Hell, he was already moving, consequences be damned. Only in having her, having one intimate moment with her, would he be able to get on with things, even if it meant piling more trouble on top of the trouble already at hand.

She led him through the main room of the house and down the hallway without stopping at any of the rooms or using the stairs to the upper floor. Grant didn't question this. Her words echoed inside his head.

Not my room...

From the kitchen, she exited through the back door. She led him across the fenced backyard and toward the bunkhouse where he had lived before Andrew Hall died. In the doorway of that rustic building she stopped, turned to him and offered a weary smile.

But she had not changed her mind.

Shoulders rippling, chest on fire from withholding the swift rise of an exquisite kind of passion, Grant moved to the doorway where she stood and put a hand to the wall for support. Inches from Paxton, he breathed in her heady scent while watching her expression alternate between acceptance and defiance, her features changing mercurially, second by second. She knew nothing about

Were imprinting, or the factors behind their almost dizzying attraction, but she was game, nonetheless.

The gentlemanly thing for him to do would have been to wait until she landed on one of those emotions so vividly expressed on her beautiful face. A gentleman would have allowed her all the time she needed to realize where she was and what she was suggesting they do…and been offered an out. But being this close to her had its disadvantages in terms of his behavior. With his body calling for action, Grant could hardly keep from taking her right there in the open doorway.

Paxton was the first to end the temporary standoff. Rising on tiptoe, she brushed her mouth over his. No touching or meeting of their bodies this time, just those warm, supple lips, featherlight on his.

Grant pressed closer, sandwiching Paxton between his body and the wall. Moonlight flooded the room beyond the doorway, streaming in from the yard through a series of windows to cast long shadows across the floor. Grant would have felt the moon's presence without having to see it. Though his insides shuddered in recognition of the moon's presence, the light illuminated Paxton with a silver caress.

He liked everything he saw and everything he was going to touch. Paxton had become as addictive for him as the moon was. And, like Madame Moon, the woman whose scent and body he craved had lured him into a dangerous and possibly permanent relationship.

Her fingers breezed over his face as if searching for something she couldn't see. Only Grant would have seen the irony in that.

Their mouths parted. His eyes bored into hers.

"Just for tonight," she said with a whispered breath.

"Tomorrow we're those other people needing different kinds of answers."

And…well…who was he to argue?

Everyone had a weakness. Patience was his. Although Grant would have preferred to take things slowly, appreciating every move and gesture between them, that kind of control wasn't in the cards. Time was a luxury they didn't have.

He tugged Paxton's shirt over her head before kissing her again. The rough wood wall behind her might had been uncomfortable for her with his weight pressing in, but that thought fled as she snaked her arms around his waist.

The damn internal flutters he had been experiencing in her company rushed to meet her hands as she ran them up his back. His skin moved beneath her touch. Desire for her became unconquerable. With a snap of his fingers and a well-balanced move, the woman in his arms became braless. Through his shirt, Grant felt the hard, round tips of her breasts pressed against his chest and the little quakes that shook her.

Slipping his thigh between her legs, he widened her stance. Her hands now slid to his waistband, searching for a way inside.

Grant gracefully swung Paxton inside the bunkhouse and closed the door. One more tug and she was back with him, hip to hip and half naked, her mouth as demanding as his.

They were standing in the middle of the lofty space, surrounded by beds and brown leather chairs. The closest piece of furniture was a long, narrow dining table.

"Good as anywhere," he said, stretching Paxton out on top of that table's dusty surface, leaning over her to soak in the beauty of her bare arms and torso.

"We've gotten this far once before, Paxton."

He vowed not to let anything stop them this time, and hoped she felt the same way. The atmosphere in the bunkhouse buzzed with a sense of urgency he couldn't explain. Paxton was here with him, and willing, but timing had become an internal pressure.

He had experienced this moment once before—his eyes on hers, his fingers on her zipper. That zipper now whispered down its metal track, filling the night with promise, while Paxton remained quiet, on her back, on the damn table.

She never once took her eyes off him.

Grant wished he had the ability to twist minutes and hours to their advantage. He had been hard, aching and erect, since Paxton had turned to him on the front porch steps.

Forgetting about his superhuman strength, Grant tore open his shirt, losing the buttons that remained from earlier that evening. With wolf-gifted hearing, he listened to those buttons hit the floor.

Paxton smiled up at him. She opened her arms wide, giving him an unimpeded view of her perfect breasts and issuing an invitation for him to join her on the table.

As alpha of a Were pack, he was used to being in control, and yet that control was slipping. This small woman was besting him in ways he'd never dreamed of. All she had to do was wet her swollen lips with the tip of a pale pink tongue and let a sigh of impatience slip from between those lips…

He couldn't get to the rest of her fast enough to suit what throbbed beneath his waist. He had to stop kissing her and tasting her mouth if they were to do what they had come here to do. With her mouth this hot, he couldn't imagine what sliding into her soft, feminine folds would be like.

Her shoes were off. He removed her jeans. She let him do all the work. Wildness continued to blossom in her eyes.

One small scrap of black lace remained to cover her—the same nearly transparent dark strip he had encountered earlier at the motel. Black lace, he decided, was even sexier than her black silk skirt. Seeing her like this was a turn-on.

Grant tore the lace panties from Paxton with a simple closing of his fist, eagerly anticipating what would come next. Lying in complete stillness, Paxton's eyes roamed over every inch of his shirtless anatomy, appreciating what she saw. He was happy he could please her.

Her long, silky legs parted, as if he needed to be guided to what lay between them. He snapped his belt open. After discarding his boots and jeans, Grant stood before her completely naked, open to Paxton's inspection. Her eyes were wide and gleaming. Her torso glistened with a light coat of sweat. It had to be ninety degrees in the unused bunkhouse, and it was about to get hotter.

Between Paxton's slim, shapely thighs, a small patch of blond fur beckoned to him. And that was just too much. Grant was with her on the table after one more unsteady breath, on his hands and knees.

As Paxton lay back again, Grant lowered his mouth to one of her rosy-tipped ivory breasts and ran his tongue over the pink nipple. Paxton tossed her head from side to side and bucked. His weight pressed her down.

No time for exploration, his mind warned. *No matter how hungry you are.*

"All right," he said soberly, after sampling the delights of her other straining breast, the light suckling making a direct connection with his groin. "Are you with me, Paxton?"

Eyes closed, she answered in a tone indicative of the same need spiking through him, "Yes. We have to…"

Her remark dangled unfinished. Her breath rushed out as Grant entered her body gently with his rock-hard cock. All the while, he studied her face. Braced on his hands, he moved his hips, inching deeper one small push at a time, relishing the fire of Paxton's moist inferno.

She was far hotter than he had imagined. Molten was exactly how he would have described her. As Paxton began to move, raising her hips to meet his, making way for him to find the spot she wanted him to find, their tongues danced and their lips burned. Hips slapped against hips as Grant built up a rhythm that took him deeper into her plushness. He dipped in and out of her body with a series of plunges, thrusts and withdrawals that drew moans of delight from her.

He stroked her, worked his way deeper and deeper toward what lay nestled at her core. This is where a wolf's soul resided, and by God, he'd have that, too.

When he touched that sultry spot, Paxton closed herself around him. A growl tore through him that he almost couldn't swallow. Grant wanted to howl, throw his head back and put sound to the extremes of the pleasure he was finding, locked between her sleek legs. But the woman beneath him needed him to be a man for a while longer, at least for tonight. Any sign of Grant's wolf would have hindered that.

Pleasure came at him in waves, tilting, churning with incredible speed. The rhythm of his fiery physical assault matched their breathlessness. Grant shut his eyes as his thrusts became faster, harder. She took it all, and all of him, urging him on. As he made love to her, Grant crooned to her with words that lay beyond the realm of his comprehension. Words like *love* and *chains* and *futures*.

Seconds later, he hit the sweet spot he had been seeking. Rigid beneath him, Paxton gasped. The distant drumbeat he'd been aware of for some time got measurably stronger and rushed to meet him there.

He touched that spot a second time, and a third, backing off long enough to make her claw at him for more. Nonsensical sounds bubbled up from Paxton's throat. She started to tremble, her interior quakes indicative of an imminent climax.

She wrapped her legs around him as if fearing he might finish before she could reach the peak marking the culmination of this union. Deep internal pulses inside her drove Grant on. Merging with that rising beat would possibly seal their fates, and at the moment, he didn't care. Paxton's body was issuing demands he had to satisfy. Their mating had to be complete.

His desire to possess all of Paxton Hall, body and soul, woman and wolf, was the impetus for one final thrust, and that triggered an immediate response. Paxton came hard. She cried out, shuddered, writhed beneath him, gripping his shoulders, digging into his flesh. Bodies locked together, they rocked in unison as a tsunami of pure sexual bliss crashed over them. Peaking together, their bodies arched, strained, as they fought to hold on.

And then it was over.

Tangled together on a table in an unused bunkhouse,

and with the possibility of danger outside, Paxton's sexually sated cries faded. Her heartbeats slowed.

When the opportunity arrived for a full breath, Grant looked down at his lover, not sure what would happen when Paxton opened her eyes. They had scaled the heights of pleasure together, but a rocky road lay ahead.

It wasn't hard for Grant to imagine how beautiful Paxton would be once she had shape-shifted. How gracefully she'd move. How it would feel to have her stretched out beneath him, opening to him over and over again. He would have given a lot to start that future right then, and grew hard again just thinking about it.

But a replay of what they had shared here wasn't to be. Not yet. This one session had been dangerous enough. They both had caved to desire.

Tomorrow, he thought, pressing the fair hair back from her face before kissing her forehead, her cheek, her mouth. *In the middle of all this potential danger, we'll see what you are and what will happen next.*

For now, their time together was up. These wonderfully private moments were over.

Someone is heading this way, my beautiful Paxton, and that presence will demand my attention.

Although the real world had been temporarily set aside in favor of touching the sublime, it now returned with a vengeance.

There's a monster to catch and a full moon on its way. There's a pack to protect and a potential new member. That new member is you, little wolf.

As Paxton's lashes opened, Grant whispered out loud, "Welcome back to the Wild West, lover. Only the hardy can make it here, and I'm hoping you are one of them."

Chapter 15

Ignoring the whispers and sounds flowing through her mind, Paxton found Grant Wade studying her when she opened her eyes.

Speech was difficult with white-hot nerve endings zinging. Although she wasn't a beginner when it came to sexual escapades, she had never experienced anything like what had just happened. She had never felt like this. Never been left panting.

Was it merely the incredible sex or was it something else entirely? Because sex like that didn't belong to this plane of existence.

Grant was composed of waves of electricity, and the charge was ongoing. The explosive climax he had given her had been similar to detonating dynamite, and was taking its own sweet time to recede.

He wasn't relaxed or smiling, in spite of the release. Grant's tenseness had returned with a speed she hadn't anticipated, signaling clearly that their time together was over.

Had sex been all Grant Wade wanted from her?

Even so, it had been worth it.

"You okay?" He asked her this as if he actually expected her to answer the question seriously.

"Yeah," she said, since he was waiting to hear her confirm that she was all right. "Fine."

She assumed Grant would get up, take his clothes and leave. If he thanked her, she would give him a good kick. She'd take a cold shower and try to wash off his scent, knowing she would have to put this little indiscretion behind her, like strangers often did after a one-night stand. Because the truly awkward part of all this had arrived.

Grant nodded as if he, too, understood this.

To ease any potential embarrassment either of them might be feeling Paxton said, "This doesn't have to be strange. It happens all the time."

"All the time to you?" he asked, studying her.

His face was close enough for her to feel his breath on her cheek. Her body continued to quake inside, craving more of everything Grant had to offer.

Damned if she'd let him see that.

"I mean random meetings between two people attracted to each other for whatever reason," she clarified.

Instead of responding to that statement, Grant turned his head to look at the door. His broad, bare shoulders rolled in agitation.

Paxton followed his gaze, alerted by the kind of glance he'd settled on that door. "Is someone out there?"

"Yes."

That explained one possible scenario for his sudden nervousness. She was a little bit relieved.

"I didn't hear the knock," she said. Then again, that wasn't really a surprise, since she hadn't been able to pay attention to anything beyond the sensations of their exquisite coupling.

Grant smiled warily. The expression told her he was holding something back. Was there a jealous woman outside, ready to burst in?

Paxton reminded herself that she wasn't part of his life and therefore didn't need to know everything Grant did. But his wary expression bothered her.

"I have to check on something," he said, his gaze swinging back to the door. "And I don't want my departure to seem to you like avoidance or insult."

"Thanks for telling me," Paxton returned drily. "Now I won't think that at all."

It was her turn to stare at the door. "Go," she said, giving him permission to find some distance. "It's all right. I'm all right. I'll get dressed and…"

Her remark was interrupted by a sound she clearly heard, coming from outside. She sat up quickly as Grant got to his feet. His demeanor had changed again. She noticed he had fisted his hands.

In the moonlight streaming through the window, Grant's picture-perfect face suddenly seemed more angular than chiseled, and much more defined. His expression had grown darker and resembled a scowl. He was seriously anxious about what might be out there, beyond the bunkhouse door. Paxton also figured he truly was loath to leave her like this, so quickly, because he didn't rush over to the door.

"Go," she repeated firmly.

Slipping off the table, she hastily gathered up her clothes.

The knock that came soon after startled her, though

Grant appeared to have been expecting it. Without giving a damn about being buck naked, he opened the door and spoke in a low tone to whoever stood there.

"More trouble," she heard the person outside warn.

Grant threw her a worried glance before turning to pick up his jeans. Once he had donned his pants and boots, he came back to her.

"You can't stay here, Paxton."

"I'll go to the house," she said, monitoring his change in attitude. He seemed so much more formidable. Warier. More dangerous.

His head shake was firm. "It's too late for that now. The trespasser I mentioned is sniffing around, so I can't let you out of my sight. Please get dressed. Sorry about the shower you might be anticipating. You'll have to come along."

Pulling on her jeans, she said, "Where are we going?"

"To Desperado."

Paxton stopped moving halfway through the act of getting her shirt over her head, thinking she might not have heard Grant right. After stuffing her arms into the sleeves, "Now?" was the only thing she could come up with to say.

Thing was…

Grant really didn't quite look like himself. Half in and half out of the shadows, he seemed bigger, more muscular and somehow larger than life. Shadows hugged his bare chest, creating valleys of light and dark. His arms were corded with the same kind of tension that made his shoulders ripple.

Was the lack of light making her think those things? Was she imagining things that weren't there?

His tension was contagious.

Her hands shook.

Then she noticed the mark on Grant's left upper arm for the first time—a small silvery circle that could have been a recent tattoo.

She stopped moving with her gaze riveted to that mark, and touched her own arm. She'd been born with a similar circle in the same spot.

Coincidence?

Tossing her hair back from her face, Paxton remembered that there was a hell of a lot she didn't know about her old home and about Grant Wade. Actually, she knew next to nothing about either, and again felt afraid.

She felt sick.

Glancing from the open door to Grant, who stood bathed in moonlight and was visibly on edge, Paxton fought off a second wave of nausea. Reaching to the table for support, she closed her eyes, counted to ten and said, "It might be a good idea if you explained a few things first."

"Grant?" Ben said from the doorway, showing respect for his alpha and friend by not mentioning Paxton, Grant's nudity or what so obviously had gone on in the bunkhouse.

Careful to keep a rein on his inner beast, Grant didn't dare go to Paxton. His reaction to Ben's warning had been swift, causing his wolf to slip its tether for a brief partial appearance.

Had Paxton seen it?

More trouble, Ben had said, which left no time for explanations, either the short or the long versions, Paxton was asking for. The monster they'd been seeking had returned to the area, as he'd feared, and was closing in on the ranch.

Damn persistent sucker...

"Later," he said to Paxton, relieved to hear the even tone of his voice when the rest of him was in flux. His skin undulated like the surface of a disturbed pond. Claws, fur and teeth had to be monitored. Now wasn't the time to give Paxton the second fright of her life.

"We'll talk later, I promise," he said to her.

Paxton had backed into a corner with one hand gripping her upper arm. Her fingers covered her moon mark as if it was something foreign. She was unable to hide the fact that she had seen his mark without understanding what the similarity meant. To the human portion of her mind, none of this made sense. Of course, it made sense to every other Were on the planet.

Only pure-blooded Weres bore moon marks and passed them on to their offspring. The fact that Paxton had one was proof, as Grant had thought, that Andrew Hall had to have been a werewolf. Not only that, Andrew's lineage had to have been pure enough and strong enough to pass the wolf and the mark to his daughter. It also meant that both of Paxton's parents had to have been Lycans.

Christ. This was incredible news.

Andrew's daughter was a Lycan.

And, as fate would have it, Grant would be the one to tell Paxton her mommy and daddy had been werewolves, and that Arizona was a magnet for Weres, both good and bad. Once she knew this, Paxton would have to rethink her entire existence and consider the possibility, as Grant had, that her father had sent her away for more reasons than just wanting to be rid of his family.

Grant just wasn't sure what those reasons would have been, since Desperado was a werewolf Mecca and Paxton would have been at home here, among others of her kind.

The whole thing felt off, somehow, now that he thought about it. Still, would having more facts help Paxton come to terms with the long-term loss of her dad?

What would she do when she found out what she was? Would she pass the test all Weres had to go through during their first transformation, not-so-lovingly called The Blackout for good reason?

"There's danger all around us tonight, and we have to head straight toward it," he said to her, hating that she looked so pale. "I'm sorry to involve you. That wouldn't have been my choice."

Paxton didn't appear to be buying this. Stubbornness was often a she-wolf trait; he had learned that from his dealings with Shirleen.

She said, "Someone found the bear?"

Grant shook his head. He kept his hands behind his back in case his claws slipped through. Even now, his body wanted a rematch on that damn table.

"I'm pretty sure there is no bear," he said.

In response to that statement, Paxton's eyes blazed angrily. The hand covering her mark dropped to her side. "Then tell me what that thing out there is, and why you're so concerned."

"No time to explain. We have to go," Grant reiterated. "Now."

She pushed off the wall, a little steadier on her feet than she had been the minute before, and said smartly, "Okay. If you say so."

Damn it. Did everything have to be so difficult?

Nevertheless, Paxton was dressed and standing. Ben was waiting for them outside. They'd take the truck to Desperado and see who turned up looking for a fight.

Surrounded by his pack, Paxton would be safe. Grant would see to that.

Paxton didn't take the hand he offered her. The honeymoon was over as far as she was concerned, when it had been, well…it had been everything he'd ever hoped making love to a woman would be, even considering the time constraints. He sincerely hoped there would be a round two.

Paxton preceded him from the bunkhouse looking disheveled. Her porcelain skin was a shade lighter than it had been. She had pulled her T-shirt on backward. Anyone looking at her right then would have been able to tell what they'd done in that outbuilding, and maybe even how good it had been.

For the record, he wanted to tell her that it had been damn good.

She walked without help, gaining strength from her anger. Yet he would have liked touching her. After being with her intimately, wanting more of her was expected.

"Paxton, this is Ben," he said when she faced his tall, dark-haired packmate.

Ben nodded in acknowledgment of the introduction, then turned toward the house where Shirleen waited for them at the back fence. Ben spoke as if Paxton was one of them and in on what was taking place before Grant could urge caution.

"He breached the fence less than a quarter of a mile to the south," Ben explained.

"A human trespasser?" Paxton asked, drawing a long look from Ben, who continued speaking without addressing her query.

"Nothing about this guy is usual or explainable, Grant. He might be heading here. I can't hear his chatter. Maybe you can?"

"I'm not sure why he'd come to the ranch," Shirleen said. "What's in it for the bastard? There are no cattle or horses here for him to steal. Maybe he wants to chew on something else for a change?"

From two feet away, Grant felt Paxton stiffen. However, it was too late to take back those remarks. Everyone here was angry that their lives had been disrupted.

As they moved through the house to the front yard, Paxton remained quiet. Without a single request for fresh clothes or a bathroom break, she climbed into the truck. Ben and Shirleen slammed the front door and loaded themselves into the truck bed, taking up positions on opposite sides to keep watch as they drove the short distance to Desperado.

In essence, Paxton was getting exactly what she wanted, give or take having a monster on the loose. They were going to Desperado, and she was about to have a very rude awakening as to the town's purpose.

"There is something out there, as I said earlier," he finally explained. "Whatever it is has been killing cattle and causing an uproar with the ranchers. It's dangerous, and so are those ranchers wielding rifles when they give chase."

She gave him a brief sideways glance.

"There's more to the old ghost town than meets the eye," he went on. "It's protected on all sides."

Paxton said, "Protected by what? Fences?"

"Electric fences," Grant replied, keeping the rest of the explanations about the town's protections to himself. No use going there until he had to.

"You believe Desperado is safer than the ranch?" was her next question.

"More of us are gathering there, and there's safety in numbers."

"Why not gather at the ranch?"

"Desperado is the place we've designated as a meeting spot."

"These gathered people are your friends?"

Grant nodded.

"And you will go after this person or thing that has been bothering ranchers in the area?" Paxton asked.

"Not this time. I don't think we'll have to."

"You assume the trespasser might come to you?"

"That's what I expect, and I could be wrong. I'm sorry you're in the thick of things, Paxton. The timing sucks. I'm also sorry about the interruption back there in the bunkhouse. We needed more time to enjoy the company and figure things out."

"I'm pretty sure we covered everything," she said.

Grant took his focus from her when Ben tapped on the back window.

"Someone else thinks they've seen our beast," Ben said through the sliding window. "Listen."

Sure enough, the sound of gunfire was like an explosion of firecrackers in the distance. And maybe, Grant thought, Paxton was starting to believe him about the danger. She slid closer to him as she stared out at the night.

Chapter 16

The sounds Paxton heard in the distance had to be gun-fire, making Grant's explanation about ranchers going after trespassers seem real. But she couldn't figure out why they were on their way to meet Grant's friends at Desperado, and what made an old ghost town a better bet for a rendezvous than the ranch, when she would have thought the opposite.

More secrets? These people were feeding her half-assed explanations that didn't actually explain anything. What wasn't Grant telling her?

Images of that old abandoned town from her child-hood flashed through her mind, though most of her memories were long gone with time. She remembered the electric fences surrounding the town that had been meant to keep out trespassers even back then.

If given half a chance, determined tourists would have run off with shutters, floorboards and any other pieces of the place they could pry up, she recalled her father telling her. She supposed some things never changed, and that an off-limits ghost town was likely to be an even bigger target for that kind of thing.

Still, if this was one lone trespasser Grant and his neighbors were after, a gathering of the clan seemed a little like overkill.

Just as she remembered, the road leading to Desperado had no streetlights. This far out of the city, the roads were only partially paved. The streets of Desperado itself were dirt, as tourists would have expected from a relic of the Old West. What electricity there had been in the town itself when she was a kid had been minimal, for emergencies, and carefully hidden in a tribute to the full Western experience.

She stared out of the truck's closed window, expecting to see the town's main gatepost any minute, no longer sure how to gauge the distance from the ranch to Desperado. It couldn't be far. At six years old, she had ridden her pony over this same road.

Night in the desert would have been beautiful if things hadn't turned so serious. Moonlight and stars in the clear night sky lit parts of the scenery. Saguaro and other types of cactus cast long shadows over the white, sandy ground. In the distance, a long, low mountain range stretched dark and colorless in the night. Though Paxton had no idea what time it was, she figured it had to be very late. Temperatures had cooled considerably, but she hardly felt the chill with her metabolism revved up by adrenaline and tonight's hot, sweaty sex.

A shower would have been nice. Her skin and clothes were saturated with Grant's scent. She smelled like sex. Like him. The fact that he was a few inches away from her at the moment didn't help her concentration much, either. When Grant wasn't looking, she gave him fur-tive glances.

The guy looked like himself again...all bronze and brawn. His shirt, open in front due to the missing but-tons, showed off his shape. Fair highlights in his au-burn hair glinted in the moonlight each time the truck swept around a curve.

Paxton rubbed her eyes and withheld a sigh, believ-ing she had imagined the changes she had seen in Grant at the bunkhouse. However, his anxiety, so like a living thing, permeated the cab.

Uncomfortable with the silence, she spoke. "Those ranchers wouldn't actually shoot a person for trespass-ing, would they?"

Grant's attention remained on the road. "This idiot has been stealing their animals."

"He dares to come back for more?"

"Seems so."

"What does he do with the cattle?" she asked.

"He kills everything he steals."

Paxton sat back on the seat. "Why would he do that?"

Ignoring Grant's reluctance to answer this line of questioning, Paxton pressed on.

"What did Shirleen mean when she suggested this guy might want to chew on other things for a change?"

Grant's gaze, drifting to her, felt like a tractor beam. Paxton made herself stay put.

"Might as well cough up some real answers," she said. "I'm nothing if not persistent, and I'm not going anywhere, it seems, except into the heartland of a bunch of secrets you don't think I have any right to know."

Paxton met his eyes defiantly.

"You have every right to those secrets," he said. "It's just that, as I said before, the timing sucks. Bad timing means it's unlikely that you will believe anything I say. Until you experience some stuff for yourself, you will remain in the dark."

"That's rather cryptic and pretty damn ominous, Grant."

"Yes, well, the world, it turns out, holds many more secrets than anyone would assume. Most people wouldn't be ready for a close look at those secrets."

"As far as cryptic goes, you're getting worse by the minute," Paxton argued.

"I get that."

"Yet here I am, in this car, on my way to Desperado, and you won't trust me with a close look at whatever it is you're hiding."

"What if you didn't like what you saw?" he asked.

"I believe that's entirely up to me."

"All right. Let's test the concept of sharing, shall we? How about if I start by telling you we believe the guy we're searching for out here isn't human."

"In my book, no one who kills animals for sport can be considered human."

Grant glanced away briefly before looking at her again. "That's not what I mean."

"Okay. What do you mean?"

"Not human, as in this guy is from another species altogether. One you're not yet familiar with."

Paxton shook her head. "This is nowhere near Roswell, New Mexico, and you're suggesting this guy is an alien?"

She was ready to either laugh or jump out of this truck if Grant answered that question positively. It would definitely make her think twice about secretly desiring him on a level that could very well make her do something stupid. Again.

He was curiously tight-lipped now.

"You are going to have to explain. Especially now," Paxton insisted.

Without letting his gaze linger longer, Grant spoke in a voice that took on the aspect of a deep rumble.

"The truth is that we aren't sure what this guy is," he said.

"*What* he is?"

"Signs suggest he might be a werewolf."

Paxton turned on the seat and answered with a not-so-hearty laugh that didn't make her feel any better about what Grant had just told her. In fact, the grim expression on his handsome face let her know that he was deadly serious.

Hell, if Grant believed in werewolves, he had to be out of his mind.

"You wanted in on our secrets," Grant said, noting the way Paxton stared at him.

She had no immediate response to that remark, so he went on.

"Of course, this sucker might not turn out to be a Were. In that case, however, he'd have to be something dreadfully similar."

"Like a bear?" Paxton quipped.

Her lips were as bloodless as her face. Grant had expected that kind of reaction and guessed the time had come for revealing a few more things. If the beast out there showed up at Desperado, Grant wasn't sure how they could keep its existence hidden from Paxton. Sooner or later, she had to have more details about her species.

"This guy is unusual," he said. "Maybe he's not an idiot all of the time, because I've heard him speak."

She said tentatively, "Then you've seen him up close?"

Grant shook his head. "Never up close. I heard him speak to my mind."

Paxton's hands were on the dashboard as if she was bracing herself for more bad news. "So you came up with an alternative to alien and made him the next best thing? A werewolf?"

Her voice reflected her disbelief and also a few new suspicions about his state of mind.

"You're thinking I'm crazy," Grant said.

"Don't you think what you've said warrants that?" she fired back.

"As a matter of fact, I do not, unless you have an explanation for the reason that mark on your arm matches mine."

That was harsher than he had meant to be in breaking the news to Paxton about her hidden heritage, but it was too late to stop now. He had been driving slowly, with Ben and Shirleen in the back of the truck, and yet they would reach Desperado in a few more minutes. Time was short for any kind of believable explanation.

Paxton's voice was hushed. "What does the mark on my arm have to do with you imagining the guy you're after is a werewolf? Come on, Grant. I can't wait to hear what you'll say next."

"It has plenty to do with what I'm trying to tell you. You see, if the guy we're chasing is a Were, and using his abilities is how he has been avoiding capture, it's almost certain he will have a mark like ours, too."

Paxton's tone tightened. "Maybe you'd like to start making sense?"

Grant reached out to touch her arm. "Only full-blooded werewolves have this mark. We're all born with the same one."

Paxton's hand again covered her upper arm, as if

doing so might make the mark disappear. Her face had gone paler, and Grant wasn't sure how that was possible.

"It's called a moon mark," he explained, hoping she would listen to him. "The marks resemble the leftover scar of an old wolf bite for a reason. That reason harks back to the first bite a wolf gave to a susceptible human being centuries ago. A human whose genes carried a defect allowing a specific wolf virus to infect them."

She said in a clipped tone, "I've never even seen a wolf up close."

"You not only saw a wolf up close, you inherited some of its traits."

Her hand moved to the door handle as if she'd use it to escape what she had to assume was a conversation comprised of madness.

Grant lowered his voice. "The only bear around here is the fact that you bear that white ring on your arm. You bear it because you are one of us, and a child of the moon."

"Get real, Grant," she snapped, though it was no more than a whisper. "You believe you're a..."

"Yes. And so are you."

Completely speechless, Paxton stared at him with her lips slightly parted for an argument she couldn't quite access.

"We're all werewolves here, Paxton. That's why your father left Desperado to me. He knew Desperado was the perfect place for werewolves to find solace in a world where people would hunt us down for sport if that world became privy to the fact that Homo sapiens aren't the only species on the planet."

All Paxton said was, "You're actually serious."

"Completely," he confirmed.

"You're a werewolf."

Grant nodded.

"And Shirleen? How about the guy with her? Both of them are werewolves, too?"

"They're part of this pack, yes."

"Pack?"

"A tight-knit group of..."

"Don't tell me. *Werewolves?*" she said.

Grant waited for her to go on, sensing she had more to say. Paxton wasn't taking this well, but who would? Who, outside of select insiders, could possibly have believed what he was asking her to believe?

"Don't you suppose I'd know if I was something like that?" she countered adamantly. "I mean, truly, Grant. This is absurd."

"I understand how it sounds, Paxton. And I know you have a hundred questions, which we will eventually get to. Until then, the quick fix to the question you just posed is to say that you obviously weren't told about your background or your family's special inheritance for a reason, and that omission was terribly lax on everyone's part. Unheard-of, actually, if you want the truth. Hell, you're worrying about the kind of inheritance that's written on paper, when there's been something so much more pressing in need of your attention."

She started to argue, then gave up in frustration.

"You haven't shape-shifted yet," Grant continued. "That's ground zero for belief in all of this. Holding your wolf back for so long is highly unusual for someone your age."

"I'm only twenty-six."

Grant nodded. "Most she-wolves transition at or around the age of sixteen. Earlier, if puberty hits before that."

She muttered, "She-wolf. That's rich."

The conversation was far from over. Actually, it had just started, and wasn't sitting well with Paxton. But they had reached the gate leading to Desperado, and two of his packmates stood beside the entrance.

"I suppose those guys are werewolves, too?" Paxton's tone dripped sarcasm, with a little fear thrown in.

"As a matter of fact…" Grant started to say, but his remark was cut off when the two Weres guarding Desperado's front gate whirled toward something Grant couldn't see from the cab of the truck, and Ben and Shirleen jumped out of the back.

"Damn it." He opened the door, understanding the sudden directional shift, and muttered, "I'm hoping this guy is a werewolf, rather than some other rendition of the word beast," sensing Paxton's frozen reaction to those words.

Paxton sat without moving, fairly sure she had lost the ability to control her limbs. Several choice cuss words passed her lips when Grant left her to join the party at the gates. Not just any party. One for werewolves. A pack of werewolves. And according to Grant, she was one of them.

Yeah. Right.

She had made love to a madman and was trapped in his truck. If the other people in Grant's little circle of friends also believed themselves to be *Weres*—as Grant had called them—she was in the middle of nowhere at the moment with a pack of crazies.

Her next move?

As she saw it, she could either play along and wait for Grant to take her back to the ranch, or borrow the blue truck and get the hell out of there before the craziness spread to her.

Keys dangled in the ignition.

Through the windshield, she saw that the two new guys by the gate were gesturing. Those guys looked like people. There was nothing furry about them. Everyone had turned in the direction they were alluding to with a series of hand gestures, possibly trying to pinpoint the location of some creature straight off the pages of mythology books. According to Grant, the grand-master madman, all of the people present believed they actually were furry on the inside.

Shuddering at the thought, Paxton slid sideways a few inches at a time until she was behind the wheel. Turning the truck around to face the city wasn't going to be easy, and maybe even impossible with Grant so close. Her only real option was to go forward and hope she could locate another way out of Desperado in the dark.

She saw with some relief that the road into the old town was lit by small globes of light supplementing the light of a receding, nearly full moon. The outline of the open gates stood out, easy to see, as well as at least twenty feet of dirt road beyond them.

Five people stood to the side of the gates, not far from the truck. They were ignoring her for the moment, their attention elsewhere. Would she be able to start the engine without those people stopping her from stepping on the gas?

Have to try.

She leaned forward. The keys felt warm to the touch.

She wasn't up for playing at being a goddamn werewolf, no matter how hard Grant tried to convince her.

Now or never...

Foot hovering over the gas pedal, Paxton turned the key in the ignition, thanking God the truck was an automatic. Grant turned his head to look at her with a puzzled expression on his devastatingly handsome face. The others with him glanced her way.

Heart in her throat, hands shaking big-time on the steering wheel, Paxton hit the gas. The truck lurched forward, tires spinning and tossing up clods of dirt and dust. It was a powerful machine and well tuned. She was through the gate and heading for Desperado in seconds, distancing herself from the strangers and their oddball beliefs.

Chapter 17

Staying on the road was easier than Paxton had imagined. The last time she had come this way was on the back of her pony. That time, she also had been trying to distance herself from bad news.

Now, as then, she was running away, seeking solace in the old ghost town. She had loved her father and Desperado...at least, that's the way she remembered things looking back. Now, she was getting away from a man who tried to tell her she was a werewolf.

Desperado's outline appeared a short distance ahead. Paxton's heart was heavy. Part of her had been left there years ago, along with more questions than Grant could possibly have answers for.

She drove at a crawl through the town's main street, surprised to see that the place wasn't empty. Every curse word she had ever heard slipped from her lips in a long stream of syllables as Paxton processed the idea that the people gathered here weren't ghostly apparitions, but quite possibly more of Grant's werewolf cult.

The old town called to her as she passed through, in the way it always had. History and age had been kind to the buildings, and Grant had mentioned making repairs.

She had loved this place once and considered it her personal property. She had been familiar with each empty store and alleyway, and by the looks of things, not much had changed. As fate would have it, Desperado was never to be her personal property, because the town now belonged to someone else.

Shirking the desire to stop and look around, Paxton wished she had arrived in different circumstances that would have allowed her to lay her hands on the old boards of the saloon. Strolling through the mining office and general store would have been like walking into the past. All of that was out of the question now that she was a fugitive for stealing Grant's truck.

The truck garnered stares as she rolled by the people on the street. Grant had been expected here. Seeing someone else at the wheel was a surprise for the onlookers.

"See ya," she whispered, passing the old hotel, unable to resist a quick peek at the place.

No one stepped into her path or tried to hail her as she passed them. She'd have to pick up some speed soon. If Grant was in the kind of shape his body, with all that muscle, indicated, he might possibly be able to catch up with her before she left Desperado behind.

She could add car theft to her list of accomplishments. *But werewolf... Really?*

Arms aching from her tight grip on the wheel, she tried to rationalize that the mark on her arm had been caused by childhood inoculations. Tetanus? Smallpox vaccinations? Maybe she and Grant had experienced the same kind of birth trauma, and the mark was indicative of that.

Who knew why or how such things happened?

Moon mark. Did she really care if birthmarks had a name?

Yes. Damn it. All right. The similarity of those marks was one mystery too many.

Desperado was behind her now and merely a series of dotted lights in the rearview mirror. There were no little light globes on this side of town. Darkness enveloped the truck. An alley of skeletal trees hampered what moonlight there was.

Paxton could no longer see past the headlights, but if memory served, somewhere out here was the electrified fence marking the town's boundary. With people in town tonight, that fence would be turned off. The truck was probably strong enough to barrel through a bunch of wire without too much damage.

No one had chased her down. Grant hadn't shown up. It could be that he was letting her go without a fuss, glad to be rid of Andrew Hall's daughter and her endless queries. Possibly he was as sorry for what had happened in that bunkhouse as she was.

Oh, yes, she was sorry.

Sorry she had liked what they had done on that table. She was regretful over how badly she had instantly wanted more of the same, and that with everything that had happened since then, how suspicious she was of the way her body quaked each time Grant's name crossed her mind.

Thoughts about Grant dissipated suddenly, overpowered by a loud crashing sound. Paxton applied the brakes, nearly missing the tree that had fallen across the

narrow, single-track road. Falling trees weren't a rarity
in the desert, given the parched state of their roots, but
this was a holdup she didn't need.

The truck idled as she sat there, staring out, considering her options in light of this latest hindrance.
Going around the tree was bound to be a terrible idea
for the truck, given the tough landscape's giant ruts and
chasms, invisible in the dark. Without the truck, she'd
have to walk, by herself, with no flashlight. Since there
was no way she'd make it to the city, miles away, in any
case, she'd have to go back to the old ghost town and
face the consequences of running off with the truck.
Maybe Grant would lock her up in Desperado's jail and
throw away the key.

Something else that crossed her mind stopped her
from getting out of the vehicle to see if she could budge
the damn tree. The word *beast* resonated there, along
with Grant's explanation that they did not know for sure
what category of beast their trespasser was.

Paxton didn't want a replay of her meeting with the
thing she'd thought was a bear. Grant had told her the
creature that had jumped on her car might be a werewolf. She didn't believe that was possible, but damn it,
was everyone in this part of Arizona insane?

"Go to hell, Grant," she shouted.

As those words echoed in the truck's cab, the sensitive skin on the back of her neck chilled as though
someone had dropped an ice cube down the back of her
shirt. Red flags of warning began to wave, telling her...

Oh, God...

She wasn't alone.

Grant's chest had tightened as he had lunged for
the moving truck, aware that the special speed he pos-

sessed wouldn't get him to Paxton in time to stop her from whatever she had in mind by taking the vehicle. Surprise had made him hesitate a beat too long.

Paxton was long gone.

Ben, on his cell phone, barked a quick heads-up to the pack members in town. Shirleen raised an eyebrow when Grant whirled to face her—she was waiting for instructions on how to handle the situation.

"Headstrong," Grant muttered, taking off at a brisk jog toward Desperado.

Too damn headstrong for her own good, he silently added.

"At least she won't get far," Shirleen called after him.

As for the not-getting-far business, Grant wasn't so sure about that, given the possibility of Paxton's memories of the area and how many details a six-year-old kid's brain would retain.

He didn't remember much about his own life prior to his first shape-shift. When a body temporarily closed down for a complete system rewiring, more than just a few nerve cells were fried.

Room had to be carved out for a long list of new senses and abilities that included a wolf's enhanced sight and the power to smell things no other species could. His body had been loaded with new muscle for both protection and the kind of speed he could have used now to chase down stubborn she-wolves who hadn't yet experienced their own physical awakening.

Turning on the heat, Grant raced on, his legs churning on the dirt road. He had to pay attention to his surroundings and was glad moonlight exposed what lay in the shadows on both sides of the road to town. Desperado was only a mile ahead of him. He heard Shirleen, always light on her feet, running behind him, and he swore out loud, fearing that his pack might be in trouble because of the attention needed to handle Paxton's breach.

"Paxton. Stop. Wait for me. Keep out of the dark spaces. I don't understand your need to run."

He sent that silent message on a closed channel reserved for personal things in order to keep other Weres out of his thoughts. Chances were good that she wouldn't hear him, because Paxton retained most of her humanness at the moment, and old human habits were often hard to break.

He glanced up at the moon, well aware that last thought wouldn't be true for much longer. To most of the Earth's population, the moon overhead already appeared to be full. Werewolves knew better. However, now, tonight, the big silver disc tugged on his will to remain in human form. Emotion was ruffling his skin, bringing chills.

In a fully morphed state, he could have reached Desperado faster, arriving seconds after Paxton did in spite of the truck's massive engine. But he didn't want to scare Paxton. In any case, the rutted road they hadn't bothered to repair would help to delay her departure.

"Don't hold back on my account," Shirleen sent to him, reading parts of the thoughts he hadn't purposefully hidden. "All right. Done deal," Grant said aloud, changing his mind about shifting in order to catch Paxton sooner, knowing he'd have to shift back when he did.

Claws popped at his invitation. Layers of muscle began to seize, shimmy and quake. His arms burned beneath the layer of chills. So did his legs. Facial bones began to rearrange. A dusting of fine brown fur sprang from chest pores, and the hair on his head lengthened to brush his neck with what should have been half a year's worth of growth.

With a larger lung capacity, breathing was easier and required less effort. Embracing his true nature brought him an exquisite sense of freedom. He didn't have to ditch the open shirt or his jeans and boots, being in full control of how far he could take this shift.

Running was easier now. Sprinting through the landscape was like experiencing a suspension in time and space. In Were form, he always had the feeling of being pasted onto the world rather than being part of it. Always, when wolfed up, he imagined he could hear, far off in a distant time, his four-legged ancestors howling.

This was what being a werewolf meant, and nothing in polite human society could have covered it.

Without the ability to speak, Grant sent his thoughts winging through the night. *"Paxton. Wait. There are so many things I need to tell you."*

Another shape-shifting perk, aided by his connection to Paxton, was Grant's ability to tap into her emotions. He knew her heart was racing and that she felt lost. Hell, she *was* lost. Paxton had been stranded for far too long in a form that didn't truly explain her. She'd been lost to part of her family and to her heritage, ignorant of what lay ahead for her in less than twenty-four hours, now that she had come home.

"Stop," Grant sent to her again as the town came into view. *"Wait. I'm coming to get you. I can't protect you if you don't listen."*

Shifting to his human form again would be necessary before he reached her. She couldn't see him like this. Not yet, before she believed the things he had told her.

Near the first building on Main Street, he found nine Weres waiting for him. One of them shook his head and pointed north. Grant growled his acceptance of the news that his truck had already passed through town.

Worry set in as his pack gathered around him. All of these Weres were tense. Sharing his emotions made them more anxious.

"She just blew through," one of them said.

"Where are you, Paxton?" Grant silently called before growling again. Her fear had spiked suddenly in a reboot of what had happened earlier that night—her brush with an animal she had assumed was a bear.

He had to find her. Tonight was off the charts in terms of oddness, and Grant had a terrible feeling that Paxton really might be the focus of this latest series of close calls and mishaps.

He wasn't sure why he thought so, though the sour taste in his mouth meant trouble awaited him around the next corner. There was a new pressure in the atmosphere and a needling sensation on the back of his neck. His discomfort sang to him, urging him to find Paxton, pressing home the point that she might be in peril.

"I'm coming," he repeated for the tenth time, heading in the direction she had taken.

Chapter 18

Paxton stood beside the truck, gauging the viability of finding an exit from Desperado's vast acreage in the dark after so many years. She had grown rigid, sure she was being watched. Nerves were prickling.

Her body quakes had returned in full force. She called out, "I know you're there, so you might as well show yourself," hoping in this instance she might be wrong about having unwelcome company.

"Actually, I insist," she added, whirling around every time there was a noise in the brush.

No one met her challenge. No intruder appeared in the truck's headlight beams. Yet she sensed a presence. Inching sideways, toward the truck's open door, Paxton tried to calm herself down. But when a different kind of awareness came that was more like a feeling than a series of spoken words, she imagined a voice say, *"I'm coming."* And *"Hold on."*

The sensation the tone gave her was one of familiarity, leading her to believe it was Grant's voice.

With her back pressed to the truck's warm metal, Paxton glared at the nearly invisible landscape, searching for this other presence.

"You're scaring me." She spoke, not to the distant idea of a familiar voice, but to the closer presence she sensed hovering in the dark. "What do you want? Are you one of Grant's friends? Can you help me move this tree off the road?"

She suppressed a gasp when she heard the snap of a twig, followed by the shuffling sounds of someone or something moving just beyond her field of vision.

"Show yourself," she insisted, not liking the way her voice wavered.

The next sound that reached her was one an animal might make—deep, guttural and very much like a growl. Rather than adding to her discomfort, the thought of this visitor being nothing more than an animal came as a relief. *Wolf, then*, she thought. Real wolf, since Grant had nixed the idea of a bear. And yet that growl resonated in the night, too loud and too deep to have come from a wolf.

Turning swiftly, Paxton climbed back into the truck. More chills came. More icy waves. Her head felt light. Movement out of the corner of her eye made her swivel, wishing she had taken the time to close all the windows. With shaky hands, she felt along the inner surface of the door beside her, looking for a button that would seal her inside.

When the screech of something scraping against metal came, her fear escalated to nearly overwhelming proportions, freezing her on the seat with one hand on the steering wheel. Pulse exploding, she watched the dark blur of a moving body pass by the open window too swiftly to match it to an image.

Scared out of her mind, and unable to deal with the latest state of fright, Paxton screamed.

Grant heard Paxton. She was in danger, scared.

Doubling his effort to reach her, he flung silent curses that did nothing to alleviate his own budding fear over what might be happening to her.

He felt responsible.

If he hadn't picked her up at the airport like an inquisitive ass, and had let her find her own lodging and make her own way, maybe these feelings of extreme connection to Paxton Hall could have been avoided and she would be safe. Certainly, she'd be nowhere near Desperado right now. He had brought her here, where a trespassing son of a bitch, whatever this rogue bastard turned out to be, could get a peek at her.

Imagining Paxton was the key to solving the latest version of this mystery was probably absurd, and yet he couldn't shake the idea. That beast had shown itself to Paxton and hadn't harmed her. Something had been at the motel where she had checked in, and Grant had a bad feeling about that, too.

"How could you know about the motel?" he asked across silent Were connections. *"You spoke to me once, so why be silent now?"*

He didn't actually expect a response and wasn't surprised when none came. And he was an idiot for trying to reason with an unknown entity responsible for doing plenty of damage in the area. But, really, all he and his pack needed was one pertinent clue as to this sucker's location.

There was light ahead that had to be from the truck's

headlights. Changing from his werewolf shape to a more user-friendly appearance, Grant raced on through the slap and sting of yet another downshift in too short a time.

His face reverted to its human semblance with a swift recall of power. The sting he felt was due to his fur being sucked back inside his skin. His shirt flapped in the wind created by his sprint. Claws were the last detail to go. His human shape would be best for Paxton, and worse, in theory, for facing whatever had frightened her.

He saw the truck. Found Paxton inside. His relief over finding her unharmed was monstrous. She didn't turn her head when he came up alongside. Nor did she acknowledge him at all. Paxton was ashen-faced, stiff and staring into the distance with glazed eyes.

When he spoke to her, all remnants of his wolf had gone. This was the voice Paxton would know. This was the guy, at least on the surface, she had made love to.

"You could have been hurt," he said softly, yanking the door open, waiting until she looked at him.

She spoke in a voice weakened by what had made her heart thunder. "No bear. Not even close."

Grant searched the dark, more concerned for Paxton than anything else. He sensed no one. Nothing jumped out at them. Paxton appeared to be alone. The only obvious details out of place were the tree blocking the road and the new two-foot-long scratch running the length of the truck's left rear panel.

Had Paxton gotten too close to the brush in her rush to beat him to an exit out of town? Grant didn't think that would explain this kind of damage. The scratch was deep and looked to have been created by a very sharp object.

In even more of a hurry now, Grant climbed into the

truck, gently shoving Paxton aside. Throwing the truck into reverse, he drove backward, his eyes on the road through the rear window. The last spot wide enough to turn the truck around was some way back, and he was determined to reach that spot as soon as possible.

His next uttered curse, whispered vehemently through clenched teeth, drew Paxton's glassy gaze.

"What was it?" he asked her. "What did you see?"

The tires kicked up dirt and other desert debris, but Grant knew where he was headed. He was familiar with every inch of land surrounding Desperado, as well as most of the territory in and around the distant city. Weres often roamed far and wide, driven by the wildness inside them, before returning to their homes. *Sort of like you, Paxton, moving to the other side of the country before returning to the land of your ancestors.*

"Okay. No bear," he said aloud. "So, what did you see?"

In a slightly stronger voice, Paxton said, "I'm not sure."

She was telling the truth, which in this case might not have been such an odd response, since no one around here seemed to know exactly what they were chasing. Even the word *Lycan* covered a lot of ground.

"Describe what you saw," he said.

"It was the same damn thing."

He nodded. "The thing that jumped on the other car?"

"Yes." Paxton's eyes were huge, her pupils partially dilated. He saw no evidence on her face of her earlier stubborn streak.

"And?" Grant prompted.

"And, as crazy as it sounds, I think it might have

been expecting me. I think whoever is out there put that tree in my path to keep me from leaving."

Grant slowed the truck mid-turn and faced Paxton, anxious about her reply. "What was it?" he repeated.

"I swear I don't know. I didn't see it. Not clearly."

"But you did see something?"

She nodded. "Something."

Her pallor told him Paxton had reached the end of her ability to describe what she'd witnessed and that it would be useless to keep pressing her. However, she wasn't quite finished, and the next words she spoke pierced Grant's soul.

"It wasn't human," she whispered breathlessly. "And if this is your trespasser, we're screwed."

Chapter 19

Paxton expected the man sitting beside her to blanch at what she had just said. At the very least, he should have questioned her judgment and current mental state. Grant Wade did neither of those things, which led her to assume he was one step ahead of her.

"You believe me." She watched Grant for any hint of a reaction.

He nodded.

"Damn it, Grant. Has the world come unglued, or are there things I'm obviously missing? When did the word *inhuman* become shock-resistant?"

His sideways glance, there and gone, might have been an example of avoidance. He had the truck turned around and was heading back toward Desperado.

"Maybe I should be the one asking the toughest questions," she suggested. "Like what the hell is going on around here?"

After a deep breath, she continued the interrogation.

"Why do I imagine I can hear you speaking to me at times, when you're not close to me? Am I nuts, or is there a reason I think this?"

He seemed to be concentrating on the road, and that wasn't going to do it for her.

"You could do me the honor of an honest reply, since it appears I'm not going anywhere, anytime soon, and that rescuing me is your current MO."

He threw her another sideways glance that showed no expression of anger or gave her a clue about what he was thinking. He gave no indication of believing he might be dealing with a madwoman. And that, Paxton decided, spoke volumes about his belief systems.

When he spoke, it was in a low tone reserved for passing along a secret he wanted no one else to hear, even though no one else was present. "We believe this trespasser is unique."

"That's putting things mildly," she snapped, bristling with a desperate need to understand the things presently eluding her. Fear tickled her nerve endings. Her stomach again turned over.

"So how about telling me what else you know, Grant?"

"I'm not sure you're ready to hear what I have to say," he returned. "Especially since you didn't believe the last few things I've mentioned."

"Try me."

"At the moment, I'm acting as your guardian and attempting to keep you safe."

"I didn't ask for you to watch over me, only that you deal with my father's goddamn will."

"You're absolutely right, Paxton. And you're safe

now, so you can calm down. I'm not going anywhere and I will answer your questions one at a time."

Paxton sat back. Telling her to calm down after everything that had happened so far in Arizona was like telling a child not to cry when it fell down. Nevertheless, she managed to steady her voice, and gathered her thoughts together in spite of how fast her pulse was racing.

"What do you mean by unique?" she asked, attacking that comment first. "You said you think the thing out there is unique, and also that it's a werewolf. If you're a werewolf and your pals are werewolves, what would make that thing out there different?"

Desperado's lights were twinkling. They would reach the center of town in minutes, and then what? With other people around, Grant might postpone the explanations she was waiting for.

"I was born here," she added tonelessly and out of context, her voice exhibiting the weariness she felt.

"Yes, this was once your home," Grant conceded calmly. "And now it is home to a few others who need this place as much as you're about to."

"Nostalgia has no place in dealing with my father's will," she countered. "Presently, I can take this town or leave it. What good did it do me, in the end? I loved the place and it was taken away. I had forgotten about it, and yet here I am again, reliving pain that goes way back."

"Pain?" he said.

Paxton hadn't planned on confessing any of this to anyone. Some things were too private to see the light of day. But now that she had begun, she said, "Everything I loved was here at one time, Wade."

The man beside her stopped the truck at the edge of town and let it idle. Turning to her, he spoke slowly in a tender tone incongruous with the situation that was like a brush of silk over her tired, sensitive skin.

He might have been crazy, but Grant Wade, in that moment, was more gorgeous than anyone else on this planet.

"There are things in the world that are kept apart from it for a reason, and out of necessity," he said. "Some of the old barriers between worlds have been broken, and yet as time passes it becomes more and more difficult to maintain the few remaining secrets. Those of us living in this town need a sanctuary just as much as anyone else does. Maybe more. People in this world are not kind or sympathetic to those unlike themselves."

"Any minute now, you'll start making actual sense," Paxton said, repeating an earlier sentiment.

Grant hesitated before speaking again, as if trying to think of the right words to say.

"There are over a dozen beings living in this town at the moment and calling the old ghost town home. More come and go on a regular basis."

Paxton wasn't about to let such a cryptic statement get past her and jumped in. "What do you mean by *beings*? Are you talking about people? People with problems? People with a past in need of someplace to go? Homeless people who would otherwise live on the streets of the city? Are you saying you don't want to sell Desperado so that those people won't be displaced? Oh, and please tell me we aren't circling back to the werewolf theory."

Grant rubbed a crease from his forehead.

Paxton went on. "Which is it, Grant? Pick an answer for one of the questions I've just asked."

He ran his right hand over the back of the seat and

touched her neck lightly with warm fingers that had pleasured her less than an hour ago. Paxton wasn't immune to how that touch made her feel. She hadn't forgotten how much they both had wanted that session in the bunkhouse. It was, however, a pity that Grant couldn't come through with a viable way to explain any of the strange things that had happened since she stepped off the plane, other than to make up a few fantasies.

"Here's what you're missing and what you think you want to hear," he said, feathering his fingertips across the bare base of her neck, which, for Paxton, was a toss-up for the second most sensitive place on her body.

"I'm all ears, Grant."

She had to close her eyes. The electrical jolt that hit her each time Grant laid a hand on her threatened to send her right back into his arms. Problems or not, being in the same space with Grant Wade was erotic. Breathing in his scent made her chills scatter.

His voice broke the spell.

"The beings living in this town aren't *people* in the strictest sense of the word. The beast we're chasing is a threat to more than just the neighboring cattle, because if Desperado's neighbors were to catch that beast before we do, this town's secrets would be out. Desperado would be exposed for what it has become, and would likely be razed to the ground."

Paxton looked straight at Grant, expecting the half-truths to become real explanations requiring no stretch of the imagination, and thinking he might need an extra push in that direction.

"What secrets stand to be exposed?" she asked. "That you're werewolves and a pack, and that you hide out here to maintain some distance from everyone who isn't a werewolf?"

Ignoring those questions, he chose to relay other information she had asked for. "I wasn't lying, Paxton. Chances are better than good that the animal you encountered tonight is a wolf of some kind."

He held up a hand to stop her from interrupting when she was about to do just that. "Not just any wolf. One with the special designation of Lycan," he said.

What he said was so absurd, Paxton laughed to offset a sharp stab of panic. Grant's face, his expression, his eyes, showed no sign that this was a joke, when it had to be. Clearly, he wasn't going to let up on the werewolf thing.

"Lycan," she echoed, not liking the turn this conversation had taken any more than she liked the direction the truck was facing. Grant's friends were on hand tonight. Maybe insanity was contagious.

In the silence that followed his little dissertation, Paxton groped for a connection between reality and the extraordinary words Grant had offered her. *Werewolf. Lycan.* Thinking back, she recalled the loud thump on the roof of the rental car and the dark blur on the hood. She pictured the big scary eyes that had peered at her through the windshield, relived the hallucinatory awareness of feeling a strange presence at the motel. Moments ago, she'd had the same kind of eerie awareness on the road out of Desperado. And then there was the dark blur she'd seen out of the corner of her eye.

Long tentacles of fright returned. In spite of that, Paxton went over the thoughts again, freeze-framing the moment when she'd thought she heard voices whispering to her in her mind. Grant had mentioned the same thing. He'd told her the beast had spoken, not in person, but in his thoughts.

"Werewolf," she repeated, tasting the word, finding it sour and completely unacceptable as an answer to her dilemma. She couldn't fathom what would make Grant assume she'd believe what he was telling her.

Was this a ploy to throw her off-balance? Grant trying to gain some advantage in their negotiations over the property her father had left them?

He'd go so far as to suggest that Desperado was haunted by, not ghosts, but half-man, half-wolf creatures out of legend?

Quite obvious to her, when Grant spoke again, was the fact that he favored continuing with this game.

"The beings living in your father's town are werewolves," Grant said. "Although tonight you'd never know it, never believe it. They can only shift their shapes to become something else on the night of a full moon."

Paxton felt sick, not for the first time since arriving in Arizona. She felt sicker as she stared at the handsome, enigmatic man sitting beside her. It was so blatantly apparent that something was wrong with him mentally, something not so obvious because of his spectacular looks.

Then again, her mind nagged…

Hadn't she imagined subtle changes in Grant in the doorway of the bunkhouse? The longer physical frame and more angular features?

What about that?

She said, "I think you might be in need of meds," in a voice that hardly carried over the sound of the truck's idling engine.

Grant shook his head. "There's more."

"I can't wait."

"It involves you, Paxton."

"You've already told me that I'm a werewolf. Could there conceivably be any other incredible information about me to divulge?"

At this point, there was no laughter in her, regardless of the absurdity of the situation. As she saw it, the immediate problem facing her was how to get out of the truck without Grant chasing her.

Any way she viewed things, she was trapped. Grant's captive. One possible direction would be, as she had figured while en route to Desperado, to let Grant go on with this ruse. Pretend to believe him about werewolves until another opportunity came to get away. Could she do that? Make it work and keep a straight face?

God. If she had been to bed with this man, and had loved it, what did that make her?

What did it say about her that she had loved everything they had done and had to work hard now to forget the fever caused by Grant's talented mouth on hers? She had to breathe shallowly to dispel the memory of having his warm breath in her lungs. Crossing her legs wouldn't have stopped the tingling sensations that came from remembering how his hand had pleasured what lay between them.

And now he was betraying her trust.

Grant Wade was showing his true colors.

He had more to say, and she had no option but to listen.

"Sometimes, reality is a bitch, Paxton," he began. "At times, life can read more like science fiction. I get that, because I'm living on the bridge that joins both worlds."

"The human world and the world of the werewolf,"

she said to clarify his meaning as she moved toward the door to get away from Grant's touch.

"Your father left Desperado to me in order to protect the Weres living here and those in need of assistance regarding how to deal with what they've become. Desperado is a safe haven for the werewolf species. The only one I know of in the West. Your father knew about us. Leaving Desperado to me was no fluke, and no purposeful slight to you."

Paxton met Grant's eyes. "You said *us*. So I'm truly a werewolf?"

"Yes," he replied.

"And my father believed this? He might have thought so, too?"

"Completely, just as you soon will."

"Sorry. I'm afraid that would take a miracle," Paxton said.

"Then we'll have to show you one," Grant returned.

Defiance took over her ability to speak as calmly as he did about issues so nonsensical. Crossing her arms, Paxton uttered a challenge. "Okay. Go ahead. Show me that miracle."

Grant's focus was intense. His eyes were luminous in the moonlight coming through the window as he pointed at the moon. "Tomorrow, when the moon is full, everyone here will change shape, including you."

Paxton shoved aside the return of the chills threatening to bring on more quakes. "I've seen the movies. Nevertheless, if what you say is true, and we all require a full moon to do its particular brand of voodoo, why didn't the thing I saw tonight look like the rest of us do right now?"

I have you there, Grant Wade. Try to explain that.

While Paxton waited for him to try, it was easy to

note how that line of enquiry bothered Grant. She wondered what kind of sordid, fantastical tale he'd invent next to cover his ass. As her stomach roiled and her hands fisted, she dreaded hearing what he would come up with.

"Some of us are different," he finally said.

"That's all you've got? Really, I expected so much more."

"Did you?"

She glared at him.

"As far as we can guess, the beast out there can shape-shift without the moon's help," Grant said. "Few Weres possess that trick, and that's what makes this guy so unique."

He was looking at her strangely, perhaps beginning to understand that she wasn't going to fall for any part of his explanation.

"I understand this is hard to process, and even harder to believe," he admitted.

"Next to impossible," Paxton agreed. "And let me state again for the record that if I was a werewolf, I'd know it."

He said, "I might have thought the same thing if my parents hadn't schooled me about it early on."

Grant's expression hadn't strayed from being completely serious. "You'd know about your status unless both parents decided not to tell you about it."

Opening her mouth to protest, Paxton closed it again when the crazy conversation was interrupted by an eerie sound that echoed through the car. It was a horrible, haunting, gut-wrenching howl, and very much like the sound a goddamn werewolf might make.

The truck rocked into motion so quickly, Paxton was thrown backward. The only thing she could offer before they had reached the center of Desperado's main street was one word.

"Impossible."

But there truly was more, as Grant had predicted. None of it good.

One sideways glance told her that Grant Wade was no longer there. When that distant howl began to fade, Grant had simply melted into someone else.

Something else.

The shock of witnessing a real shape-shift tipped Paxton over the edge of reason and into a horror story.

God help them all...

Grant Wade had been telling the truth.

Chapter 20

It was a hell of a time to prove to Paxton the hard way that he had not been lying. Ready to jump out of her skin before his shift, she was now as white as a sheet.

And although Grant felt for her about learning of her heritage in this manner, he had other things to worry about—the damn Lycan interloper being foremost on that list.

That roar hadn't come from far off, which meant the slippery beast had penetrated Desperado's perimeter, somehow managing to slither past Ben and two of their best guards, or else finding another route inside. Moreover, it had to have been close to Paxton again, near that downed tree.

Anger crowded his thoughts.

His vision darkened.

The pack was already on the move. No one could afford to ignore that son of a bitch's challenging howl. By

now, every Were here would know this sucker might be
related to their species, if not exactly like them.

His desert pack was made up of strong, confident
Weres who would protect their secrets with their lives if
they had to. Grant hoped none of them would be pushed
that far. This confrontation was going to end up being
one lone rogue against another Lycan and fourteen desert Weres used to dealing with half-crazed newcomers.
Surely the sucker out there would calculate the odds and
either give up or go away.

Paxton was dead silent as she stared at him, and he
had no way to appease her. No voice with which to comfort her. It was sink or swim time for Andrew Hall's
daughter, and not in any way Grant would have planned
for her big awakening.

When they got to Desperado, he jumped from the
truck to join the others massing in the street. Everyone
was concerned, keyed up and ready to rumble. But as
he had explained to Paxton, without the presence of a
full moon, his packmates were stuck in human form.

Although they all possessed superhuman strength,
these Weres didn't have the extra punch of power embedded into Grant's DNA that allowed the full extent
of his abilities to be at his beck and call. Tonight, in a
standoff with a creature with similar abilities, he'd have
to be the front man. Everyone here was aware of this.

"Bring it on, you filthy bastard."

Shirleen took his place in the truck as the temporary
guardian for the female frozen there. Ben, still at the
gate, would get the message and respond if he hadn't
heard the cheeky trespasser's yowl.

The rest of the pack was scattering to take their
places. One or two of them would search along the fence
near where he had found Paxton. If the bastard had been

there, the atmosphere would still be disturbed in a way
that would be easy for other Weres to pick up on. Grant
hadn't had the chance to investigate, since getting Paxton away from danger had been a priority at the time.

Two or three packmates would position themselves
near the end of the main street, while others had designated areas to watch over. Moonlight, though unhelp-
ful to these Weres tonight in other ways, lit the street
with an iridescent glow.

Grant stood in the center of the main street waiting
for all hell to break loose, certain it would before long.
In the months leading up to now, the rogue hadn't ventured close enough to breathe down Grant's neck, but
something had changed that.

He glanced at the truck, refusing to believe the creep
they had been chasing could have anything to do with
Andrew Hall's daughter. The theory he'd been hatching
seemed to be a wild one, given that Paxton had only arrived that day. Yet the damn beast had tracked her twice
after their initial meeting and was hanging around here
now. Doing what? Biding his time? Looking for a way
to get past the pack?

"What do you want?" Grant sent, figuring only two
things might send a werewolf into tracking mode in
spite of the potential danger involved. Those two things
were piqued interest in a potential mate and a desire to
challenge the alpha of a pack for that title.

"Which one of those things are you after?"

Of course, the answer to that question didn't really
matter. He wasn't going to allow any other Were with
big ideas to get near Paxton. Nor was he about to turn
the guardianship of this pack over to a butcher.

When Paxton left the truck and approached, her
closeness wafted over him like a hot August breeze.

He had to look at her. Couldn't help himself. She was so damn beautiful, and so very pale.

She stopped several feet away, speechless. He wanted more than anything to go to her, hold her, make love to her, chase away the demons he had helped to set in place. A firm hold on his resolve was what it took to keep from doing any of those things.

He morphed back into a more familiar shape and said in his human voice, "I'm needed elsewhere. I'm sorry."

Explaining Paxton's presence in the street, Shirleen said, "Can't keep a good woman down, it seems."

Grant stifled a human-sized growl. His wolf was still close to the surface, wanting to be freed. His pulse was pounding dangerously, but not because of the rogue he needed to find. With chaos all around, Paxton was the larger draw. She stood motionless. Her tousled hair shone in the moonlight like spun gold. Delicate features were set in a grim expression, but no longer frozen in disbelief.

He took that for progress.

As her emotions settled over him, he knew that fear made up only a portion of what Paxton was feeling. Curiosity tangled with other emotions that weren't so easy to read, and Grant was heartened that one of those elusive emotions wasn't disgust.

"It's true," she said softly without budging. "All of it."

Sink or swim, Grant repeated to himself, raising both hands to display leftover claws that had never looked as lethal as they did right then. Nerves burned across taut interior wires while he awaited Paxton's reaction to the only part of him at the moment that hinted of wolf.

"And I…" she started to say, without finishing the remark. Paxton was thinking over the fact that she had screwed a werewolf. She was considering the possible ramifications of that.

There was so much he needed to say to her and tons of information to impart, when none of that would have appeased her. Seeing him shift shape in close quarters had been step one in her introduction to the moon's cult.

There was no time to commiserate on the fluctuations of reality. Seconds were ticking away and he had a job to do. Paxton wasn't the only treasure he had to protect. His pack depended on him to help set things straight.

Would Paxton have understood any of that if he had explained?

Each cell in his body protested when he backed away from her. He faltered when she stumbled forward as if she'd been caught in his wake, and Shirleen put out a hand to stop her. Side by side the two females watched him tear off what was left of his shirt.

He dislodged his human countenance for the fifth time that night with a twitch and a series of shudders. When his spine began to lengthen and his bones snapped, Paxton whispered, "No." She said, "God, no," as his muscles bunched and began to mound with the sound of raw meat being slapped on a counter.

"Welcome to my world, little wolf. Our world," he sent to her as their eyes met.

He watched Paxton stagger and raise a hand to her head, possibly to feel for an injury responsible for making her see things. With his shift complete, Grant filled his lungs with night scents, searching for the one smell among them he needed to find…the scent of an entity that was taking him away from Paxton because that rogue quite possibly coveted things that belonged to someone else.

"Impossible," Paxton repeated, as stone-faced as a statue.

It was too late now for cover-ups and illusions. Wildness was calling. He'd found the scent he needed, and it was too close to ignore. Grant turned from Paxton, who just might have been the love of his life if they had met some other time, whether or not imprinting chained them together.

He looked back at her only once to view the stunned, shocked expression he expected to find frozen on her face. Again, he found that he was wrong. Stunned? Yes. She was registering that. Strangely enough, though, Paxton didn't sway, faint or run the other way. Her expression had turned thoughtful, as if she might have been thinking back and piecing together the events that had taken place since her arrival in Arizona, through the lead-up to this moment.

He let her have those thoughts.

Her big eyes never left him. Her attention was focused and extremely hot. But he could not turn back. Didn't dare. The beast out there was tampering with his pack and this beautiful, as yet undeclared she-wolf, and he was the only barrier standing between them.

Don't you see that, my lover?

Power soared through him. Impatience flared. Feeling strong, fed up, angry over having to leave Paxton and his friends, perhaps at the expense of one or both of those things, Grant let loose a fierce, feral growl that rolled like an aftershock through the dirt beneath his feet.

Then he was off and running, sensing the beast nearby, determined to end this game of hide-and-seek once and for all.

* * *

"Impossible."

The word didn't begin to describe what Paxton had witnessed, but she kept repeating it anyway, needing to expel the shock icing her limbs.

Grant Wade really was a werewolf…which led to the possibility of other things he had told her being true. The beast. Desperado. And what about her?

She might have believed she was dreaming if it hadn't been for the pressure of a hand on her arm—a real pressure that helped to keep her grounded and belonged to a werewolf named Shirleen.

God…

Managing a slight turn of her head, Paxton found an expression of empathy on Shirleen's pretty face. Gathering words together, Paxton asked, "What is this place?"

"Our sanctuary," Shirleen replied.

"Whose sanctuary?"

"Beings like us. Like him."

"Werewolves." Paxton had a hard time saying the word out loud.

"Yes. Werewolves."

"And you?" Paxton asked.

"Not exactly like him, but a close enough rendition to be here with the rest."

"How does this happen, Shirleen? How could it possibly be real?"

"It's a long story, Paxton. Centuries old."

"Then maybe you can start that story now."

"I'll let Grant do the honors," Shirleen said. "Filling you in is the alpha's place."

Alpha.

Hell.

"Where did he go? Where did they all go?" she asked.

"I believe you had a run-in with the wolf they've gone after. Did Grant tell you about this guy?"

"He tried to tell me what that trespasser might be. *Rogue* was the word Grant used. Killing cattle, he said."

She couldn't remember much else with her mind issuing warnings about getting out of there in spite of how dangerous they all seemed to think this rogue was.

"Rogue. Yes." Shirleen waved to the closest building. "It would be best to get off the street now."

The woman who had just admitted to being a werewolf kept one hand clamped to Paxton's arm, so that running anywhere was not an option, though Grant's truck wasn't far from where they were standing. Besides, where would she go if she could run away this time? As far as she knew, and after what had happened to her with the downed tree, the roads in and out of Desperado would probably now be guarded.

Look where trying to escape had landed her. Inside a den of wolves.

The motel in the city now seemed like a stupid place to retreat to, and the airport was too damn far, especially when somewhere between here and there a mad werewolf lurked.

Werewolf.

True.

Several small globes of light winked along the sides of the street. Moonlight on the tips of her shoes made Paxton want to cringe. In all the movies she'd seen, moonlight was the catalyst for werewolf transformation, but the moon wasn't full tonight, so the woman beside her still looked like Shirleen.

Grant had told her about that, too.

This wasn't how she remembered Desperado. As a kid, she had explored every corner of this town without even once coming across a goddamn werewolf. As far as she knew.

"Twenty years," Shirleen said, as if reading her mind. "That's when Desperado first opened its gates to the likes of us."

"That's right after I left it," Paxton mused, briefly closing her eyes to try to assimilate that news.

When Shirleen urged her to move with a strong tug on her arm, Paxton accompanied her to the old general store, where the windows were boarded up and nailed tight. In the past, she had pretended to be the proprietor of this store. When tourists came, she had handed out candy to other kids. Now the tourists were long gone and the town had been taken over by a species of beings that turned furry in the moonlight.

This was hard to believe. Impossible to believe.

She was one of them? Could Grant be right about that one little detail?

They stopped on the store's threshold. The space inside was dark, but not completely. Paxton saw that it wasn't only the missing seasonal residents that had changed Desperado over the years. Where there had once been a counter, a woodstove and some chairs, there was nothing but the gleam of cold steel bars.

It took a minute more for Paxton to understand what she was seeing. Those bars were on cages. The kind of cages that contained wild animals at the zoo. There were two cages, each of them large enough to house a small elephant. On the walls beside them, thick ropes of silver chain hung. Closed metal boxes were stacked near the door.

"It's not pretty, but sometimes necessary," Shirleen said.

Paxton didn't ask the question screaming for an answer in her mind. *Necessary for what?*

Because, deep in her soul, she already knew.

Aiding werewolves going through a tough transition is what Grant had said. But the place looked like a torture chamber, and viewing it made her feel ill all over again.

Chapter 21

Grant followed the scent of wet fur across the rise just north of Desperado. It wasn't usual for werewolves to carry an odor when furred-up. Then again, this one ate cows and, on at least one occasion, while nestling in a dank cave, gnawed on human bones.

Grant grimaced at the thought. He'd never heard of such a thing, yet he knew that bad-guy Weres with grudges against humans existed. He had forgotten to check with Ben about asking the sheriff for a list of missing hikers, and that seemed more important than ever.

Walking at a swift, purposeful pace, he noted how quiet the night was, and that the sky was filled with stars. Desert heat seeped through the soles of his boots. Too bad there was no time to stop and enjoy any of those things.

His packmates guarded the fence line. Grant nodded

to them as he passed. Those Weres were silent, diligent, watchful and used to seeing him in his current form. In a fight, he could count on any of these Weres to have his back. They trusted him to eventually find the crazy rogue who was twice as dangerous as anything they had encountered to date.

Near the section of fence where Paxton had encountered her second fright of the day, Grant halted. Ben had been there and gone, but the place reeked of another, more feral presence.

That elusive sucker hadn't disappeared after all. He was still here.

"Come out," Grant sent.

A response came in the form of a deep, guttural growl, reminiscent of a wolf's stern warning to back off.

"Can't do that," Grant said. *"Since you've been hanging around for a while, you know why."*

The next growl was louder and more menacing than the first one, and raised the hair on the back of Grant's neck.

"Come in and set things right," Grant sent. *"You're causing too many problems that can't be overlooked. Half of the residents in the area are looking for you. We both understand why they can't actually be allowed to find what they seek."*

Sounds came to him of something heavy being dragged over the sandy soil. Christ, had the bastard tagged more cattle?

Waves of chills met with Grant's elevated body temperature. He swore inwardly and turned in a tight circle for a good look around.

"Show yourself. It's not as if I haven't seen the likes of you before."

The voice that responded to his invitation echoed in

his mind with the muffled clang of a rusty bell. The surprise for Grant was how old and weary it sounded.

"You believe that, wolf, about having seen the likes of me?"

Contact.

Grant ran a clawed finger across his left thigh, slicing through his jeans in a show of anger as he spoke.

"I'm guessing you're more like me than I'd care to admit, though I'm leery of your fetish for thievery and teething on things that don't belong to you."

"Then, as I said earlier, you know nothing," was the reply.

"I know this can't go on," Grant warned.

"Who is going to stop me? You?"

"I'm here now for just that reason."

Another growl came from the bushes beside Grant. His muscles tensed, readying for whatever this guy was going to do. Another round of chills rapidly melted behind the heat of his revved up metabolism.

"In a fair fight between us you would lose," the invisible bastard taunted.

"Why don't we test that theory?" Grant raised his hands to prove his willingness to try.

"You have never been my target. If you had been, you would not be here now to defend your little pack of wolves," the trespasser said.

"All the same, you're bringing unwanted attention that none of us can afford."

"Shall I take my hunger elsewhere, then? Bother someone else?" the cheeky bastard said.

"Wouldn't the consequences be the same wherever you went, if stealing animals is your MO?" Grant suggested. *"Not to mention your nasty habit of pouncing on the occasional human. That was you, I assume?"*

Silence fell for several long minutes before the beast spoke again.

"You know about that kill and still believe we're alike?"

"I can smell the power in you," Grant said. *"But I claim no kinship. Your actions sicken me."*

"All wolves once hunted in the wild."

"Until some of us evolved," Grant countered.

More silence, then the rogue said, *"The difference is that you try to fit into a world that would kill you as soon as they found out what you are."*

"Yes." Grant nodded. *"So I'm curious about how you've existed this long, given that you don't seem to give a damn about how anyone might react to your actions."*

"My actions aren't completely selfish, I assure you."

"Prove it. Show yourself. Come in and accept our help."

"I can't do that."

"Then, with so much at stake, it will have to be a fight," Grant challenged.

"Perhaps some other time," the beast said.

Grant shook his head. *"After you've satisfied your need to bring more trouble down on us? Do you even know what we do here?"*

"I know what you do," the beast in the bushes conceded.

"We help our kind deal. We give Weres a place to land when they spin out. Why do you think we can't help you?" Grant asked.

"Because," a human voice said, as if the beast had shape-shifted in seconds to press home the idea of how much power he truly did possess, and to get these last words in, "no one can help me now."

The scent of this newcomer dissipated along with his words, as if the sucker had simply blown away on a stiff breeze. After a minute, nothing of its presence remained.

For Grant, this newest disappearing act was not going to cut it. He moved several paces north, then south and west, inhaling deeply, striving to gain an awareness of where the rogue had gone. He felt like the being he chased wasn't as insane as he'd imagined. In fact, that Lycan had seemed lucid and in control of his faculties.

Grant couldn't fathom why the creature had not wanted to fight. There had been no challenge for the leadership of the desert pack, when if that beast had won, a new alpha could have walked into town that night. The creature he still thought of as a monster hadn't harmed Paxton near the fence, either, which made the tally three for three in benign Paxton sightings.

"What the hell do you want?" he sent far and wide in frustration.

Perplexed, unsatisfied with this meeting, Grant went after the other Lycan. He swept through the area looking for anything that might lead him to the rogue's whereabouts. Eventually, his search paid off. Kneeling down, he ran a claw over the thin red trail that had appeared almost out of nowhere and ended several feet ahead. The blood trail was puzzling, but didn't offer up any real clue as to the Lycan's actual direction.

"Who the hell are you? Houdini?"

Standing, scanning, barely breathing, Grant let out a howl of irritation that was answered by every coyote between where he stood and the ghost town behind him. The blood on the ground didn't belong to any missing steer. Not this time. So what poor, unsuspecting human being had lost it?

* * *

Paxton shrank back with a shoulder to the doorjamb. The room, and what it contained, was scary. What were the cages for? What was going on here? Worse still, in terms of causing a hair-raising adrenaline rush, was the way Shirleen suddenly bolted for the door, nearly knocking Paxton over in her hurry to get outside.

Loath to be alone with those ominous cages, Paxton followed Shirleen, supposing the woman was tuning in to a sound Paxton couldn't hear. Two others joined them in the street. People? Weres who hadn't shape-shifted tonight? They were large guys, tall, relatively young, very well built—and examples of a world that had gone mad.

All three of her new companions were facing west, so Paxton whirled to stare in that direction, fighting the desire to duck in case more bad news was coming.

"He found something," Shirleen announced, and the men beside her backed into the shadows hugging the buildings.

Anxious, Paxton said, "Grant?"

Shirleen nodded, then turned again toward the entrance to town, visibly tensing. "Shit," she whispered.

If Shirleen's body language hadn't caused Paxton's nervousness, that one word would have done the trick. It didn't take a psychic to understand trouble was in the air and headed their way, although Paxton had no idea what kind of trouble everyone here was expecting.

By the time she began to consider this, strange feelings began to take her over. She couldn't have described them. In spite of the fact that she couldn't see anything past the old saloon, she somehow knew...yes, she *knew* Grant was returning.

His nearness brought unexpected heat. A spot deep

inside her began to quiver, as if Grant would again soon touch her there. Limbs began to quake, as they had when wrapped around Grant's waist. Her stance wobbled. Her head hurt. Grant was coming back and she wanted to run out to meet him, but couldn't.

Grant wasn't a man in the strictest sense of that word. He was something else.

Beside her, Shirleen spoke. "Now isn't the time to distract him."

Paxton had seen Grant go from man to werewolf and still hadn't been able to grasp the full meaning of that. She had seen the claws and the face that, though changed, still had the same baby-blue eyes. Not a mindless monster's eyes, but eyes glowing with an intelligent gleam.

He appeared at the end of the street now, as if she had conjured him. As Grant walked, he began to change back to the man she recognized. But truthfully, his alter ego wasn't so far removed from the human persona's glorious package. It was somehow more of the same.

As he headed toward her, Paxton's knees weakened. Her heart slammed against her ribs. Grant was coming for her and something had upset him. He was broadcasting concern in ways she easily understood.

"Paxton."

She was sure she heard him say her name.

"Yes?" She inched forward.

And then she was in Grant's arms, tight against that marvelous muscle, enfolded in his incredible heat. All the while, her mind urged her to be careful and to stop the madness. Warnings came to break away because Grant wasn't normal. He wasn't even human.

Breathing was difficult. With her head pressed to his chest and her resolve on hiatus, Paxton heard him speak in thoughts to Shirleen. His words and sentences were like whispers from a far-off place.

"Dangerous," he said. *"More than we thought. So far beyond what we had imagined."*

Grant had found the trespasser he was hunting. Possibly that trespasser and the creature she had, early on, believed to be a bear were one and the same.

Concern wasn't the only thing Grant was telegraphing to her through their closeness. He wanted to protect her, save her from having to face what he had found. That goal was paramount in his short list of objectives. Save her. Save his friends. Save Desperado and whatever he did here with those awful steel cages.

Nerves that ran along the wires under Grant's skin seemed to fire hers up in an invasion of blistering heat. The hardness of his body and the realization of how much she noticed it became another insurmountable obstacle to regaining her wits.

Thinking seriously about pulling back, and about reexamining her mental state, Paxton knew that yelling for help was completely out of the realm of possibility. Who would hear her and come to her aid when this man was their leader? Which of these werewolves would challenge or defy him?

She felt him begin to shake. She felt his heat spike to a degree well beyond impossible range. And, still, she did not run.

When Grant tilted her head back to look into her face, there was no claw on his index finger. When he forced her to meet his eyes by whispering her name seductively, Paxton obeyed.

Their bodies were pressed tightly together, and Grant didn't seem to mind that there were others present. Holding her hostage with an apologetic gaze and an unspoken promise, it was a man's lips that rested on hers lightly, briefly. Except that the kiss didn't feel light or brief to Paxton. It felt like goodbye.

When Paxton opened her eyes, she found herself being lifted into Grant's strong arms. "I'm not a baby," she protested. "And I'm perfectly able to take care of myself."

Swear to God, she would have said more if Grant's hungry mouth had allowed her to. His lips kept returning to hers, sampling, tasting, as if he couldn't get enough.

She was in Grant's arms and they were moving off the street. Light disappeared when they went inside the old general store. She wondered if he was going to take her there, on the floor. If the kisses didn't stop, she might even allow that, in spite of what he was.

After several more steps his mouth finally withdrew from hers, but Grant continued to hold her.

Finally, he set her down.

Their eyes met again. His were filled with regret. Was this the goodbye she had anticipated, felt, sensed? Would he head back out to continue his search for the bad guy, maybe without hope of returning?

Grant backed away from her slowly and spoke to her for the first time since his return to town minutes ago. "I'm sorry for this. It is necessary. You will have to trust me on that."

"What do you mean?" Her voice was raspy with hunger for Grant Wade, whatever the hell he was.

The sound of metal clanging on metal filled the space. Following that came the sound of a bolt sliding into place. Still, it took more time for Paxton to comprehend what had just happened, and by then Grant had moved out of sight.

Dread struck. Panic hit with sheets of ice that replaced the former heat of her internal furnace. *Had he? No. He couldn't have.*

Shoving both of her hands forward, Paxton took hold of the steel bars keeping her from accompanying Grant's departure. They were the cold steel bars of one of the cages she had seen.

Her head swam with the uncertainty of the situation. Her mind protested over and over again. Hell, had she been wrong? That kiss, hot, insatiable, had not been meant as a sad temporary goodbye or been evidence of the pleasure of a blissful reunion between lovers.

It had been a distraction.

A lie.

And a trap.

Chapter 22

Grant's heart hurt. But his reasons for caging Paxton had been sound. She would be safe until the time came for an all-clear. That stubborn streak of hers could get her into trouble, when trouble is exactly what they didn't need more of.

His body continued to ache from too many shape-shifts in the span of a day. Even Lycan bones and tissues had their limits. Part of his discomfort also stemmed from another source, however, and that was from having to leave Paxton like this.

She didn't call out to him, scream or shout obscenities. Silence accompanied his exit from the building. An absolute absence of sound. Bless her, Paxton might actually be trusting him. Either that or she was too stunned to react.

He wanted to go back in there and explain why she needed to be out of the picture for a while. He'd tell her that cage was as much for her protection as it was for everyone else's, and that the rogue out there had more on his mind than waylaying hikers or cattle. The bastard hadn't been able to hide from another Lycan the emotions driving him toward Desperado.

That wicked creature was interested in Paxton. Too interested. While the beast's brief conversation hadn't resulted in an explanation of what that rogue wanted, his mind had offered up the first real clue.

Paxton was the unspoken name that had filled the creature's mind.

Since there had been ample opportunity in the past few months for the rogue to have headed into the old ghost town and he hadn't, Grant might have done them all a disservice by bringing Paxton here. Actually, it turned out that he had ended up using Paxton as bait to corner a madman.

There was no way he could he have told Paxton this, frightening her more than he already had by shifting in her presence. No. She had to remain ignorant of this new turn of events.

"Paxton, I'm sorry," he said, knowing she wouldn't hear that or the sincerity of his apology.

One good thing was in their favor. His fair-haired lover was stronger than she looked and had wolf blood in her veins. They had mated, man to woman, forming a bond that went beyond anything in the human world, and no good-for-nothing Lycan with foul habits and evil tendencies was going to set foot here or have face time with her again.

I promise you this, Paxton. He will not get to you.

"Was that necessary?" Shirleen asked, coming up behind him. Shirleen had confessed to liking Paxton, so she would be wondering why he had locked Paxton in that cage.

"She is the draw," Grant replied. "He wants to come for her."

"Strange how you all seem to think so," Shirleen said thoughtfully.

"Yes, well, you're already taken, so what kind of extraordinary she-wolf does that leave?" Grant teased.

"You think he will come here for her?" Shirleen pressed. "In spite of how many of us there are?"

"I think he might."

"To do what? Why her?"

"Lycan," Grant said, uttering the one word that possibly explained what that rogue wanted.

Shirleen's eyes widened. "Andrew Hall's daughter is Lycan?"

"Afraid so."

Shirleen let that go. "It isn't that rogue's blood I smell on you. Whose blood is it?"

"He left a trail to throw me off the scent. It worked. I lost him."

Shirleen looked past him, toward the building housing the cages. "How long will she be in there?"

"As long as it takes to get to the bottom of this creepy escapade."

She blocked his path when he began to walk. "Full moon tomorrow. Paxton might actually need that cage then."

Grant shut his eyes to ride out the sensation of falling through space without a parachute. Shirleen was right about Paxton. Who could predict what would happen when that full moon rolled around and how it might affect the woman he'd started to think of as his mate?

He'd have to be watchful on two fronts if that thing—

that mad beast out there—caught a whiff of Paxton in
the middle of her first shape-shift and decided to do
something about it. Even worse would be for the rogue
to come after her tonight.

Shirleen spoke again with the kind of logic she always displayed. "If he waits until tomorrow night to
confront us, it will be better for us all. Half the wolf
power this pack will have under the full moon would
surely be sufficient to contain one Lycan."

Grant had to agree. But he felt nervous about how
much damage a rogue Lycan could do, whether or not
his friends were furred-up and ferocious.

He said, "Don't you suppose he will have considered that scenario?"

"Then if he has any plans to come here, he would
implement that plan tonight when we're more vulnerable. Right?"

And that, Grant thought, was the reason for his anxiousness and the impetus for caging Paxton. The bastard out there could shift without the full moon, and
that trick could cost this pack dearly.

He glanced to the end of the street, aware of the posi-
tioning of each member of his pack. With his eyes shut,
his abilities allowed him to locate Ben and the others
at the fence. Given that the beast out there had similar abilities, the rogue would also know those things.

It wasn't safe to think about Paxton. It wasn't safe
to feel anything for her. He had to close down all channels that led to her and hope the sudden silence would
be sufficient to keep a monster out.

That was the plan.

Such was his intention.

Until Paxton, just twenty feet behind him and en-
closed by a metal cage meant to withhold the strength

of a male Were in the throes of a life-changing event, touched his mind with a call that was a plea for help. A call he couldn't refuse in spite of the obstacles facing this pack because they were so completely connected.

Holy hell!

His mind reeled. She wasn't just a she-wolf in the disguise of an unsuspecting human. Nothing so simple as that.

Paxton was much, much more. And tonight, after all these years, without a full moon in attendance and in a scene complicated by the added bonus of having a mad wolf knocking at their door…Paxton Hall was coming into her heritage one damn claw at a time.

Sickness twisted Paxton's stomach with a grip so tight, breathing was nearly impossible. Thinking was out of the question. Standing up was no longer an option.

Sinking to her knees, blinded by the onset of pain so sudden and intense she wondered if she had been shot, Paxton cried out. The onslaught of agony was all-encompassing and not focused in any one spot. Her head was being crushed in a vice. Strength left her limbs. Her heartbeat fluttered weakly and she couldn't lift her head. She felt as though she were dying, one desperate, insufficient breath at a time.

Vision tunneled, blotting out the small globe of light that had been her lifeline. But moonlight flooded the space, cutting through the dark to reach her from the open doorway and creating a dappled pattern on the front of her thighs. With it came a wave of cold almost as terrible as the initial strike of pain that had driven her to the floor.

She had to be dying. But why?

"Grant!"

Had she said his name out loud when breathing was a stretch?

"Grant…"

He had promised to protect her. Or had she imagined that?

"It's killing me," she whispered, doubling over without any real idea about what *it* was.

Moonlight touched her face now with a cold caress. She shrank back from the only light left in the dark, having nowhere to go and no way to escape her steel prison.

Inhaling the moonlight brought up bile that made her choke. Paxton felt her pulse take a dive. As a nurse, Paxton understood what those symptoms meant. She was going into shock and had never felt so sick and so completely alone.

"Grant. Please."

Why did she think Grant Wade might swoop in to help her when he had put her in this cage and left her here? If someone was to blame for her current state, it was Grant.

Not true…

She had wanted to come here. To Desperado. All along, she had pushed toward the events that had befallen her.

There was no energy left to raise a shout. Her blood pressure had plummeted. The first convulsion arrived swiftly with a nasty body wave that pressed her against the steel bars for support. Paxton's forehead slammed against metal highlighted by a beam of silvery lunar particles, and she hardly noticed the impact. Her back arched dramatically. Bones crackled. Inside her, more trouble was brewing. Something deep in her gut was clawing its way upward from her stomach to her chest, wreaking havoc along the way.

The second convulsion sent her to the floor, curled up in a fetal position. She shook so violently, the hard surface she laid on scratched through her clothes, bruising tender, stinging skin. She was sinking beneath a wave of darkness streaked with those damn light particles.

And then, as though someone had flipped a switch, the remaining light went out.

Eyes shut, pulse faint, Paxton thought she heard shouts in the distance. Her mind buzzed with static. She breathed fresh rounds of pain, shook with pain, absorbed each wicked example of extreme physical torture by curling up tighter and trying desperately to hold on to the remaining vestiges of life.

"I don't want to die here," were the last words she got out before that darkness became nearly total.

But she wasn't gone yet. Thoughts still blinked in and out, though the breaths she groped for were inadequate. Only one tactile sensation remained—the icy burn of the steel bar her fingers were clamped to.

Refuse to give in.

Refuse to give up.

Sharp screeching sounds rang in her mind... unfamiliar noises of no particular concern when she faced pain so encompassing.

Was someone approaching?

Maybe she imagined that.

Wait. Yes. Someone was there. Her fingers were being pried from the steel bar, and she didn't want to let go. If she did, all sensation would be lost.

"Paxton," a deep voice crooned. "It's okay. I'm here."

Grant's voice. He had returned after leaving her there.

You put me here, you bastard. She could not say this out loud.

The stronger voice overrode her unspoken thought. "This was for your own good. I left you here to keep you safe. Please believe me. I had no idea this would happen now."

Bastard.

A set of instructions followed that she had to consider.

"Don't let your mind slip away. It's important that you hang on to what makes you *you.* That might sound strange, but I'm sure you know what I mean. Can you open your eyes, Paxton? Open your eyes and look at me?"

Hurt. She couldn't have said that out loud, either, because her lips were numb. Fear of seeing a face that might no longer resemble Grant was what kept her eyes tightly shut.

"I know you hurt," he sympathized. "I understand what that pain is like. However, you must do as I ask. Open your eyes. Trust me. Take a chance and open them now."

Her lashes flapped once, twice. She couldn't communicate the fact that she lacked the strength to do what was asked of her.

Can't.

"You can," he directed, as if he had heard her reply. "You bear the mark that indicates a strength you might not yet comprehend. Remember? There's a mark on your arm like mine. It's there for a reason. Only those of us from a long-lived family line of survivors possess that mark. When you open your eyes, you'll see that."

More cold rushed in. Shaking ensued, along with more convulsions. Paxton again had the sensation of being about to leave her body, and she picked up the inward chant that had become her mantra.

Refuse to let go.

Refuse to give in.

"Yes. That's it," the deep voice applauded. "Fight, Paxton. I've seen that fight in you. The pain is temporary. Rise above it and become what you're meant to be. There's no going back or holding back the tide once it has begun, so you must stay with me, little wolf. It's time for you to understand who and what you are."

Don't like what you're suggesting, she protested in silence, unable to argue. Was she supposed to place her trust in a man who hadn't been honest with her from the start? A man who wasn't actually a man at all, but a creature straight out of late-night TV?

Grant was here with her. Who else would know about the mark on her upper arm? His voice had the ability to move her.

Excitement jump-started her heartbeat, and yet Paxton still felt half in and half out of the world, as if she floated somewhere in between two places. *A bridge between two worlds,* Grant had said.

She feared one more quake might do her in.

"Paxton."

Grant's authoritative tone served to gather up her rapidly fraying attention.

"It's a good life," he said. "You'll see. You have to want it badly enough to get through this phase. Most of us with the mark can. You can. There is no acceptable alternative. Now open your eyes and see the world as it really is."

Having no idea where the energy came from to do as

Grant asked, Paxton opened her eyes. The light hadn't gone. Grant Wade's broad shoulders were blocking it. He was beside her on the floor, looking completely human and cradling her against a bare chest that supplied enough warmth to burn through her tremors.

The icy fear began to melt. Her body's tightness eased slightly. Paxton blinked up at Grant, wanting to thank him for coming back, but unable to do so because his human semblance was a disguise that hid the secrets beneath his bronzed skin.

Not a man...

Still, God, his heat was soothing and necessary. Paxton wanted desperately to curl into him and hear Grant tell her there was nothing inside her that didn't belong there, and that the sickness rolling through her wasn't related to him and what he was. She needed him to confirm this was a dream from which she'd soon wake up.

But he called her a "little wolf," and the words rang in her ears with a discordant sound. Those words were a mistake. Grant was the wolf. Werewolf. She was Paxton, and that was all. Next up would be to get out of there the minute she could move her legs.

"This is just the beginning," Grant said slowly, as if trying to soften bad news. "There's just a little more. The next flash of pain will be worse. You might want to die. But you will withstand that pain, Paxton. You must not leave me. Handle what she will throw your way, my beautiful lover."

"She?"

When she asked that question, Paxton heard Grant's reactive sigh of relief.

"The moon," he said. "To me, the moon is female. For you, it might be different."

She felt Grant lifting her. He was rescuing her after

putting her here in the first place. Before her next breath, she was in his arms and they were moving toward the doorway, toward the light shining there.

That light wasn't the final white glare that sick and dying people mentioned in hushed voices, because she had not died in the cell. Already, she could breathe easier and move her arms. Fresh air filled her oxygen-starved lungs.

More of the terrible tunneling darkness receded as Grant carried her onto the covered porch outside the building. Moonlight lit the street, slanting in from a position low over the top of the nearby mountain range. Though the light was weaker now, it was in a perfect position to have reached her inside the room behind them through the open doorway.

Grant carried her into the empty street, holding her tightly, probably realizing she couldn't have stood on her own. Whereas she had always been fiercely independent, Paxton now felt like a child.

"If this has already started, moonlight might aid the transition, might make things easier. Are you ready to see?" he whispered with his face close to hers.

Grant's face. No mistake. Big eyes. Chiseled cheekbones. Expression of concern.

"And may fortune be in our favor, Paxton, so that the damn beast sniffing around won't get wind of this before it's done."

Paxton had no idea what he was going on about. Concentration hadn't caught up after sliding into a caged abyss. Her face and lips tingled, coming alive after being numb. Her body felt brittle and way too rigid.

The way Grant held her suggested that he thought she might break if he set her down. Maybe he thought she'd pass out. His energy buzzed through her as if he could, by some kind of fancy transference, shore up her energy with some of his own.

It was, of course, too late for anyone to help her. When Grant leaned back and moonlight touched her again, the thing nestled inside her soared to the surface.

Chapter 23

In his arms, Paxton shuddered once more.

Grant shored up his grip on her.

Her head was thrown back, exposing a smooth expanse of pale ivory neck he wanted to nuzzle. Her legs, clad in dirt-speckled jeans, dangled over his arms. Paxton felt so very light; he feared there would be no room for her small-boned frame to graduate to the next phase of her first shape-shift.

But her body was trying to do just that.

He wasn't going to let her go or let her die. Silently, he sent her one message of encouragement after another, backing up those messages with a push of his own personal power. She didn't scratch at him or fight. Her hands covered her face because the light was hurting her eyes. On her upper arm, below her short T-shirt sleeve, sat the ring of silvery tissue that looked like his.

Who the hell knows where your moon mark comes

from or how Andrew kept it a secret? he mused, not wanting to mention Paxton's father's name. Andrew Hall had never set foot in Desperado since Grant took over as caretaker and alpha of the desert pack. Though Grant had bunked in the guesthouse, Andrew had seldom been in residence, preferring another, undisclosed location for his long-term illness.

They had never crossed paths or spoken face-to-face. After word of his death arrived, Andrew's will had been the only remaining link to a legacy directed at werewolves…from a man with knowledge of the species who, for some reason, cared enough to help.

Paxton had to be that reason, Grant surmised. Her father had brought her here and had sent her straight into Grant's arms. He hadn't been wrong about Paxton's wolf blood—it had to have come from family. There was no way to copy a mark like hers. Although he didn't have proof of her father's heritage, and Andrew Hall had certainly never admitted to being part of the species he protected, the man had to have been a pure-blooded werewolf.

If Andrew had been a Were, it explained *her.* This. Now. What it failed to address was how Paxton had held off her wolf for so long and how she could be going through the change without a full moon present. Those things would suggest she was Lycan, and also that he had been an insensitive idiot for not picking up on it when sensing Weres was his business.

Damn it, he was anxious for Paxton, who was in the dark in so many ways. If offered the choice, he would gladly have changed places in order to take on her pain. At the moment, with her shirt torn open and what remained of her flimsy lingerie exposed, the belief that she could be a Were seemed ludicrous.

He wished they'd had more time in that damn bunk-house and that he could have explained to her what to expect. She wouldn't have believed him, of course. Not many people could have, in her place.

Grant's heart skidded in anticipation of what would happen next. Paxton would be enough like him to be able to stay with him if she chose to. She would be free to love him if that's the way her heart ran after just one day together.

One frigging day that felt like years.

Imprinting was a hell of a thing to have taken hold of him so quickly. Taken hold of both of them, it now seemed to him.

New shudders rocked Paxton, punctuated by her muffled groans of surprise and pain, before her body went limp in his arms. Grant anxiously waited for movement that didn't come. For her big break from human status to manifest. Paxton didn't open her eyes or acknowledge where she was. Her breathing again was shallow. So far, other than a few good quakes, there had been no real hints of a big reveal.

But he wasn't wrong about what she was going through. Any werewolf could have recognized the signs.

As if his last thought had nudged a reaction, Paxton suddenly kicked out with both legs. She squirmed and began to fight his tight hold. Her head came up with a snap. She opened her eyes.

Their gazes met and held long enough for Grant to see a reflection of the moonlight in those amber irises seconds before the golden color began to darken.

Next clue. The flash of gold all Lycans possessed.

The time for ignorance and denial was over.

Paxton's face began to alter like soft sand sifting into a new shape. Slowly, and with the moon granting his plea for leniency on Paxton's behalf, her pale cheeks sharpened without making her scream. Deep hollows formed, and the angles made her thin face seem twice as delicate.

Moonlight melted on her skin. Her face and bare neck shone with a silvery luminescence, as if she had swallowed moonlight and it shone through her pores. Because breathing was difficult for her, she panted, taking in air through her mouth. As her chin began to elongate, her moan of discomfort was a barely perceptible sound.

"Yes," he said to her. "Let it out."

She had larger eyes now, and a longer neck. She had taken on an otherworldly look that was ethereal, yet backed by steel. Her arms were defined. Long blond hair flowed down her back.

Paxton was shifting in his arms and hadn't cried out or doubled over to retch her guts out. Her overall size hadn't changed. Some of her features hadn't yet rearranged because she had paused part of the way through her transition. And though Paxton no longer looked quite like any human on Earth, and didn't resemble Shirleen or any other she-wolf he had ever known or seen, she was a Were in her very soul. Different. Beautiful. Unique.

Lycan.

Grant stared at the result of the moon's purposeful early caress with his heart thundering. The wolf in him begged to respond to Paxton's wolfishness. She was the wolf of his dreams. His wishes for a mate had been answered.

"You are beautiful," he said to her, slightly in awe, meaning every word.

But the face-altering business was only a moment of

calm before the storm. After another racking shudder, Paxton again went rigid. The familiar crack of bone on bone came as her spine snapped to a new alignment. Soon after that, her struggle to get free intensified.

Though Grant wasn't so sure about obliging that request for freedom, or what she would do if left on her own after the shock of this new identity, he loosened his hold.

"What if you get away? What if you run?" he said. "Danger lies beyond these walls, Paxton. Tonight, if the beast out there has his way, everything might come tumbling down around us."

She couldn't speak. Her body had changed in this second wave of shifting, but not tremendously, and she was still breathing.

Paxton Hall, she-wolf, was breathtaking. This close to her, Grant's wolf was not to be caged. His claws, face, chest and spine, morphed in seconds as he continued to hold Paxton close. The look on her new face when she witnessed this was priceless, but she couldn't protest, argue or feign disbelief. There were two werewolves here. Paxton's inner self, long in captivity, had finally been set free.

"Damn!" Shirleen's tone was one of surprise. "What the hell?"

Fully shifted, Grant's senses strengthened. While he wanted to deal with Paxton, something else dared to vie for his attention. He looked west with sudden interest. Silently, swiftly, Grant set Paxton down, ruing the need for a few inches of distance when he wanted to go at her in animal-to-animal fashion and solidify their bond. His need to possess her was so strong, he backed up a few more steps to keep from touching Paxton again, afraid he'd never let go if he did.

Paxton didn't run away. She sank to a crouch, attempting to deal with new parameters for balance. Her eyes were damp when they again met his, and reddened by the pain she had not yet put behind her.

"Welcome to my world," he sent to her. *"To our world."*

Soft growls of protest escaped from her throat.

"The beast comes," he sent to her. *"Can you hear me? Can you feel his presence out there, somewhere close?"*

In spite of her quakes, Paxton stared back.

Bless her, she was on board. Paxton was Lycan, another term for strong and fierce. However, there was much more to come, just as he had promised her.

His first instinct was a primal one—an urge to throw her on the ground and possess her. They could imprint their brains out if he showed Paxton everything a Were could do with a mate, twice over.

The ache he carried inside for finding a real partner had intensified a thousand times, and at the moment there was nothing he could do about it. Whatever he and Paxton had to work out had to be postponed. His terrible, gnawing need for her had to be ignored.

"It will be okay," he promised.

But could he keep that promise? She might be stronger as a werewolf, yet she remained a fledgling, without the knowledge of how to access and wield the new power she possessed. Christ, she couldn't even stand up.

Paxton was vulnerable, sick, and he had to leave her. Had to. He was alpha. Helping Weres come into their own was his gig and what he had signed on for, but they were all stuck in the middle of a mystery only partially solved by Paxton's arrival and late transformation.

What happened to you all these years, to keep you from this? How have you postponed what your heritage demanded?

Big freaking surprise.

By fornicating with Grant the werewolf, she had caught his disease, and she could have killed him for that—if she didn't want to ravage his body first.

The only sound Paxton could dig up was a growl—the kind of sound wild animals made when angry, threatened and in distress. That was appropriate as hell, she supposed, since it seemed like she *was* an animal.

The world had tilted off its axis, and she was hanging on by her claws. She had somehow been treated to an unwelcome physical software upgrade that had tripped her system into uncharted territory, and she didn't know what to do or how to react.

The shock was not only staggering, it was slowing her defenses and leaving her afraid to even try to comprehend what she had become. Her skin was on fire. Nerves were frying with each upward degree of core body temperature. Her legs felt like someone else's legs. She didn't recognize her trembling hands.

But Grant was on the move, and she could not lose him. He had the answers to this riddle. If he had given her this disease, perhaps he knew how to reverse it.

Without knowing how, she found herself shadowing him, somehow able to walk, quickly finding her balance, if not her sanity. He didn't like having a shadow and growled a warning for her to stay back. Without him, though, she was in limbo. Fear clenched her insides. Desperado's buildings seemed darker, more sinister, when she had long ago loved this place.

Was she going mad?

Grant strode toward the end of town, halting twice more to issue sounds of displeasure when she ignored his warnings about being left behind. Paxton prayed he soon would wake her up.

"Help me."

His shoulders tensed as if he heard her thought, yet he kept moving toward the darker places beyond the old wood walls.

Paxton's shock was making way for a litany of strange new sensations. The warm breeze ruffling her hair was unusually sensual. Desert heat slid down her body to slip inside her jeans, leaving her thighs tingling. She wanted to tear off her clothes and run naked through the dark, cool off and mate with Grant on blistering desert soil, rutting like animals.

Off came her shirt, tossed aside. The mark on her upper arm felt like it had been made by the kind of hot iron brand ranchers used to mark their animals, and it seemed larger, deeper, more visible. Scarier still, it did look like leftover damage from a large animal bite.

Moon mark was what Grant had called it. Bearing the mark was proof she was like him, he had said. If that were true, it had taken having a sexual liaison with Grant to find out she was something unimaginable. Something inhuman.

Stumbling twice before getting her stride down smoothly, Paxton refused to slow until she reached the edge of town, near the old mining office. Grant had stopped there and was looking at her over his shoulder. His expression was one of regret. It took her a few seconds to register that he had shifted again, so fast she hadn't had time to notice. The human face he presented to her was a camouflage, as was his hunky cowboy body.

"Not a lie," he said soberly, in response to her thought. "This is the face I was born with. It's the one I present to the world most of the time so that we can all get along."

Paxton shook her head, but was sorry she did. The piercing pain behind her eyes was excruciating. The inability to speak brought more panic. *"Not the real you, Grant."*

"Both faces are me," he corrected. "I'm the same guy who picked you up at the airport and..."

He was hearing her thoughts, however absurd that idea was, and he wanted her to understand what was going on without having the time to tell her exactly what that was.

"Show me the other one," she said to him in her mind. *"Change again for me."*

"I have to stop a beast from getting here, Paxton. He is too damn close, and though you're a Lycan, you are new at it and much too vulnerable to help in this fight. You'll have to stay here and keep back. A stint in that damn cage truly was meant for your protection."

Paxton's hands stung so badly, she growled in terror. Hearing the sound made her want to cry. As she stared at the sharp little claws working their way through the tips of her fingers, she vowed not to faint.

Never been weak...

This is only a dream.

She ventured another silent question. *"Does that beast have something to do with this place? Does it have anything to do with me, since I've encountered it twice?"*

"Damned if I know what it wants here," Grant replied. "Nor do I really want to find out after everything I've learned about this creature. But I have to find him. You do understand that, after what I've told you? You do see how necessary it is to keep Desperado off human radar?"

He wasn't telling her the truth. Paxton leaned forward. The inferno inside her was taking its toll, driving her crazy, making her twitch. The wolf in her was outrageously issuing X-rated demands in spite of the appalling situation she found herself in—this unshakable dream that seemed so real.

And Grant was withholding secrets that pertained to her.

She saw the same level of lust she was feeling reflected in Grant's blue eyes, but it seemed that his ability to control it was a hell of a lot better than hers. Fear, lust and greed were like a sudden heat wave coloring the space between them.

Grant was upset, nervous and preoccupied. When he turned to sniff the air, the scent he was after hit her like a flying brick. In that breeze was a smell she recognized.

Paxton dropped to a predatory crouch. With one hand in the dirt and the other on the mark on her arm that burned like a sharp-tipped arrow had been embedded in her flesh, she glanced up in time to see Grant shape-shift again in a fast ruffling of time and rippling flesh.

Screaming was not an option. Arguing took a back seat to the sheer amazement of what she was seeing for the third time. In this form, the intimacy of their connection blossomed. She had a new appreciation for the large, formidable werewolf whose face exposed the anger he was feeling and whose skin undulated continuously as though unsure of which form to take.

"I know that scent," she sent to him, and he nodded without asking more details.

The creature Grant was expecting was none other than her bear...the bear that wasn't a bear at all, but something everyone here expected to be far worse. Hell, her instincts shouted, what could be worse than a god-damn werewolf?

Still, now, as she inhaled the scent of the stranger out there beyond Desperado's walls, bits of memory, sharp as broken glass shards, came crashing back. Memories tied up with that same scent in a not-so-pretty red bow, suggesting that Desperado had always been strange, and she had just been too young to notice.

Grant ran, skimming the ground with a burst of speed.

In his mind, he had connected with Paxton's vision of what this intruder was, and that picture left a bit-ter taste in his mouth. This creature she had mistaken for a bear was a werewolf, all right. He'd pegged that early on. What he had not foreseen was the immensity of power connected to that wolf and the sheer force of the creature's oncoming presence.

Grant felt as though he'd been hit with a battering ram square in the chest as Paxton's haunting howl rang from the town behind him. She was in need of help, but she hadn't followed him. Paxton hadn't moved from the spot where she crouched to duck the fear coming at her from an awareness of that unseen creature's approach.

The air again was filled with the odor of damp fur, nearly missed because Paxton's sweet scent still filled his lungs, taking his mind off business.

Sour odors grew stronger near the fence. Ben was there, watching, waiting, with another pack member, equally alert. Neither of those Weres would be tuned in to this. Their wolves were tucked away and buried deep for one more day.

Lycan to Lycan was how this would happen, with Paxton included in that scenario. She had noticed the scent. She bore the mark of her Lycan lineage, however unfortunate that might have turned out to be. Her transformation without a full moon kept the puzzle of her existence foremost in his mind.

Ben nodded a silent greeting. As soon as Grant cleared the gates, he took off running.

When he reached the small rise of earth and sand he had stood on the month before, Grant stopped. The foreign pressure was growing stronger by the minute. Edgy, and with his nerves charged, Grant's silent internal alarms tripped. How much harm was this beast hoping to inflict? It was here again, so soon.

"This gets tedious. Where the hell are you, beast?"

The desert was the same unusual quiet that didn't bode well in terms of surprises. Claws ready, Grant dragged in a raw, ragged breath and widened his stance. Time seemed suspended as he flexed his muscles and rolled his shoulders.

From a pool of darkness no longer blessed by moonlight, the damn beast finally showed up in the flesh.

Chapter 24

Paxton was a kid again and reliving the past.

She had never been afraid of the ghost town that had been her special place, at least in secret. Back then, each moment spent on her own in the town had been stolen and short-lived. Just her and her pony, breaking rules.

Rarely had she been allowed here after dusk, even with others around. Never alone. Never when it was dark. That rule had been at the top of her father's long list and set in stone. Her father's rules were to be obeyed.

But she had always been a rebel, even at an early age.

Now, a certain familiar scent had triggered an uncanny resonance with the past. The buildings around her began to shift the way Grant had, growing, darkening, wavering, until their shadows stretched to find her…as if reaching out to the shirtless freak with a new face whose hands were decorated, not with rings, but with the markings of an animal.

Paxton shook off a bout of lightheadedness and concentrated hard, realizing that something unusual had been here then, too…breathing, hiding, watching. Kid senses had perceived the anomaly and filed it away because to a six-year-old, not much in the gray area registered as either good or bad.

Desperado was the gray area, she now knew, and always had been.

More shards came, sharper, slightly out of reach, as Paxton thought back.

There had been sounds in the afternoons beyond her pony's hoofbeats on the packed dirt road. Whispers. Chatter that mimicked the wind passing through cracks in the old boards. She was bothered by a similar kind of chatter now, in the present, and this anomaly served to temporarily link both time frames.

Her ability to stay in the past was disturbed by Grant calling to her in his thoughts. He hadn't really told her what he wanted from her. There hadn't been time. What, then, would happen if she pursued her objective to sell off this town, now that she was one of the creatures Desperado housed?

Impossible had become her key word of the day.

In the span of a few hours, everything had changed. She had changed, literally. Desperado not only held Grant's secrets, it held some of hers, if she could only find them.

Grant was regretting his hasty departure and needed her to know that. But other whispers returned to tug at her thoughts with more remembrances of older days, as though those old secrets were just out of reach. Inside those memories, it seemed to her now, someone other than Grant had spoken her name with determination—not out loud, but as a thought sent

directly to her mind, similar to the way Grant sometimes communicated with her.

Those two worlds Grant had spoken of were merging with a dizzying display of overlapping sights and
noises. Underneath it all, the ringing in her ears sig-
naled a possible imminent loss of consciousness that
she wasn't going to allow. *Not now. No way.*

"Paxton?" a voice called out.

She couldn't decide if this voice was real or imagined. In the present or from her past.

"Paxton, can you hear me? I think you can. It's
Shirleen. We've got to move out of the street. Take
cover."

Shirleen was interrupting her search for the missing
part of her past Paxton was determined to find. She had
to know what had been hiding here back then and what
she hadn't seen.

"Can you change back, the way he does?" Shirleen
asked, strain evident in her tone.

Paxton had no idea if that was possible.

"The rest of us are strong and mostly human tonight.
In Grant's absence, we're charged with your safety and
the safety of this town," Shirleen said. "You, like this,
standing in the middle of the street, doesn't help the
cause."

Paxton got that with the force of a sucker punch to
the gut. Desperado was being threatened and Grant
supposed she was part of that.

Four-letter curses stuck in her throat. Her palms were
bleeding from fisting her claws. Without Grant there,
the agony of her shape-shift felt far worse, and she had
to survive when that, too, seemed impossible.

Her father had set a strange series of events into motion with that damn will. She wished she could give him a piece of her mind right now.

Shirleen stood ramrod straight, waiting with the patience of a saint for Paxton to move. Paxton wasn't sure she *could* move. Grant's pull on her wasn't only physical. Despite his warnings, every fiber of Paxton's being clamored to go after him, as if he had taken part of her with him.

The street scene was clearer now that her vision had sharpened. Incredibly, every board and nail stood out on Desperado's exterior walls. She noted that the dirt road she stood on had a waffled appearance from too many shoes recently trampling it down, and that the old wood on the buildings had a decadently aged odor that threatened to again toss her back in time.

Shirleen wasn't going to allow that. "It's important," she warned.

Thawing from their former numbness, Paxton's arms felt heavy and foreign. Her legs ached. Yet she was sure she could have run faster than she ever had, if given the chance.

Any minute now, I will wake up.

In the event this wasn't a nightmare, she had to deal.

"Can't leave," she sent to Shirleen.

"It isn't safe in the open, Paxton."

"A memory is here that I have to find."

"Can't you find it later?"

It was too late to find out anything from the past. The elusive whispers had gone, chased away by Shirleen's insistence that they get going.

Paxton offered Shirleen a dangerous glance that resulted in silence. But that silence lasted mere seconds before Shirleen jerked to attention and two more strangers came running.

* * *

"You have found me."

The beast, trespasser, Lycan rogue, stepped into Grant's sightline in human form, dressed in dark clothes and a hood that hid his face. He was so tall, his presence alone made him formidable.

Grant fielded a thought about whether to shift back so he could speak, and whether that might put him at a higher risk. He decided to wait.

"Don't bother," the other Lycan agreed, attuned to Grant's dilemma. "I can hear you perfectly well, either way."

"Why have you returned? Have you changed your mind about coming in?"

"I have no intention of submitting myself to closer scrutiny. Surely you know this by now?"

"You're a wanted beast."

"And you're lucky I'm here."

Grant failed to appreciate that remark.

"Anxiousness is an emotional state that broadcasts over quite a distance. Yours is particularly strong," the Lycan warned.

"Where do you come from and what do you want here?" Grant tossed back, hoping to get a glimpse of the Were's face.

"I want what you want," the Lycan said.

"Is that a joke?"

"Like you and the others you watch over, I need to be free. I must not be caught. That is imperative for all of us. You must stop looking."

"It's too late for anonymity. If not us, the ranchers will find you."

"They won't find me, no matter how hard or long they try."

"We know about the cave," Grant said.

Silence, then "Yes. There is a cave. Several of them actually."

Grant refrained from taking a harsh breath as he adjusted to that news.

"Who are you?" he repeated sternly.

"Need to know basis only," the Lycan replied.

"What do you want with Desperado? Why come here now?" Grant asked.

"The town contains something dear to me."

Grant rolled his shoulders. *"Dear to you? What could that possibly be if you have never set boot or claw there?"*

The Lycan facing him didn't bother to answer that question.

"I believe you said I was missing something, earlier tonight," Grant said. *"Maybe you can explain now that we're face-to-face."*

"What I meant was that there is danger all around, wolf, and it's not what you're expecting."

"That's supposed to be a surprise, when you're central to that danger?"

"I was right. You know nothing."

Grant sensed the frustration mounting in this creature. The air had changed again, thickening more, carrying the scent of anger and another hint of blood.

The Lycan had turned, so that only his silhouette was visible. He was looking to the west, as if he also smelled the blood.

"Perhaps you can enlighten me," Grant suggested. *"After leading us a merry chase, I'm assuming you wanted me to find you tonight for a reason. Am I supposed to be your next meal? Is that what you're think-*

ing? Get rid of the competition, knowing I'll use all resources at my disposal to find you?"

"Honestly, I'm not thinking anything of the sort. I came to warn you about what's coming, and that's the only reason for allowing this conversation."

"What is coming? More of your wicked antics?"

The Lycan brushed that remark off with a wave of his hand. "What's coming is the worst thing you can imagine. Maybe even worse than that."

"Presently, you hold that honor."

"If I did, you and your pack would have been dead long ago. As you know, none of you are."

That, Grant thought, was an odd thing for a challenger to admit. As taunts went, it was pretty benign and a complete mystery. He was having a hard time wrapping his mind around the possibility of this creature not wanting to harm the pack. Honestly, he still wasn't sure what was going on. This meeting with the Lycan wasn't going the way he had anticipated it might. There had been no attack or move in Grant's direction.

"Besides you, what else is coming?" Grant asked, expecting another cryptic remark that wouldn't lead anywhere. Strangely though, the Lycan answered.

"Old enemies have come back, multiplying too fast for me to keep up or stay hidden."

"Are you talking about humans?" Grant asked.

"Not humans," the Lycan replied in a thoughtful, civilized manner that went against the rogue cattle rustler image Grant had pictured. Also, the scent of the blood he had detected couldn't have been due to anything this sucker had done, since the Lycan was in his presence at the moment.

What wasn't he getting?

Perhaps the bastard was trying to throw him off-balance.

When another rustle came from the bushes, Grant readied his claws in case the Lycan had an accomplice. That could have been the terrible thing this guy was alluding to. Not one rogue, but two. Three. A dozen.

"What's left if you're not talking about humans?" Grant demanded. *"If you know about the nearby pack and have no bad intentions toward us, what have you got to lose by accompanying me back there?"*

"Maybe I would prefer to be my own master."

"What is coming?"

"Old enemies," the Lycan repeated, turning his head, interested in whatever he had perceived in the wind.

"How much longer do you think you can avoid those rifles and search parties? This desert isn't as large as you might think. Both ranchers and a wolf pack are on the hunt, and they'll find you eventually. You've been a wild card inflicting too much damage, bringing too much notoriety."

"Yes, I've inflicted some damage, as you say, though I doubt if it's the kind of damage you're assigning to me."

"Cattle. Maybe a hiker or two. Bones in a cave. Months of hide-and-seek. I can smell the blood now, Lycan," Grant said with an edge to his tone.

He could have been wrong, had to be wrong, but Grant thought he detected the same kind of weariness in the hooded Lycan's voice that he had heard earlier.

"Blood is the key, the direction," the creature said. "If you follow the trail, you won't find me as the cause."

With that bit of questionable insight, Grant sensed he had again been left alone and that the mysterious Lycan, with all his cryptic secrets, had gone.

Grant charged into the brush after the rogue. Pulse racing, he searched for footprints and scents, utilizing the full scope of his supernatural senses.

He turned into the wind to soak up the iron-rich odor he had perceived. *Blood is the key.*

The key to what? To where to find that sucker? Follow the scent and this rogue will be waiting? The rogue whose voice had not reflected the complete derangement everyone had expected?

What could be worse than an intelligent opponent?

More sounds filled in the quiet. Among them, Grant picked out the faint swish of boots in the sand. Growling, he glanced behind him, where the lights of Desperado's gates held a welcoming glow and Paxton Hall's wolf called to him in a language he understood on so many levels.

But he had to see this through. A man had placed his trust and property in Grant's hands for the sole purpose of keeping Desperado and its inhabitants safe. His pack trusted his decisions. A new she-wolf needed him. And now there were two anomalies to face. Paxton was one of them. The other was a Lycan he had to continue to hunt. He had to either bring this rogue in, or take him down. *"I'm sorry,"* he sent to Paxton. *"Hang on, lover. I don't know what I'd do if you…"*

Unable to finish that sentiment, and with the nebulous warning the Lycan had given him about what was coming ringing in his ears, Grant took off, doing exactly what that Lycan had suggested by allowing the scent of blood to guide him toward whatever awaited him in the dark.

Chapter 25

Paxton smelled what the others had caught a whiff of. That scent permeated the air.

Her strength returned with a rush of adrenaline as she took a step toward the darkness beyond Desperado's buildings. Aware of Shirleen and two others behind her, Paxton swiped at the air with her claws to warn them back.

Claws.

Blood was rushing through her arteries, ramping up her blood pressure, skyrocketing her pulse. Her heartbeat echoed loudly inside her head, leaving scant chance of hearing much else. But the onset of an enhanced sense of smell was another matter altogether, and Paxton was familiar with the iron tang of blood, just as every nurse was. The blood wasn't hers and had not originated from the Weres behind her. So, whose blood was it?

Grant's?

Although she was already filled with dread, another persistent idea needled. She knew Grant's scent, so this couldn't be his blood she smelled.

When she closed her eyes, she could almost see an image of him, upright, half wolf, perfectly all right. It seemed to her that some of her racing heartbeats stemmed from their strangely attuned connection and had to do with Grant's current state of agitation.

There was no way to call him. Trying to further their unique and uncanny bond might distract him from his objective of seeking out a madman. Shirleen had warned her against being a distraction.

Shirleen and the two other Desperado inhabitants were maintaining several feet of separation from the new werewolf in town. Their wariness over what was happening to her tonight, without that damn full moon, radiated off them.

Paxton swallowed the urge to scream.

According to Grant, everyone here was a werewolf, and this was his pack, so she couldn't help wondering where that left her. Her world had radically changed with a terrifying turn of direction. If this wasn't a dream—or, hell, if it was—she could fall down and whimper over the hand she had been dealt or get on with it. If she was dreaming, she would eventually wake up. If she was dreaming, she couldn't really be hurt by anything she did.

With a cursory glance at the others, Paxton strode forward, as Grant had done, getting better at balance with each step as she headed out of town. Once Desperado was behind her and darkness filled the empty spaces, she willed her new body to run.

That wasn't so easy with new muscle and sinew.

Stumbling often at first, Paxton shored up her determination to find Grant and get the hang of her new body, a feat made more difficult by the way her eyes processed the dark. Even without extra light, she easily saw where she was going. Everything around her took on a dull red outline, like something in the infrared spectrum. There was also a subtle layering of scent, vision and awareness that told her exactly which path Grant had taken.

Utilizing those resources, Paxton ran. Her nerve endings sparked, squeezed by muscle that seemed to have been replaced by thin sheets of steel. Her hair, longer, darker in color than usual, flew in her face as she moved.

She didn't dare look at her hands.

The pain of her shape-shift hadn't disappeared. Her head ached. So did her chest. Both legs burned like they had been dowsed in fire, and all ten fingers stung. In spite of that, Paxton kept moving, desperate to find Grant, the creature who held all the answers she needed now, more than ever.

When she detected him some way ahead of her—a wavering mirage of joining senses—she saw that Grant repeatedly looked over his shoulder, toward Desperado. Toward her. Her mind told her that he was keen on getting back to her and that he had feared she would come after him.

How right he was.

Their astoundingly intimate connection was a heady reminder of the moments they had shared in the bunkhouse. Their insatiable passion for each other hadn't been tapped out by multiple explosive orgasms, but strengthened by the keenness of their fervor.

She still felt him inside her, penetrating deep, sending her soul to new heights. And in the process, he had unleashed a wolf. Her wolf.

Werewolf.

She felt feverish, new, different…and also the same. She felt stronger, fierce, feral and angry. Hell, yes, she was furious over being caught up in someone else's nightmare. Grant's nightmare. Because it was obvious Grant had instigated all of this.

Running churned up clouds of dust that got stuck in her mouth. Leftover desert heat brought moisture that dripped like falling tears down her cheeks. She was fast now, incredibly fleet as she covered ground on two long legs like a heat-seeking missile. Possibly all she had to do was call to Grant with her mind and he would hear her.

She didn't make that call.

He was on a mission, and she wanted to know what and who the beast was as much as Grant did. She didn't want to meet that beast again, but being left alone with a bunch of strangers in the ghost town she had once considered to be her safe haven wasn't a comforting thought, either. Neither was staying in this new shape for much longer.

This could be a dream.

In a dream, she'd be free to experience all that life had to offer without repercussions. She could again run without fear of being found by her father's minions. No longer a kid, she got to decide how she spent her time and who she climbed into bed with, even if that person wasn't actually human.

"Grant."

The thought slipped into existence before Paxton could withdraw it, and the red mirage in the distance halted as if Grant Wade had run into a solid brick wall.

* * *

Some said that curiosity killed the cat, and that, Grant thought, might be expanded to include she-wolves too suspicious for their own good.

Paxton on the loose was adding significantly to the problems at hand, and he couldn't leave her on her own out here with a rogue Lycan on the loose. Taking her along on his search could lead her directly into harm's way.

Paxton's imminent arrival also put him at odds with his vow to figure things out, and no muttered curse he could think of was good enough to describe how he felt about being at this crossroads.

He turned toward her without backtracking. They were less than a half mile from Desperado's gates, following the dry, sandy wash that ran east to west toward the outskirts of the city. Cactus silhouettes stood like prickly soldiers on all sides of him. All but the rim of the moon had sunk behind the mountain range. Daybreak wasn't too far off. In the time between now and then, the night could potentially hold more surprises.

"Okay, Paxton. All right."

She was going to be burning with anger. He had put her in the cage, and that hadn't worked for either of them. Making love to her might have helped to catapult her wolf into existence, but couldn't have been helped, given their attraction to each other.

"In my defense, I couldn't help myself. You are so very alluring. How was I supposed to resist?"

"Wait," she sent back. *"The others don't understand. Can't possibly understand."*

Grant knew what she was saying. Paxton's past had been tied up with Desperado in ways she had never guessed, and in a few hours she had learned a lot. More than anyone would have cared to learn. She might now know firsthand about the existence of werewolves, yet had only an inkling about what was going on. And he was no better at piecing together this puzzle.

The intelligent rogue's warnings had been steeped in mystery, and he was here somewhere. Grant could feel him. Paxton had fled Desperado hoping to find answers of her own without realizing she might be doing exactly what that rogue wanted.

They were treading on treacherous ground.

Life was about to get real.

She ran toward him, easily covering the distance, already at one with her new physical form. Confusion ruled her thoughts and emotions, though. He was her focus. If she assumed he could offer her complete enlightenment, she'd be grossly mistaken.

Paxton was also counting on this being a dream. The kind of dream where anything goes. He wished that was true and that they would all wake up.

Appearing suddenly, as beautiful as anything he could have imagined, she stopped inches from him. Minus the ability to speak, she slapped him hard on his wolfish face.

Lord help him. In spite of everything, Grant smiled. Ignoring for the moment the night and all its wicked possibilities, he pulled her close to him with a slight tug on one arm.

Paxton shoved him back, then again stepped close. With her chest still covered only by a useless scrap of lace, her heat scorched his bare chest. She looked up with gleaming golden eyes.

"Wolf to wolf, at last, and no time to finish this, little wolf," he said, encircling her with his arms while

damning himself for each second stolen from his reason for being out here.

Standing there, wrapped up in each other, craving each other, they were sitting ducks ripe for plucking. He had never been so lax in regard to issues of safety. And yet, having this she-wolf in his arms and her eyes trained on him were all the proof he needed that they would find no way to outdistance their affections. Paxton would stay in Arizona with him…if they lived long enough.

Now, his body shuddered with a desire for her that he could not express or act on until they were safe and Paxton fully comprehended her new reality.

Her eyes were changing color from amber to gold and back as her desires melded with his. She had temporarily forgotten what shape she was in, with her wolf ruling her emotions. Her wolf sensed kinship, sought her mate, craved contact. That was the way of the wolf.

"Must get you back," he sent.

"No," she responded. *"Tell me how this is possible."*

"There's no time to explain," Grant replied. *"We're too far out here, and I have met the rogue."*

"Show me how to change back."

"Not yet. Not here. I'll help once you're safe. We're faster like this. Stronger."

She tensed. *"We're not alone."*

She was right.

A new scent reached Grant that was foul, fetid and reminiscent of a decomposing animal carcass. Sounds disturbed the quiet, odd noises of something skimming the ground.

Grant's heart began to race as he took Paxton's hand, whirled and encouraged her to run. The rogue had warned of trouble coming. Grant hadn't considered that the Lycan might have been hinting of a return visit to finish what he had started.

That rogue might have seen Paxton all wolfed up, and was coming back for her.

With Paxton in tow and a hold on her hand that would have broken bones if she had been in human form, Grant aimed for Desperado's gates. Jolts of electricity sparked through him each time he glanced at Paxton. He reaffirmed his vow that nothing would happen to her on his watch.

But tables had turned, and the hunters were being hunted. Alone, he would have waited for whatever kind of creature was going to show up. But he wasn't alone.

Flapping sounds, the kind giant birds made, reached him. No clear picture formed in his mind as to what he and Paxton were running from. Although Lycans possessed a lot of talents and special abilities, flight wasn't one of them.

The strange sounds came from several directions, too many for this to be any one person, creature, abomination. Maybe that Lycan actually had accomplices. They could have been waiting for the bastard's signal to attack.

Negating that was the fact that there was no scent of wolf in the air. With more than one Were on the loose, Grant would have read the signs. This scent was new and uncategorized in his databanks, suggesting that after all this time, a new species might have turned up.

Old enemies, the rogue had warned.

For the life of him, Grant didn't know what that meant.

He and Paxton ran like the wind, utilizing the reflexes handed down by their ancient ancestors. Paxton kept up as if she had been born to race, all balance and grace now. They reached Desperado's gates in minutes. Ben and his companions came to meet them.

Grant began his reverse shift as he and Paxton slid to a stop, shaking off the discomfort of realigning bones that had grown worse in the last few hours and now plagued him no matter what shape he took. This reversal left him sweating and out of breath.

"Don't know what's out there," he said to Ben. "Can't tell what it is."

"The Lycan?" Ben asked, anxiously scanning the desert.

"That bastard is as intelligent as he is wily. But he's not alone. Something else is haunting the desert tonight. The Lycan warned me about it."

Ben continued to search the area. "If you don't think this is him, do you have any ideas about who is out there?"

Grant shook his head. Paxton's clawed fingers slipped from his and everyone's attention turned to her, sensing the she-wolf had something to say.

"Not wolf," she sent to him, frustrated with her inability to speak those words out loud.

"What else is there?" Ben was quick to ask.

Grant waited to see if Paxton, so new at this werewolf gig, had the answer to that question when he didn't have a clue.

"Dead," she said.

Red-hot bolts of nerve fire roared through Grant, knocking on his skull, vibrating his ribs, as Paxton repeated the word.

"Dead."

Any queries he had about that remark had to be postponed. Paxton had begun her reversal and sank to her knees in the sand.

Chapter 26

*D*ead.

According to Paxton, the thing or things out there were dead. Grant would have worried about her mental state if it hadn't been for the look of abject horror on her face, added to the rogue Lycan's power of suggestion.

The words *old enemies* bothered him. And anyhow, he couldn't figure out how Paxton might know things he didn't or how she had come up with a word that united the sounds and smells pervading the night so eerily.

Paxton couldn't say more. Reversals were new to her system and this one was taking longer. Doubled over, she sucked in breath after breath of air as if each of those breaths might be her last. In this state, she wouldn't have heard his assurances that she would be all right.

He wasn't sure what *dead* meant in this case. Maybe Paxton had come up with the word because the scent of blood had intensified. The flapping sounds had vanished, and yet the air around them seemed heavier, as if the area had become crowded with things none of them could see.

This was downright spooky. Grant's skin prickled with warnings to get out of there fast. Tucking an arm around Paxton's waist, he hauled her up and stood her on her feet. Supporting her with his body, he pressed the hair back from her face and cupped her chin with his palm.

"Can you run?"

Golden lashes fluttered over closed eyes when he spoke to her. Paxton's face had regained its human characteristics and worrisome lack of color. Spine bones popped and snapped as each of her vertebrae found its groove, most of those sounds bringing a groan.

As he waited for her to acknowledge him, the wind picked up, blowing sand in their faces. Enough of his senses were working to tell him this wasn't good. With an arm protectively around Paxton, ashen-faced and weak from her recent ordeal, Grant whirled to face the expanse of darkened desert beyond the gates. Ben and the other two packmates joined him, wielding clubs that resembled baseball bats.

What was out there?

He kept his attention on Paxton's white face. "What do you mean by *dead*?"

In answer to that question, a deep, familiar, unwelcome voice filled Grant's mind. *"The dead rise again,"* the rogue Lycan warned, his voice an unwelcome whisper, as if the bastard stood right next to Grant, understanding everything that was going on by the gates.

Grant felt the blood drain from his face. Paxton had heard that warning also. He had to pull her tightly to him to strengthen his support. As the Lycan's voice in his mind retreated, Grant's brain shuffled random details into a pattern he hoped to be able to access.

Blood.

Slaughtered animals.

Human bones in a cave, scratched by tooth marks Ben couldn't identify.

Words the rogue had spoken earlier that night came back to him: *What's coming is the worst thing you can imagine. Maybe even worse than that.*

And finally, *The dead rise again.*

With a snap of insight, centuries of data began to add up, and the image that data presented made Grant blanch. "We have to get the hell out of the open," he said. "Right now."

"What?" Ben asked nervously. "What is it?"

When Grant could speak again, he turned to Ben. In a harsh, gravelly voice, he said the word that would have made anyone who heard it wish they never had.

"Vampires."

Paxton's ears rang with the word Grant had spoken.

There wasn't one place on her body that wasn't plagued by pain, and on top of the skin-tearing horror of her own shape-shift, a new terror had been introduced.

"Vampire," Ben said. "You've got to be kidding." His expression conveyed that he was waiting for Grant to renege on that statement.

It was a ghastly idea but, given that werewolves were real, why not fang-bearing dead people who drank blood?

Grant hustled her through Desperado's gates with an arm still wrapped around her. "No dream," he said.

"Should I wait?" Ben shouted after them. "Shouldn't someone wait to see if it's true?"

"Hell, no," Grant replied sharply. "Come in. Get them all inside. I can almost guarantee that Lycan was onto something."

"What if he comes back?"

"Let him," Grant muttered. "Let him come."

Somehow, Paxton kept up on unsteady legs. Back in her human form, her real shape, she felt heavier, awkward. Grant's unhealthy buzz of fear had become hers, but could vampires actually exist?

"Can't take a chance," Grant said to her as they trotted toward the lights in the distance.

"He could be lying," Ben said, following behind. "That rogue could be pulling one over on us."

"Yes," Grant returned. "There's always that possibility."

"The bastard eats cows," Ben said, pointing out the mental imbalance of anyone who could do that.

"Suddenly, I'm not so sure he does," Grant argued.

"What can...a vampire...do?" Paxton asked in disjointed syllables as they reached the first light globe leading into town. "Out here?"

"I'm not sure," Grant admitted. "My knowledge of bloodsuckers is next to useless."

"Do we have to worry, then?" Ben called out. "Because the wolf out there said so?"

Really, none of this was making sense to Paxton. Ben was right to question Grant's enthusiasm for trusting the wolf they had been after. No one could imagine why Grant might believe anything like that.

Was that rogue the thing that had jumped on her car? Grant was letting some information slip through his carefully monitored net. She saw the rogue's outline in his thoughts—the size of their opponent and the hood that covered his face.

"I think we have to believe it," Grant said, reading her thoughts clearly. "Just don't ask me why that Lycan seems willing to help us out on this occasion."

They were halfway to town when another harrowing howl stopped everyone in their tracks. It had come from behind them, near the gates. Not too far away.

Paxton faltered when Grant tugged her ahead, before catching herself. Fear overwhelmed her. Her stomach turned over as the sound the beast had made rang in her mind.

Not just a sound. *No.*

God...

Was she the only one here who knew the damn beast's howl had been meant for her and her alone? And that inside that awful sound, curled up in a wolfish disguise, the beast had called her name?

She sent her mind outward, reaching, searching for the thread tying her to that beast. When she felt that thread snap tight, Paxton leaned forward to reel it in, imagining her hands rolling up that thread, willing herself to find what connected with her on the other end.

When another, sharper image came, it rocked her backward. Paxton stumbled with a hand over her mouth. The connection she had searched for was with the creature that had dented her car, the thing that had looked at her through the windshield with unblinking eyes. She saw that thing now in her mind—big, dark, furry and ferocious. She relived the fright of seeing it in person.

Grant's beastly Lycan—it had to be the same—had just made contact with her on a personal level. She had never been so afraid. She was petrified.

"We can't stay here," Grant warned. "Paxton, are you all right?"

Hell, no, she wasn't all right. She was as far from all right as was humanly possible, because she wasn't human and neither was anyone else around her. Out there in the desert was a beast that had her number. Knew her name. Knew how to disrupt things so utterly and completely by flooding her mind with a memory so clear she could have touched it.

Paxton was so white and dazed, Grant shook her gently to regain her focus, determined to carry her back to town, if necessary.

There was a faraway look in her eyes that he didn't like. She swayed slightly on her feet. Paxton had turned inward.

He wondered if fear caused her glassy-eyed state, or if it was due to the shock of her first shape-shift. She had retreated, and all he could do was try to make her understand the danger they might be in if they dallied too long in the open.

"Talk to me," he said to her.

"Grant," Ben warned. "Pressure is building out there."

"Go on," Grant directed. "Get to town."

"Not without you," Ben said.

With a firm hold of Paxton's shoulders, Grant said, "Damn it, Paxton. Where have you gone? Tell me what you see."

Her large amber eyes didn't meet his or show any indication that she'd heard him. Shifting again in order to carry Paxton the rest of the way to Desperado at a sprint wasn't a trick he'd like to perform with his body already quaking from the inside out, but he was game to attempt that if he had to. Still, saving strength was necessary, and he figured he had only one more good shift in him tonight before his body gave out.

"I can take Paxton," Ben said.

The jealousy Ben's offer induced was vastly out of proportion with the situation they found themselves in. Grant couldn't stand the thought of anyone else laying hands on his she-wolf. He wasn't going to allow that. Could not allow it.

"No one will touch you," he sent to her, adding aloud, "You were right when you said that no one could possibly understand what you're going through. You didn't know. No one told you what to expect."

Her skin would be supersensitive and feverish. She would feel like she had been through hell and back. Paxton's insides would feel like they had turned to jelly, and he could see she was having trouble regulating her breathing, due to the extreme distress of the shock to her system. Grant had a feeling Paxton was also fighting something unrelated to that shift, and as new to the game as she was, had found a way to cordon that other thing off from him.

"Grant," Ben said in a low tone meant to get them moving.

"Yes," Grant returned with his gaze steady on Paxton. "Time to go."

But, by then, it was already too late.

Chapter 27

The night began to roll toward them. That was the only way Grant could have described the sensation of being trapped inside a moving pressure cooker.

Ben and the other Weres beside him circled their alpha and the newest she-wolf, hands raised, wooden clubs ready to do some damage to whatever was using the darkness for cover. They didn't wait long before their belief that this was a lone rogue attack was shot down. This was no wolf attack, and *vampire* was a term no one wanted to accept.

Sections of the landscape around them grew darker with a black mist that blotted out scenery beyond their small circle. From the mist came high-pitched chattering, the kind of sounds made by old telephone wires. The strangeness of those sounds brought a terror that Grant quickly shook off.

"Who are you and what do you want here?" he called

out, realizing that any attempt to run back to Desperado now would be futile.

Bracing himself, Grant gathered Paxton closer, feeling the warmth and temporary comfort of having her body pressed to his. He withheld the impulse to shift, waiting for the right moment when his strength would be needed most.

Everyone with him understood that this new dilemma facing them was evil and were at a loss to conceptualize it. When a white face appeared like a glow light in the middle of the traveling black mist, they all took an involuntary step back.

Gaunt to the point of being skeletal, with red-rimmed black eyes in deep sockets and malice in its emaciated expression, the white-faced creature that appeared before them brought a whole new meaning to the word monster. *Freak* was the description Grant's mind dug up. Combined with the term *death*, the existence of vampires became a terrible reality.

There was to be no discourse. Grant supposed the abomination facing them couldn't talk. He had no idea what animated the dead or the kinds of characteristics vampires possessed. But he could sense the thing's raging, insatiable need for blood.

As the black mist floated closer, more faces appeared. Two. Three. The pressure these walking corpses caused on Grant's system was outrageous, squeezing his lungs, compressing the rest of him. Tight against his side, Paxton chose that moment to move. She shivered and tensed as if only then becoming aware of where she was.

She looked up at him with beguiling amber eyes, and he could not comfort her or tell her things were all right. He couldn't allow himself to think of her at all when the situation was grim and his promise to protect her was about to be tested.

The black tide swept forward. Those awful chattering noises filled Grant's ears until he wanted to cover them with his hands.

"That's right. Come and get us," he snapped. "Try."

Beside him, wooden clubs swung at the creeping blackness with powerful strokes. Grant heard Ben swear. Someone else groaned as the clubs, singing their own kind of violent song, connected with an enemy's arm or shoulder. The time had come for him to jump in, but in order to fight he'd have to let go of Paxton, which was his worst fear.

In the end, she instigated the separation by stepping back. Her shaking turned convulsive. Her mind buzzed with jolts of wayward electricity that Grant felt as if they were his own. There was a sudden rise of temperature in air that had gone icy. Grant fought the cold front facing him by merging with the heat of his wolf.

Yes. Let's get this over with, freaks!

The vampires arrived too fast to track their movements, the first appallingly ugly face inches away from Grant before he could blink. Its mouth opened to show off a pair of sharp yellow fangs. Its breath was beyond fetid.

Swathed in black, the rest of this creature's body was difficult to see, even for a Were with exceptional abilities. Grant willed his wolf into existence with the human equivalent of a growl and a snap of mounding muscles. The energy accessed for this latest transition from man to werewolf threw off enough heat to prevent the vampire from immediately traversing the rest of those inches.

Duly noted. You don't like heat.

Grant filed that fact away as he raised claws sharper than the vamp's treacherous teeth and planted his feet in preparation for this meeting. Roaring a dangerous warning to the fanged aggressors, he opened his arms wide in invitation.

Undeterred, the vampires circled the Were party, snapping their fangs, seeming to float like the mist that had at first hidden them.

I have no time for games.

Tired of waiting, Grant sprang toward one pasty-faced freak with his own fangs bared. Their bodies met with a thud. The damn vampire's body felt like ice. As bony as the freak was, Grant's lunge hadn't sent it stumbling in the opposite direction.

Ben and the others were silent now, which added to the eerie sensation of having been swallowed by the dark.

With terrible insight, Grant realized his packmates wouldn't be able to fight off these vampires, and that he, being the only Lycan here and able to fight at full strength, would have to take the brunt of this attack.

"Hang tight," he sent to his pack as the tips of two razor-sharp fangs grazed first his arm, then his left shoulder, in a blur of movement.

Anger rising, Grant narrowed his focus and tuned in. With wolf energy flowing through him, he again met the white-faced freak. One good shove, followed by a fast misdirection, and Grant had a hand around the vampire's neck. The creature fought like a madman, with hatred in its dull black eyes. Hatred for the living. For warmth. For werewolves, who were the epitome of warm-blooded life.

Grant had never met a creature like this one, or knew anyone who had. Except for that rogue Lycan, who seemed to know a lot of things no one else did.

The vampire got free, ducked and parried with a series of actions almost too fast to see. Darting in and back, sideways and forward in an endless battering, the creature seemed frighteningly tireless. Grant fought the bloodsucker with an as-yet untested skill set, whirling, lunging to keep the fangs away from his neck. Those fangs would have sliced through the hide of a steer with no effort at all, and nearly reached Grant's jugular more times than Grant cared to count.

In what had to look like a bizarre danse macabre, Grant renewed his efforts. At last, by calling upon every last bit of his strength, he managed to get his claws into the speedy abomination's ragged clothes and spin it around.

Should have tried this naked, freak.

A sharp keening wail came from the throat of the vampire. The sound was magnified by the other vampires moving inside scattering mist. Two more wails echoed that one, which meant that Ben and the others truly hadn't taken any vampires down.

It was at that moment, as Grant looked into the creature's sallow face, that he saw who the damn vampire's focus was actually trained on and who that vampire wanted to get to so badly. The surprise nearly made him loosen his hold on the creature. His anger went red-hot and felt like a living thing. Paxton stood where he had left her, and the vampire's gaze was riveted to her.

As the bloodsucker struggled and worked its canines, Grant realized with horror that the vampires might not have come to face off with the Weres at all.

It seemed that everybody wanted a piece of Paxton Hall.

The only real question now was why.

* * *

With a volcanic heat overtaking her, Paxton watched the fight as if separated from it by a mile. The edges of her thoughts were blurring, just like the landscape was.

Deep, murky blackness cloaked the remnants of the memory that had been shoved aside by events taking place around her. But the epiphany had been to remember she had seen werewolves before, long ago. And she had seen vampires. What she couldn't recall were the specifics.

Paxton closed her eyes. Desperado held the key to all of this—the attack tonight, the rogue on the loose in the area and her father's wish to close the ghost town the same year he had sent her away.

How many times had she gone over this, searching for reasons for that separation? The questions had become fixtures in her nightmares. Why had she been sent away? Why had her dad never made contact with her? Why had Andrew Hall recruited an alpha wolf of Grant Wade's stature to protect the place? Because, in bringing Grant here, her father had to have known about werewolves, just as Grant had told her. And if he was up on werewolves, her dad must also have known she was one of them.

She had a sense of pieces starting to fall into place too slowly, and that everyone here had to live long enough to help her with that.

Desperado. What other secrets do you hold for me?

Paxton reopened her eyes with a start. Spectral forms were attacking and regrouping with astonishing dexterity. Only the white faces of these attackers were visible. Their death masks. She was awake enough to see them now, and that the Weres were holding them off.

As the cold these monsters brought with them met

with the fire of her anger, sparks of energy imploded inside her, waking her beast, kicking into motion another shape-shift. Paxton dropped to the dirt, dizzy with a fresh rush of adrenaline. Hands in the sand, she gasped for air and rode out what she knew was the second birthing of her wolf.

It didn't take long this time, from start to finish. In less than a minute she was on her feet. She didn't run the other way to save herself, wasn't about to let others fight to protect what was rightfully hers. The town. The ranch. Her heritage. That's the way Grant had put it. *Heritage.* She had been slow to realize he hadn't been talking about anything tangible. Grant had been alluding to her species and how she had come to be one of them.

She was not going to allow Grant or anyone else to be harmed because of her. Losing Grant Wade would be the worst thing since she had long ago lost everything else.

For several seconds more, she watched him fight. Grant the werewolf was fast and fluid. His muscles were spectacularly sculpted. His back was a thing of real beauty. He moved as if he was a principal dancer in a choreographed routine, darting here and there to keep his hold on the monster captured in his claws. In silhouette, Grant's chiseled man-wolf profile gave him the look of a pagan god.

He was fighting for Desperado. He was fighting to protect Ben, Shirleen and the others in his desert pack. And he was fighting for her.

God, how she loved him for that.

When the vampire's eyes moved to her—those terrible, empty, red-rimmed eyes—Paxton's fear levels did not escalate. Instead, she experienced a thrilling sense of rightness and of being in the right place at the right time to discover another clue to this mystery. Suddenly she felt incredibly strong. The power sparking inside her made her willing to use her new strength to stop those ghastly eyes from turning her way.

One step was all it took to channel her anger about this attack on her lover and his friends. Without thinking twice, she rushed in to join Grant. He tossed her a worried look, but her wolf ruled her actions now. Whirling, she undercut the vampire's spindly legs with her own. The monster was too wily to go down, so she jumped on its back, going for its face with both clawed hands.

Someone pulled her off. Paxton growled as she was lifted by the waist and tossed off-balance, but she jumped back to Grant to help with the sucker in his grasp.

She was too late. Another furred-up werewolf had replaced her efforts—this one far larger, much stronger, with superior fighting skills.

Grant had told her very few werewolves had the ability to shape-shift without the presence of a full moon, so who was this? Which one of his pack members also possessed this trick?

Night overlapped night. Frenzied activity created clouds of dirt. Grant's packmates were fighting for their lives now, and though she was tired, she wasn't helpless.

Paxton moved back in again with the fury of a lioness whose cubs had been taken away. She couldn't allow Grant to be hurt, to be harmed, not only because he was needed here, but because he was hers.

He was hers body and soul.

And both of them knew it.

Thawed by the energy she radiated, and not particularly adept at fighting, Paxton clawed and kicked her way back into the deadly skirmish. White faces, gaunt faces, spun inside their black camouflage until the sound of a muted explosion reached her, and the vampire that had been wrestling with Grant disintegrated in a freaky shower of dark gray ash.

Terrible shrieking wails rent the night before the white-faced fang bearers receded back into the hovering mist and the mist retreated suddenly, as if blown away by an invisible wind, taking the horror and reality of the vampire attack with it.

The night again went quiet. No one moved. Paxton's heart beat as hard and as steady as any of theirs.

Ben and the other two Weres had been left standing and were looking at each other in disbelief. A fine layer of falling gray ash coated their shoulders. More of it swirled in the air like a drift of discolored snow.

"Grant?"

No reply to her call came, and Paxton saw why. Grant stood a good distance to her left in his werewolf form, his eyes and attention fixed on a large male werewolf she didn't recognize.

He was a big sucker with a lethally powerful appearance. He had dark brown hair and mounds of muscle similar to Grant's, but was both taller and broader. Nothing else, either in his looks or his demeanor, resembled her lover. Paxton's first impression was that this Were had been a werewolf much longer than anyone else present and was far more experienced.

The newcomer must have been the Were who had pulled her off the vampire. In helping to fight off the vampires, this guy had turned the tide.

Neither of the large males spoke through their thoughts, as far as Paxton could tell. Grant didn't appear to be pleased to see this guy. He was tense, antsy. His claws dug into the sides of his jeans.

The two Weres faced each other like this was some kind of new showdown, without a ripple of movement from either of them. Then the larger Were's eyes drifted to her, pinning Paxton with the bright intensity of their interest and sending her stomach into free fall.

Chapter 28

Grant gritted his teeth as the rogue faced him—the elusive Lycan, in the flesh, larger than life, intimidating as hell and covered with scars that should have healed the way most wounds did for their kind.

Streaks of gray-peppered hair hung past a pair of massive shoulders. He wore no shirt, and Grant supposed no human-made shirt would have fit this guy all wolfed-up like he was now. They had chased this Lycan for months, and here he stood, dangerously powerful and open to their inspection.

The idea of the Were they had called a beast and a monster coming to aid this pack was curious, as was the warning the Were had given about their attention needing to be turned elsewhere. Putting two and two together, it was obvious the big wolf had known about the vampires. More of a heads-up would have been nice.

The big wolf had pale eyes that shone like lanterns in

an unrecognizable face stretched to an abnormal length by his transformation from man to his wolfish state. As those eyes landed on Paxton, Grant strained against the urge to grab that wolf by the throat if he so much as inched in Paxton's direction. Luckily, that didn't happen, and the big wolf's disconcertingly rapt attention returned to Grant.

"Those creatures are gone, and yet you remain," Grant sent. *"No running away. No hiding this time. Could it be you're waiting for something else to happen? Maybe you think those fanged bastards will return."*

Taking a chance backed by intuition, Grant tucked his wolf back inside. The pain accompanying this latest shape-shift was staggering in scope, hinting that it would do him in if he tried another one anytime soon. More beats of time passed before he got his human act together. His voice wavered when he spoke.

"The cryptic warnings didn't begin to describe this. You might have been more specific."

Expecting a response was ludicrous, Grant decided. After all this time eluding capture, the Lycan facing him wasn't apt to give anything away.

"We acknowledge your help, offer our thanks and will repeat the offer to accompany you to town. If you accept our hospitality, it will come with questions and a possible quarantine," Grant added.

The Lycan didn't nod or return the favor of changing into human form. Instead, he turned casually, without a sound, and disappeared into what was left of the longest night that Grant could recall.

Instantly, Grant was at Paxton's side. Controlling the need to touch her, in case she was already hurting, he said, "It's not safe here. We have to go."

The sun hadn't yet risen, but dawn wasn't far off.

Grant felt this in his bones. Glancing past Paxton, he wondered if novels were right about vampires being unable to move around in daylight, and if the so-called children of the night spent their daylight hours snoozing in dark, dank places, like...*caves.*

"Shit," Ben muttered from someplace behind him, having come to a similar conclusion. "This might explain a lot. It also leads me to wonder if this big guy wasn't the one killing cattle, and those fanged freaks were responsible."

Grant was in complete agreement with Ben's analysis. Problem was, given the new light just shed on what kind of other creatures currently called the desert home, plus the swift disappearance of the rogue, there was no way to classify that lone wolf now as either ally or just an enemy with benefits.

There was no justification for a rogue werewolf helping them if he was the one causing trouble.

And what was his interest, and the vamps' interest, in Paxton, whose attention was fixed on the spot where the big Were had stood? Grant had no idea what Paxton was thinking. Either she had again found a way to hide her thoughts from him or her mind was blank.

"Come on," he said to her, waving to include Ben and the others. "The sun isn't actually up, so who knows what those fang-bearing bastards might do next?"

He did know one thing, though. Paxton had chosen the word *dead* to describe what had been coming, and she had been right. While he didn't want to press her after what she had already been through, who wouldn't have had a whole bunch of questions on that score?

Paxton appeared to be assimilating her transition from human to Were. She was in pain and dealing with it. In her wolf form, she was just as untrusting as she had been as a human, and she growled when he got close.

Grant saw how tired she was. He felt the burn of the deep-seated anger that flushed her skin. Too many secrets had been revealed to her tonight. Any lesser, more fragile female would not have been able to cope. But Paxton Hall was special.

"It would be enough to drive a weaker person insane," Grant cajoled with a calmness he didn't really feel. Her pain added to his own. He could tell Paxton wanted to bend, yet stood tall.

If I could touch you...

He couldn't lay a hand on her because Paxton wasn't going to allow it.

The air near the gates remained as odorous as if vampires had tainted it and left their mark on the night. It stank of decomposed bodies and the damn gray ash they became after being dealt a final death blow.

Grant figured they had sent at least one vampire to its final resting place—wherever the hell that was. He contemplated whether the other vampires would be angry to lose one of their number and seek revenge. Heaven only knew if the undead had brains or feelings outside of the hunger that ruled them.

There was an hour at most before a new day arrived. For Grant, sunrise could not come too soon.

"Don't think about anything now, except getting to Desperado," he said to Paxton, losing precious minutes by giving her the time to recover. "You need shelter, a comfortable bed and a hot meal."

He would have given all ten claws to be able to crawl into bed beside her and sink his hard length into her lush, waiting depths. He ached to waken her each morning with a kiss, and had never wished for anything so badly. But he wasn't sure any of that would happen now that she knew about werewolves. About herself, and about him.

"Paxton, let's move," he said, nodding to the others, butting up against his she-wolf with his hip and one bare shoulder.

When she took a step, he could have kissed her right then and there. She had heard him. She was going to comply and would be all right once they reached shelter.

"I am not to blame for this," he whispered to her. "Please believe me."

Urged into action by his silent additions to the things he voiced aloud, Paxton began to walk. He saw no evidence of her fatigue in the way she carried herself. Paxton the she-wolf was the epitome of grace and courage, in spite of being new to the gig.

There was a lot more than shape-shifting in her future, Grant wanted to tell her. Chief among those things was the fact that they had imprinted. She might not want him to touch her at the moment, but she wouldn't be able to leave him, any more than he could abandon her. The first meeting of their eyes had sealed their fate as lovers and mates. Making love so blissfully had finalized the deal.

Thinking about hot, sweaty sex with Paxton, now that she knew nearly everything, made Grant hard all over. Made him ache in places that weren't already aching. Ahead of him on the road, Paxton growled again, and what he heard in that sound was, *"Over my dead body."*

Uneasy, sick and tired beyond belief, Paxton turned toward Desperado. She had kissed her old self goodbye and there was nothing she could do about it.

There was no going back.

So, all right. There were now three Lycans in the area, and she was one of them, according to Grant and her ability to shift shape without a full moon's help. The wolf they called a rogue was the third Lycan to show up, and when his eyes had found her, a strange emotion had stirred her insides. Those pale eyes seemed familiar. Then again, for all she knew, all wolf-to-wolf contact might feel that way.

She looked back at a desert that would have appeared normal to most people, and in reality was anything but. In her mind, behind the clash of leftover pain and the wish that none of this was real, the rogue Lycan's eyes continued to haunt her.

Grant was silent now. So were the others. Night birds and bugs had resumed their songs to herald a dawn that would soon light the mountain range.

And yet...

She knew the rogue was out there, and that he was watching her just like the invisible eyes she'd felt as a kid. Here, in real time, the idea was as vague as it was frightening. Older now, and wiser, she wasn't about to let that memory go, because after meeting the rogue, memories and ideas in a world full of questions suddenly began to connect. Perceptions marched into focus.

Yes, damn it. She had met werewolves before. There was no doubt about it, or the fact that she had first encountered them here in Arizona.

The surprise of that realization made her hesitate. In following the path of that memory, surely the presence of werewolves in and around Desperado was part of the reason she'd been sent away.

Beside her, Grant had stopped and was eyeing her curiously. She had forgotten about his ability to share her thoughts and hadn't protected them. Grant, however, had not been here when she was young, and therefore hadn't been privy to all the years of self-doubt between then and now. The years of believing she'd been unwanted, unloved and dispensed with by the father she had, since then, continued to yearn for in secret.

Now, Grant's shining allure was like a welcoming beacon backed by a promise of danger. She would find comfort, of a sort, in his arms and should have allowed that to happen. But those other eyes, the rogue Lycan's eyes, kept her turning to Grant.

She was learning too fast, feeling too much, when she had only begun this unbelievable journey. Her world was never going to be the same. Not even remotely close.

Shut up and deal, she told herself.

The back of her neck ached. Her stomach was in knots. So far, her reasoning seemed right, but didn't address the reasons for a rogue Lycan's presence disturbing her.

"Don't go there," Grant whispered to her, concern weighing heavily on his princely features. "Now isn't the time to consider what is or isn't. Safety comes first."

Grant's right cheek was bloody. His shoulders were crisscrossed with red scratch marks beginning to welt. Her werewolf lover had fought to protect her, was continuing to do so, and what she was about to do might appear ungrateful.

She spoke to Grant from her heart. "Forgive me, but I have to."

Spinning in place, Paxton uttered a growl that got stuck in her throat…and took off for the desert behind them, hoping this time Grant couldn't catch her.

Chapter 29

"Bloody hell!"

Grant's packmates were equally surprised by Paxton's sudden, incredibly dangerous and ill-timed rebelliousness. Grant was actually afraid of what might happen next.

"Go on ahead," he barked to the others as he started after Paxton. "Warn them about the vampires," he added over his shoulder.

He ran as if he was in possession of all of his strength and he cursed the night for taking so long to end. With the weak wind in his face and his connection to Paxton foremost in his mind, Grant raced back to the wash where he had met with the rogue Lycan.

Paxton wasn't there. There was no sign of vampires or rogues in the area.

He dared to call, "Please wait," listening to how those words fell flat. His mind rushed ahead of him at a frantic pace to test the wind, the ground and various theories as to why Paxton would believe this was a good idea.

Each avenue he mentally tried led to a dead end. He just did not get it. Frustrated, Grant ran as fast as he could, skimming the ground on human feet he willed to take him where he wanted to go without faltering.

"You're smarter than this," he muttered to Paxton, silently adding to himself, *At least I would have thought so.*

The only thing he could come up with as an excuse for her behavior was that somehow, and in some way, the rogue Lycan had issued an invitation Paxton couldn't refuse. She was going after him. The other werewolf. If being scared for her wasn't enough, jealousy was like a huge dark mouth that threatened to swallow him whole.

Once he'd have been sure Paxton would have no feelings for the bastard out here after hearing about the things that rogue had done. But Grant no longer believed the Lycan had done any of the deeds attributed to him. Vampires had stolen that honor.

So, if the big Lycan was cleared of the atrocities formerly assigned to him, Grant had to find out who that guy was. For the hundredth time, there remained the unanswered question of what he wanted here.

Any time now, you'll start to make sense, Paxton had said to him early on.

"How wrong you were," he grumbled.

As if he had demanded that Paxton's scent take a form he could see, Grant suddenly became aware of the imprint on the atmosphere she had created. Her image wavered, going in and out of focus before solidifying into the visible shape of a she-wolf slowing her pace.

His relief was instantaneous and temporary. Paxton

was there, all right, and surrounded by the same black mist they had encountered less than half an hour before.

The same damn mist that also clung to the vampires.

"I have to," she had said to the man she ached for. "Forgive me," she had whispered to him when the sentiments behind her hasty exit had seemed valid. Now, foolishness was going to be her downfall.

The black mist encased her as if she was trapped in an ice-cold pool of water. Already she was shivering and trying to think of a way to get out of the mess she had gotten herself into, but she couldn't see how that was possible.

Nightmarish faces appeared. Mentally Paxton took a count. Only two fang-bearing creatures snapped at her after hissing through the wide gaps in their hazardous teeth. Perhaps they were tentative about facing a werewolf after the last encounter, because neither of those creatures came close enough for her to spit in their ugly, undead faces.

She raised her hands, brandished her claws and widened her stance. Fighting these vampires was the only option left to her. If she was going to be cursed for her stupidity in leaving Grant and the pack, she'd make it difficult for these pricks to get at her.

Growls bubbled up from deep in her chest as one of the vamps floated toward her with a crooked grin hinting that dinnertime had arrived.

Her second wave of growls was louder, braver and like no other sound Paxton had ever heard. But a vampire had closed in and was inches away from the claws she had no real idea how to use.

She swiped at the air between herself and the freak in warning, and the vampire didn't care. It was already dead, she remembered, so the danger she represented was probably small by comparison to the initial loss of their lives. Also against her was the fact that she hadn't gotten a clear look at how Grant and the other Lycan had dispatched this guy's friend.

Once, so long ago, she had seen this. She had been here, surrounded by fanged freaks in the middle of nowhere, all by herself.

That realization inspired another memory. She had been ringed by gaunt faces with snapping fangs while her pony lay lifeless at her feet.

Another memory...

Her pony had gotten loose from its tether at the gate and had trotted off without her, frightened by something Paxton's young eyes hadn't been able to see. She had gone after him. Her father was going to be mad that she had trespassed beyond the boundaries of their ranch at all, let alone without a chaperone and so close to sunset. Riding into the desert had been forbidden. Riding into the desert near or during the time of a full moon would have been punishable by grounding if her father had caught her.

Still, in all those times she had ignored his warnings, he never had caught her, and she had been emboldened by her forbidden freedom. Until that one dusk, when her pony had become a feast for vampires, and she had watched, horrified, as sharp canines tore into her beloved animal before Paxton was rescued by...

Yes. She had it now. Everything came back in one quick vision, as if a movie played in her mind.

She had been rescued by one of the watchers she had sensed in Desperado. Not just any watcher, Paxton's mind now told her. The terrified little girl who had tried desperately to keep the snapping fangs away from her pony's carcass with every means she could think of, had been saved by another creature. A werewolf.

Pale eyes in a wolfish face.

Big as a bear.

A fierce fighter that had come, not to harm her, but to help her escape her pony's fate.

That werewolf had killed the freaks, picked her up, and taken her home, depositing her near the ranch, where everyone pretended nothing had happened and her father sent her away to make sure things like that never happened again.

Banished. Gone from Arizona and from her father after losing her mother mere months before. End of story. The rebel troublemaker got what was coming to her, and after months of promises from a child psychiatrist that she'd imagined the experience, the little girl had started to believe it.

Looking up and into the face of the vampire, Paxton's anger burned with the fire of a shooting star. In her mind, the dead pony lay at her feet once again. She saw it there. Smelled its death. Now, she had run off again and was on her own, facing two freaks in need of their next meal.

But this time, I'm not that same helpless girl.

Now, gathering herself, energized by the discovery of a truth long hidden from her, Paxton charged at the vampire that was attacking her. The bloodsucker was fast, but so was she. Kicking out, her left foot connected with the moving bag of bones and it stumbled back before coming on again. She fought like a madwoman, slashing at the creep with her claws like an angry creature with nothing more to lose.

Though she did have something to lose, her mind argued. Grant Wade.

As if dragged in by mist, Grant was suddenly beside her. Her guardian angel was as fierce as any vampire as he fought beside her in human form.

One vampire went down beneath the fury of two beings at war with the epitome of Evil. Minutes later, the second vampire succumbed to its final death when its neck was broken. But Paxton hadn't killed that one, and neither had Grant.

Big as a bear, and with its unusual eyes on her, the Lycan rogue waited until the last of the funnel of gray vampire ash had settled. She finally got a good look at him.

Struck again by how unlike Grant this rogue was, she stared. This larger version of a werewolf seemed to be from another species altogether. Nothing in his appearance, other than his eyes, hinted at anything human or what he might look like as a man.

When he raised a clawed hand, Grant took a protective step closer to Paxton. But the rogue pointed at the mountain range beside them, where the sun would soon make its case against marauding vampires. The rumble in his chest sounded like the beat of a drum. Hearing it, Paxton began to feel stranger than she was already feeling.

If this guy butchered cattle, she couldn't picture it. Scary, yes, but he had helped to save her ass twice. No maniac did things like that.

Paxton owed the rogue a round of thanks and had no way to say it. Instead, she sent a thought not fully realized until the sentiment came out. *"I'm not afraid of you."*

The pale eyes blinked. The rogue's elongated head tilted slightly, as though the Lycan might have been thinking about her little speech. There was no response from the beast. Not so much as a growl. Paxton waited for the big Lycan's next move, and that move was to turn and disappear so quickly, Paxton was left wondering if he had been there in the first place.

"No," Paxton growled stubbornly. *"Not this time."*

She was after that Lycan in a flash, sensing the big Were hadn't gone far. Fast on her feet, she seemed to fly over the ground, no longer bothered by fatigue.

She would have caught up with the Lycan if Grant hadn't stopped her. With strength more than double her own, her protector dragged her to a stop before they had reached the rocks at the base of the mountain range and spun her around so abruptly, she fell onto her back.

Straddling her on his knees, with his hands on her shoulders, he looked down at her with his handsome human face, the face she loved and needed to see because of the beauty of the humanness in it.

Grant was panting, his bare chest rising and falling with effort. His magnificently sculpted abs rippled as he bent low over her. The shaggy auburn hair she wanted to run her fingers through stuck to the sides of his face.

"Paxton," he said with his mouth inches from hers and as their gazes locked. "Change back."

She didn't fight. In truth, there wasn't much fight left in her. So she did what Grant asked and willed herself to be the person she had always believed she was. And when she lay beneath Grant, with the sand at her back and his body's warmth inviting her to relax, Paxton nodded her head, took a deep breath and began to cry.

Chapter 30

Watching tears track down Paxton's cheeks drove a nail through Grant's heart. He was sure that heart would break.

His lover was going through something he wasn't able to follow. She was experiencing an emotion hidden from him, and he had a good idea what that might be. Paxton's world had changed forever. Her future was murky and vague. Her new life experience would be positive, if he could help her see it that way.

But first he had news to share that he dreaded. Not concrete news. Not yet. It was just a feeling in his soul, the little spark of an idea that had come to him while he watched Paxton fight. *Later*, Grant told himself. *Wait for the right time.*

He ran a gentle thumb over her cheek to capture a tear and looked deeply into her eyes.

"You'll do," he said.

Such a simple statement for the immensity of his feelings for her. For sure, he was no damn poet.

She blinked back more tears and refocused on him before wiping her cheeks with an open palm. After studying her hand, she spoke. "Because we're two of a kind?"

Grant shook his head. "Because you are here in answer to my prayers."

Her eyes widened. "You don't know me."

"Don't I?" Grant countered. "Tell me, do you know me? Do you know my secret, my objectives and why your father left Desperado to me? Haven't you had your hands on my body, felt my breath in your mouth and experienced the same kind of pleasure I did in that bunkhouse?"

Trapped by his body, she made only one half-hearted attempt to move. That alone spoke volumes about her intrinsic need for this conversation.

"Yes," she said. "I know that much."

Grant nodded with satisfaction. "And do you feel anything for me, after such a ridiculously short time together? Answer truthfully."

She bit her lower lip with tiny white human teeth before replying reluctantly, "I'm sure plenty of females would answer that question in the affirmative."

"How about this one?" he pressed.

She blinked again, slower this time.

"How about you?" Grant asked.

"Will you let me go if I answer?"

"No. Not until you promise not to go after the other Lycan."

"Then, yes. Okay, I won't go after the other one. And in answer to your question, I might have a crush on you. But there are more pressing issues on the table."

To hell with the other issues, he thought. "Crush, is it? After what we've shared?"

Her expression was guarded as she said, "I'm not sure what else you might call this kind of attraction."

"I'd call it fate. Two beings meant to find each other. Although that would make your father a master designer, wouldn't it, since he brought both of us here?"

He watched her think over his remark. Once she had, her amber gaze again met his.

"What is it you see when you look back at the past? Who is there?" he asked.

The question was difficult for her, but she said slowly, "Werewolves."

That answer surprised Grant. He had to wonder how far back in memory she had gone. Bypassing the desire to probe that revelation, he said, "Is that all?"

"Vampires. The vampires were there," Paxton replied with her hands on her face.

Grant lowered his voice to gentle his tone. "The memories are from when you were a kid."

"Yes." The word resembled a hiss.

"Werewolves and vampires."

Her eyes didn't stray from his. "Yes."

"So you knew about this all along. About us and about those fanged freaks."

"I didn't remember until minutes ago. I…" Her remark trailed off, incomplete.

"What, Paxton?" Grant asked. "Tell me what you are reluctant to say."

The amber eyes narrowed as she said, "They didn't believe me. Told me I had made it up. I had to trust them in order to survive. In order to tame the nightmares."

"Nightmares starring vampires and furred-up beasts?"

The look on Paxton's face put another nail in his

heart. Her pallor was as white as the monsters that, by her admission, had haunted her early on. Someone had lied to her when she was a kid, without realizing that other species existed. Those nightmares had returned tonight, and she was personally involved. Hell, if Paxton wasn't a Were, and a tough one, he might have feared for her ability to take a next breath.

But she was a Were, and more. Paxton was a Lycan. She was his Lycan.

"What else?" Grant asked. "I can see there's more."

Paxton turned her head to break eye contact, her gaze sliding to the desert beyond them. Grant felt the first breath of dawn on his back and rolled his shoulders to absorb the relief he felt.

Possibly Paxton sensed dawn coming the same way he did and also was relieved that any minute now they'd be free of vampires and fights and big scary rogue were-wolves for a while. Back at the ranch, where he'd take her, Paxton could safely rest in his arms. He would whisper softly to her about their future together and pray that she agreed.

They would make love and satisfy the cravings so easy to read in Paxton's face amid the horror of every-thing else. Perhaps it would take days, weeks, for their passion to allow a slower exploration of what their bod-ies were capable of. At that moment, however, as Pax-ton tore her gaze away, Grant realized there was a little way to go before his dreams came true. Paxton had to trust him first. She had to believe in him. And, along with everything else, they had to find the truth about her mother and her father.

Getting to his feet, he held out a hand to Paxton, trying not to look too long at the way her beautiful body glowed with the fine layer of perspiration left over from her efforts. With the special gift of sight he had been given, he was able to clearly see every detail of her slender, nearly bare torso and the small quakes running through her.

If she accepted his offer and took his hand, whether or not she needed to, it would signal a positive first step toward the future he had mentally outlined.

She was still looking at him when she sat up. Even after all the fighting and shifting, the filmy lace thing covering her breasts was intact. He had to marvel at that. Her jeans, cut low enough to expose a portion of her flat, toned belly, were dirty, and her shoelaces were untied. Blond hair, lighter in color than Paxton's she-wolf version, hung in matted strands over both of her shoulders.

All of this was so damn hard for him to resist, and at the same time it was heartbreaking. Paxton lacked the knowledge he'd had about what he was. Her heritage had been sprung on her without any sort of advance notice.

She didn't torture him by showing further hints of the rebellious streak he had witnessed tonight.

She took his hand.

Her fingers were long and delicate. Grant felt the throb of her pulse in her soft palm. As he pulled Paxton to her feet, she said one more thing.

"I take it back."

The remark could have meant anything, but Grant sincerely hoped it dealt with her earlier comment about him not taking her to bed again. The *Over my dead body* remark she had thrown at him. Because vampire dust had to be put behind them for the night, and the rogue Lycan would be impossible to track after sunrise. That left just one more thing to fill his mind.

Paxton, in his arms.

Rest.

Comfort.

Safety for the time being.

And the chance to be together.

With her hand in his, Paxton stood upright, considering how long it would take Grant to figure out that the rebellious streak he was thinking about hadn't gone away. Rather, it was rising like an internal storm to impel her to take action.

She had to find that rogue Lycan with or without Grant's assistance, and in spite of what she had said. What was left of her sanity depended on it. Everything she had been told not to believe hinged on locating him. And though she desperately wanted to go with Grant and find a temporary respite from the night's bizarre events, she would never have a moment's peace unless she put the ideas she was forming to the test.

Only by seeing that Lycan in human form would she be able to understand the familiarity she felt in his presence. That familiarity had a taste, a smell and an uncertain texture that came at her in a jumble without translating into anything tangible.

She thanked the stars still twinkling overhead that Grant didn't fold her into his arms the way they both wanted him to. She'd be an idiot if she didn't want closer contact with something so fine. She longed for his mouth on hers and to hear his whispered assurances.

Yet accepting pleasure from her lover would postpone what had to be done. Finding that damn Lycan felt like a necessity. If Grant loved anything about her, he'd have to let her solve the mystery of Desperado.

And there were plenty of mysteries to go around. Chief

among them was the ambiguity of that all-powerful fate Grant had mentioned, and how her father could have planned all of this down to the minutest detail. She had heard Grant's thoughts on this.

"You are adept at hiding things from me," Grant said as she pondered those things.

She knew, because he did not hide the thought from her, that he wanted to brush the sand from her back, but refrained.

"You asked if I knew you after our short time together," she began. "It's weird that feel as if I do. Physical intimacy aside, if werewolves can read the minds and thoughts of other werewolves, every one of them is deeply exposed to everyone else. I guess this makes werewolves closer to each other than any group of humans could ever be."

She hadn't included herself in that statement, using *them*, instead of *us*, as if she had not fully accepted her own situation.

She went on. "Thoughts and emotions become intimate, possibly speeding up the process in a…"

"Relationship," Grant finished for her.

His eyes were luminous. She was a sucker for looking into them.

"That barely scratches the surface of what we feel— what I feel," he explained. "I can't hide that from you. So you are the question mark here. And our close bond tells me you're planning something."

"Then I suppose I'm not hiding things very well," Paxton said.

"I can't just let you go after that rogue, Paxton. What kind of partner would I be if I believed danger wasn't an issue?"

"Don't you mean alpha? What kind of alpha would you be?"

"Partner," he reiterated with a crisp head shake. "You won't find anything out here in the daylight. I can promise you that."

"Then I'll wait."

He shook his head again. "There's going to be a full moon tonight that complicates things."

Paxton felt the dawning of a new day without searching for the sunrise. She felt the last of the stars disappear. "Will you lock me up in that cage again, or try to?" she asked with the tone of a dare.

"What I will do is ask that you include me in whatever you have in mind to do, so you're not doing it alone."

"And if you don't approve?"

"We're way past that, I think," Grant said. "Aren't we?"

He was right, of course. They were past having arguments over secrets both of them wanted exposed. Grant couldn't hide from her his wish to find out who the rogue was. He wanted that nearly as badly as she did.

"We've been chasing that Lycan for four months. What makes you think you would be able to find him?" he asked.

"His eyes."

In silence, Grant waited out the time it took for her to explain the remark. She knew he was hoping she'd bring up real feelings. True feelings. But how was she to talk about a secret that had been buried so deep inside her, and for so long, that it had taken on the aspects of any other dream?

"I've seen the big Lycan before," she confessed, hat-

ing the wobble in her voice, loving Grant even more for
not arguing about how impossible her statement was.

Paxton doubled back over the automatic, uncensored,
term she had used for her feelings for Grant. *Love.* Was
it possible to fall in love in one incredibly long, seemingly endless day? Surely people recognized the difference between love and lust and animal magnetism.
Because who would believe in love at first sight, especially with all the wolf issues attached to it?

Maybe what she felt had to do with jealousy. Envy
for a man who'd had the pleasure of remaining in the
West and who had carved out a life for himself here. A
man with a family. A pack.

Her own guardians, substitutes for her missing parents, had died several years back, leaving her stranded
without emotional ties of any kind.

Grant seemed to understand her vulnerabilities
when he really knew nothing concrete about her life.
She hadn't shared any of it. Strong arms waited to en-
circle her. All she had to do was take one step. And he
knew nothing.

Paxton had never loved his face as much as she did
right then. Grant's liquid blue gaze contained the power
and the voodoo to chase away pain and nearly everything else. Looking into those blue depths distanced the
mystery of the rogue and made jumping into Grant's
arms doable.

Animal magnetism.

Yes.

Love?

"Soon," he whispered to her. "After we rest we can
talk it all over and formulate a plan."

"Before the next moon rises," she said.

His nod caused a lock of his hair to fall becomingly

across his forehead. And yet this gloriously capable, sublimely sexy creature who was picture-perfect in all ways, if no one held the werewolf part against him, would always be dangerous. Being in his world meant chaos might rain down each time the damn moon got near to showing her freaking face.

"We rest first, Paxton. Do we have a deal?"

What Grant was saying made sense. Rest. Food. Daylight for decisions. It made all the sense in the world. Besides the God-awful aches, she was bone tired, trembling and didn't remember the last meal she'd had.

"Fries." Grant supplied the answer to her unspoken thought with a smile so dazzling, so inviting after the night they'd had, Paxton wanted to forego real food and eat *him* up.

Chase away the bad thoughts…

Replace mystery with the warmth of Grant's arms.

Damn it. Damn all of this.

Paxton took a step toward him, almost ignoring the rustle in the brush beside them.

Chapter 31

Instead of slipping his arms around Paxton, Grant spun her behind him and took a fighting stance. *He* was there? Maybe the damn rogue had returned after all, with dawn on the doorstep.

No. Maybe not. There was no scent. No feel of Were presence. This was something else.

The sky was pink with a yellow glow. Mountains rising above them cast long shadows over the wash in a last mingling of dark and light. Grant's skin chilled as he faced the rustle of nearby brush. His muscles corded in anticipation.

"You are an idiot. More of one than I had previously presumed," he said, in case he was wrong about the rogue and Paxton's delicious scent was overpowering the rest of his senses.

Behind him, Paxton was shaking with fatigue, and he couldn't help her with that. It appeared that he had been wrong about finding nothing out here in the daylight. Even with the sun not fully up, their sandy surroundings would now have been visible to anyone.

The next surprise was a shock that made his nerves sing. Out of the shadows, a woman appeared. *Almost* a woman, Grant's senses immediately corrected, because the filmy apparition hovered over the sand as if slightly suspended from it.

Of course, a voice in the back of Grant's mind warned, that assessment couldn't be right. This wasn't a wolf and couldn't be vampire this close to daylight unless stories about bloodsuckers had gotten the facts wrong.

"Stay back," he warned, tired enough to hear the wariness in his voice, worried that any opponent would pick up on that, too.

The woman didn't speak. Grant didn't actually see a mouth from where he stood. He felt her eyes on him without seeing them, either. The closer he looked, the more he strained to fill in the features of a diaphanous face, the harder it was to make out anything at all… which made him wonder if he was finally losing it.

There was no real contact with this being. Without acknowledging that she actually saw either Paxton or him, the creature turned away. After gliding several feet from them, she stopped again. Grant took this as an invitation to follow her, whoever and whatever she was.

Paxton seemed to understand this better than he did. Possibly he had grown too cautious in his alpha job because he could not fathom what kind of opponent was left after rogue werewolves and vampires.

"Follow her," Paxton said. "Please."

Obviously Paxton saw the creature, too.

"Please," she repeated, leaning against him with her hands on his shoulders. Her hands were cold.

"Do you know what it is?" he dared to ask her.

"Another mystery," she replied.

"One too damn many," he muttered.

He took Paxton's hand. "Stay back. Behind me."

For once, she did as he asked.

They walked forward. As they did, the filmy creature moved again, adding more distance. Each time they tried to get close, she created more distance, until they were out of the wash and had reached the pile of rocks marking the way to the old Desperado mine.

Grant stopped. "Too dangerous."

Paxton said, "She wants to show us something."

"Could be a trap, and more than likely is," Grant argued, not liking this at all and ready to turn back toward town.

Paxton was adamant. "I'm going."

"It's not a good idea," he insisted, scenting strong Were presence that made his claws slide into place.

From somewhere nearby a deep voice said, "Not a good idea? When did Paxton Hall ever let that stop her?"

Paxton refused to let her knees buckle. Recognizing the tone of that remark was another piece of the puzzle. And, well, she'd never had the patience for puzzles.

She stepped clear of Grant's protective stance with her hands on her hips and said, "Time is up. Who are you?"

"You don't yet know?" The Were in the shadow of the mine's entrance turned.

"I'm curiously blank."

"We both know that's not true."

"What I'm thinking right now is impossible," she said.

"Who the fuck are you?" Grant demanded, looking back and forth from her to the boarded-up mine.

It was a hell of a time for the memory to return. Young Paxton had been struggling to follow a small group of ranch hands to their trucks. The people were hatless to show respect to someone who had died. Her mother was that person.

Her father was there to lead the group. Tall, broad, wide-shouldered, he towered over everyone by at least a head, wearing a long black coat that made the dirt at his feet swirl. On the pocket of that coat had been an embroidered crest. Paxton saw this as clearly as if she stood there now. Recognition of that crest made it a toss-up between laughing and crying.

"Wolf," she said, raising her face to the shadows. "Our brand was a wolf."

Beside her, Grant stirred. She was on a roll and couldn't afford to look at him.

"Isn't that interesting?" she observed, searching the shadows for the rogue she knew was watching her.

Eyes watching…

Someone waiting behind old wood walls…

Those things had haunted her.

"Especially since someone eventually turned Desperado over to a pack of wolves," she said.

Grant's anxiety underscored her fear, but also made her braver. She was close to figuring out this mystery. So close.

Voices boomed inside her head. Directions. Demands.

I forbid you to go there again, Paxton.

Your mother is no longer here to keep you in line.

Your wild spirit will get you into trouble here, so you will have to go.

She would have to go…

In memory, pale eyes glowed in the dark. In the distance, came the roar of a man who mourned the loss of the love of his life. But, Paxton wanted to shout as the fog continued to share its secrets, she had lost her mother. And then her dad.

"No." Grant's one-word protest could have brought her around if she paid too much attention to the offer of safety in her lover's voice. There was no way to block her thoughts.

Back down the hole...

Her pony had lain dead at her feet, covered in blood. And she had been sent away for disobeying her father's rules about riding out alone after dark.

Vampires had been there, in her memory, just as she had recalled earlier, and had chewed the life from her beloved pony. Someone had found her, had fought off the bloodsuckers. That someone had fought like a demon to protect her.

Wolf logo.

Werewolf.

Pale eyes.

Big as a bear.

Paxton closed her eyes as the memories faded. When she opened them again, she said wearily, "Hello, Dad. We thought you were dead."

Chapter 32

What the...?

Grant pressed himself against Paxton's side, fearing she had gone off the deep end. She believed Andrew Hall was alive. Not only that, she believed Hall was the rogue they had been chasing before knowing about vampires in the area.

"Paxton," he said, not ready to go along with her dramatic perceptions.

The Lycan came forward in the shadows as if he were part of them. And, Christ, he had been part of them, since the rogue had been so damn hard to find. This time, however, the Lycan faced them, still partially in the shade and looking more like a modern-day wizard than a werewolf clothed in a man's flesh.

"You can't be Andrew Hall," Grant said, trying hard to accept that this could be the same man who had pledged his land in order to protect the future of the werewolf species in this part of Arizona. Paxton's father. And that Paxton could be right.

"This is a joke," Grant added.

"Sorry, son," the big man said without revealing his face. "It was best to remain on the sidelines."

Paxton, silent now, was free of any hint of warm and cuddly feelings for the man in the hood. Her posture was rigid. Her hands were balled. Grant wasn't certain she actually believed this, either.

He would have whisked her away to a safe place where vampires and trouble couldn't find her, but she'd have had none of that. And, in this case, trouble was looking them straight in the eyes.

"Why aren't you dead?" she asked the hooded man.

Grant didn't actually expect the Lycan to answer that question and was surprised when he did.

"It was time to pass the torch," he replied.

"What does that mean?" Paxton demanded in a softer voice.

"I could no longer help the way I wanted to," the Lycan said.

"Why not?"

"I wouldn't have been accepted by my own species."

Uneasy with the Lycan's confession, Grant watched Paxton flinch at Hall's use of the word *species*. Tough as nails, and showing more grit, she confronted the big Were again.

"What made you think that?"

The Lycan replied, "I'm no longer one of them. Not completely."

Grant interrupted. "You're either Were or not. There is no middle ground."

When the eyes behind the hood turned his way, Grant felt heat without having to see those eyes.

"Ah, so we all think until the impossible happens. In this case, it happened to me," the Lycan said.

Paxton inched forward with her head tilted to one side, as if sniffing for the truth. "What is the middle ground you speak of?"

"I wouldn't be telling you now if it wasn't so important," the Lycan answered. "And if it wouldn't save lives."

"Go on," Grant said.

The Lycan gestured to the boarded-up mine. "They found this place and made it their nest. No one else knew this, or that I had found them. By that time, it was too late."

"Nest." Grant absorbed another chill. "You're talking about vampires?"

The Lycan nodded. "They came slowly, at first, and in small numbers. Those numbers quickly grew."

Grant glanced to Paxton. She was holding in her mind an image of a dead pony and had told him she had seen vampires before. Putting those things together caused more interest in what this Lycan, who might or might not have been Andrew Hall, had to say.

"I fought those suckers at night without telling anyone else, thinking I could take care of the problem. As the alpha here, that was my province."

Grant nodded for him to go on.

"Eventually their numbers were out of control. I had to recruit the pack, and together we came calling. The wily bloodsucking bastards separated me from the others as easily as culling sheep. My wolves were slaughtered, almost to the man, and I…"

Grant waited without breathing for the Lycan to finish his statement, already fearing what he might say. At his side, Paxton looked to have been carved from stone.

"Well, I was strong enough, different enough, to live through that massacre. I was strong enough to get my affairs in order and to send Paxton away."

Paxton spoke in a small voice. "You sent me away for my protection?"

The hood bobbed when the Lycan nodded. "Always the rebel. That was my Paxton. Never listening. Always bending or breaking the rules I hoped would keep you from a similar fate."

A punch of emotion rocked Paxton back on her feet as she recalled the werewolf who had come to her rescue. That werewolf now had a name. That werewolf had been her father.

It *was* Andrew Hall facing them.

Paxton took two more steps, feeling weightless now and only starting to process what was taking place as all three Lycans faced off.

It wasn't really a face-off, though. Even as a man, her father outweighed Grant by at least forty pounds. The hood he wore did nothing to disguise his size and bulk.

Something so bad had happened to her father that he had faked his own death. He had torn apart every emotion she'd had since she was a kid with his confession of the reason he had sent her away, but that didn't address his continued silence. She, out of everyone, could have kept his secret, whatever that secret was.

"Yes," he said, listening to her thoughts. "You might have kept those secrets if I had been willing to tell them to you."

"It was you who downed the tree," Paxton said.

"Yes. To keep you inside the fence."

"And it was you on the hood of my car."

"Hoping to keep you from venturing out in the dark."

Paxton tried hard to assimilate this news and could barely breathe beneath the weight of it.

"Middle ground," Grant said, stepping up to meet her. "What does that mean? What could be so bad that you'd fake your death and hide out here, without your pack, your daughter or other company?"

"Oh, I have company. It's just not the sort you'd expect. They keep me busy. And now, they have their eyes on…Paxton."

Grant said, "What are you talking about?"

"To get to me, their archnemesis, they will go after my daughter, knowing she is my only weak spot."

"Who will do this?" Paxton asked.

"Then why did you arrange to bring her here?" Grant demanded before her father could reply.

"Who will come after me?" Paxton repeated.

"Are you talking about vampires?" Grant asked.

Shadows had receded near the entrance to the mine, and the hooded Lycan, her father, backed into them. He didn't leave her there with her questions, but seemed to need those shadows the way she needed light.

"She was buried here, you know," her father said. "A portion of the mine caved in while she was inside."

More emotion struck, tying Paxton's stomach in knots. "My mother?" She was not sure how much more of this she could take.

Her father nodded. "You were…"

"Young," she said. "And not allowed to see her. Not allowed to visit her grave because I was told there wasn't a grave."

"You couldn't be allowed to come here, though I think you tried, sensing her soul was here somewhere. Am I right, Paxton?"

"Yes."

"And you were almost killed."

"They ate my pony," she said. "So you sent me away."

Her father lifted a hand. "You would have returned here time and time again, until one day I might have lost sight of you, and you would have suffered the same fate your pony did. That outcome would have killed me if they hadn't."

Paxton was aware of Grant's energy sparking inside him. She put out a hand to stop him from advancing on her father.

Would have killed me if they hadn't. Those words rang in her ears with a discordant sound.

"What happened to you?" she asked again, willing her father to answer the question that had become the heart of this mystery. She sent him that message over and over, bombarding his mind with her Lycan voice. "You said it's important that we know now, so please tell us the rest."

Grant, impatient beside her, said, "The vampires you hunted got to you?"

Her father nodded.

"Yet you're here now," Paxton protested. "You survived."

"I survived, but at great cost. I lost everything."

Her voice took on a plaintive quality. "You had me. Could have had me."

"No," her father said flatly, as if he had thought of the possibility so many times since he had sent her away that it no longer had the power over him it once might have. "Not you. Not like this."

"But I'm here. You brought me here."

"I'm dying, Paxton. My wolf blood wears thin. I arranged for you to come here for two reasons."

"Those reasons are?" Grant was quick to ask.

Ignoring the interruption, her father said, "Grant had to know about the danger facing the area in order to protect not only the pack, but our neighbors."

"Vampires," Grant said.

"And also because it was time for you, daughter, to come into your heritage. You needed to be here, among your kind. It was time for you to come home."

Paxton felt a tear slide down her cheek. More tears pooled in her eyes. "How did you know it was my time?"

She thought she heard a lightness in her father's tone when he said, "It was the same with your mother's line, twenty-six being the year of her wolf's birth."

"But how…?" Her question failed.

"And because in getting close to me, your wolf would respond to mine," Grant said to her. "Like calling to like, with a little thing we call *imprinting* calling the shots. Once you were here it was only a matter of time before we connected. Isn't that right, Andrew?"

Her father nodded.

Paxton turned to face her father again. "Grant was chosen to be a possible mate?"

"Grant Wade exemplifies the best in us," her father replied. "Nothing was too good for my daughter."

So there it was. Mystery solved. Paxton's head swam. She felt faint. But instead of feeling angry with her father, she suddenly felt grateful and almost euphoric. Instead of feeling lost and alone, she had found her father alive, and he had sent her into the arms of a potential mate. Grant. Cowboy. Alpha. Werewolf. Her father's chosen successor.

She wasn't sure she liked anyone choosing a partner for her. Then again…

"All right," she said to her father, almost afraid she

would collapse from fatigue before hearing more. "Now tell us the rest. Tell us about you."

Grant strode toward Andrew Hall holding tightly to Paxton's hand. The elder Lycan waited as they approached without making any move to disappear. This was what Andrew Hall wanted. He had specifically expressed to them how important this reunion with Paxton was.

"Maybe you can remove the hood, Andrew, and finish this tale, so that we can understand it," Grant suggested.

Andrew was silent for several beats before raising his hands. Long fingers grasped the edges of his black hood. As it was drawn back, Grant stared at what that covering had hidden. He tightened his grip on Paxton's hand when she swayed in reaction to what they were seeing.

Andrew Hall's face was unrecognizable as either human or Were. His features were marred by rows of white scars. Eyelids were fused to the skin above them. His mouth was pulled up on one side in a permanent sneer. The rest of his skin was mottled and as pale as his eyes. No color left. Nothing recognizable as human skin.

The big Lycan looked like an embattled ghost.

Long gray hair hung down his back. On his neck were rows of black dots, in pairs. There were so many dots, seeing them made Grant sick to his stomach. Something nasty had been attacking Andrew Hall for some time, and Grant knew what that something nasty was. Vampires.

"So you see now why I can't fit in," Andrew said sadly.

"You're Lycan, no matter what," Grant objected. "Someone could have helped you. We can find help now."

Andrew Hall shook his head. "Who would have guarded this place and other places like it, if I had left my post? Which member of your pack could have lived through what I have lived through, for as long as I have? Only you might have taken up my role while unprepared for it, Grant, and then my daughter would truly have been alone."

"Lycan," Paxton intoned.

"Yes," her father said. "Lycan, once upon a time. With so much vampire poison in my veins I'm not sure what I have become, and the fear is that I can't hold out much longer."

Grant closed his eyes. Andrew Hall had taken it upon himself to be Desperado's protector. Their guardian angel. In the background, he battled bloodsucking parasites with no one to help him, so that Weres in this part of the desert could thrive.

It wasn't a necessary sacrifice, Grant told himself, when so many Weres would have come to his aid. But the big Lycan had his own demons, and those demons had driven him.

Perhaps his presence here at the mine where his wife had died was due to his need to keep vampires from finding her remains. But that was a question Grant would never ask. What was done, was done. The rogue had been found.

He stopped processing that information when he remembered the woman who had led them here. His entire body chilled with the thought of who that woman might have been, and what she was. Andrew's wife, maybe. Paxton's mother. It seemed to him that there were two ghosts here at this old mine, and many more layers to this earthly existence than he had thought possible. It also seemed to Grant that some of those things should be left alone.

Paxton slid her hand from his and pulled away. She was next to her father before Grant blinked, and looking into Andrew Hall's marred face.

"How did you know who I was?" Andrew Hall asked her.

"It was the eyes," she replied. "I remembered my father's eyes."

Andrew Hall had wanted to see his daughter again, and had held out against all that vampire venom in his system in order to do so. He was handing Grant the torch…so that the desert pack would take over the fight against vampires when Andrew was gone.

The Lycan was a hero, of sorts, Grant decided, and would be honored among the pack whether or not Andrew showed his face there.

Giving in to emotion, Paxton put her arms around her father, burying her head against his broad chest.

Grant watched this with a lump in his throat.

Although her father did not immediately return his daughter's gesture of comfort and reunion, there was no doubt in Grant's mind that Andrew Hall wanted to, but had simply forgotten how.

Chapter 33

Sunlight slanted through an opening in the curtains. Long, thin fingers of yellow luminescence left stripes on the bed and on Grant's lover's naked body.

She had talked in her sleep, as she had nearly every night since that dark one at the mine, tossing and turning until he quieted her with a kiss on the nape of her neck. That wonderfully tender place beneath her cascade of silky blond hair was the spot he had grown to love almost as much as the woman it belonged to.

He had done this same thing every night for a month.

Paxton had not mentioned going back to the East in the weeks that had passed, showing no desire to retrieve her things. She didn't seem to care about anything except being one of the pack, strolling through Desperado and going out to meet her father each evening when he came as far as the edge of town.

And, well, she also liked Grant Wade, and *this*.

Gliding his palm over her taut belly made her stir. Slipping his fingers between her thighs made her growl in a sleepy way.

Daylight had become Paxton's friend. She rested easier after the sun came up, and who could blame her? Still, her body, in his bed, was warm and fragrant, and much too delectable for Grant to ignore his craving for her or the hardness of his erection.

Yes, they knew each other. Absolutely. He understood that she'd make him work a little harder at seducing her before she let on that she'd been waiting for him to do so. His she-wolf was sometimes adept at hiding her thoughts, but never thoughts dealing with her feelings for him. Each morning, he made love to her. Each day she told him she loved him.

The feeling was mutual.

The place his fingers found nestled between her legs was soft and lightly furred. When he dared to insert the tip of one finger into the tender folds beneath all that softness, Paxton sighed and arched her back.

"Wolf," he whispered with his mouth close to her ear.

"Bastard," she responded teasingly, leaving her lush lips slightly open in invitation.

It was always like this, Grant thought to himself. And always would be. Although they sometimes took an hour to satisfy their craving for each other, taking the time to explore each angle and curve, holding himself back was never easy. Paxton Hall was just too damn sexy. And she was his.

Gently, he rolled over to lay his body against hers. His lover didn't open her eyes. But she smiled and opened her legs.

"What? Again?" Grant asked.

Fair lashes fluttered before her eyes finally opened and she said in her best bedroom voice, "If you think an alpha can handle it."

It was his turn to smile. "I'm pretty sure I can, since you insist."

"Of course, if you'd rather not..." she began, the jest fading as he entered her with a smooth thrust that made her fingers curl.

Her eyes never left him after that, and Grant wouldn't have had it any other way. As their bodies rode out the storm that took them over with each renewed thrust, each give and take, plunge and withdrawal, Grant finally sealed his lips to hers. He drank in her groans of pleasure as if every sound were a special kind of sustenance for him.

And when he reached her core, that place where their souls met and collided amid the pulsating inferno, his lover's hard-beating orgasm spun him into his own divine ecstasy.

It was like coming back to Earth after a journey in space when Grant's mind could function properly again. He was a little out of breath and his lips were on Paxton's. Her hands were on his bare backside, frozen there as she came down from the same kind of blissful journey.

"Will that do, little wolf?" he whispered, drawing back far enough to seek the answer in her amber gaze.

"Not quite, I'm sorry to say," she huskily replied. "I expected far more from a Lycan."

So, what the hell? Grant thought, smiling widely, knowingly, happily. He was damn sure he was up for the next round, as well as the one after that...and was ready to prove it.

He had a job to do, a pack to protect and a beautiful

she-wolf in his bed. Maybe, just maybe, his mind had been changed, and being an alpha wasn't turning out to be so bad after all.

And, in the end, he had Desperado's ghosts to thank for that.

* * * * *

Can't get enough of DESERT WOLF?
Check out Linda Thomas-Sundstrom's
previous werewolf books:

WOLF BORN
WOLF HUNTER
SEDUCED BY THE MOON
HALF WOLF

Available now from Harlequin Nocturne!